Fear's Game

Walking in Freedom Book 1

Lisa Bell

Keep walking in freedom!
Lisa Bell

Radical Women

Book Cover and Interior Design by Radical Women

Paperback ISBN: 978-1-965561-01-0
eBook ISBN: 978-1-965561-02-7
Hardcover ISBN: 978-1-965561-05-8

For my daughters and all my grandchildren.
May you face life fearlessly,
knowing the One who ends all fear.

Contents

I leave the gift of peace with you—my peace. Not the kind of fragile peace given by the world, but my perfect peace. Don't yield to fear or be troubled in your hearts—instead, be courageous!

Jesus of Nazareth
(as recorded in John 14:27 TPT*)*

Chapter 1

HOME ALONE

TEARS PLAYED BEHIND VALORIE'S eyelids while she took one last glance at the porch. Michele and JR waved, jumping up and down and tugging on her dad's hands. No doubt they'd have him at the beach within minutes, eking out the last of the day in the surf—without sunscreen and not wearing life jackets. She cringed and glanced at a white van parked at the neighbor's house.

The man in the passenger's seat darted his tongue over his top lip, eyes like coal staring at her, the gaze lingering then moving down. Muscles tense, she reached for her water bottle, but the sinister look in that man's eyes stopped her.

What a jerk. Just leave.

She locked the door, rolled up the window, then threw the gearshift into reverse and backed the Volvo from the driveway, jetting down the street. At the stop sign, she breathed. Before moving, she glanced into the rearview mirror as the van pulled up behind her. She shot through the intersection and sped up to reach the main road. Merging into traffic, she looked back.

The van followed and cut off a car to move behind her.

Like runaway hoof beats, her heart pounded as she drove toward the safety of home. At one intersection, she caught the white van in her peripheral vision to the left. She kept her eyes straight ahead, sweat building on her brow. When the light changed, she pressed the accelerator and lurched forward, moving to the left lane, checking her rearview yet again.

Still there. Crap.

A horn beeped, drawing her attention back to the road as she almost hit a car head-on. Valorie steered the car back into her lane, sweat running down her back.

She sped up, praying a cop pulled her over. With two sharp turns, she raced to her house, hoping she lost the van. Unbuckling before the car stopped, she parked, turned off the motor, and ran toward the front door. The van pulled up across the street as the sun moved toward the horizon.

The passenger blew a kiss in her direction.

Stifling a scream, she flung open the door, raced inside, and slammed it behind her.

The security alarm beeped, waiting for the code. Maybe let it go, have the police come. But it might take too long. First the alarm company calling. Then waiting while they connected with police.

Call 9-1-1. Faster.

After locking the bottom knob and two deadbolts, she turned and punched in the code to silence the beeps. Then she rearmed it, punching "at home." She turned back and slid two more locks into place before moving a stool in front of the door. Sunbeams streamed across the room.

Oh no! The drapes.

She crossed the room, ramming her knee into the coffee table as she grabbed the phone.

"Ouch!" She stumbled to the window, her hands shaking as she tried to grab the pull cord.

"9-1-1. What's your emergency?"

Valorie choked back a sob. "A white van followed me home. Two men in it. They're sitting across the street. Watching my house. Please send help." She tugged at the drapery cord, yanking hard.

"Ma'am, calm down. Are you sure they aren't just visiting your neighbor?"

"No. They were at my parents' house. When I left, they followed me. One of them made lewd gestures. Please send a patrol car. Now!"

"Ma'am, are the men still in the vehicle?"

"Yes. I'm inside my house. Doors locked. Security system armed. But they're still out there." Valorie peeked out the window. The man saluted her. A whimper escaped. "Please. Hurry."

"I show you on Lakewood Drive. Is that correct?"

"Yes."

"Officers are en route. Stay inside. Don't open the doors until they arrive."

"Hurry!" Valorie knew the woman wanted to calm her, but she couldn't stop shaking. "Can you stay on the phone with me until they get here?"

"Ma'am, are the men approaching the house?"

"No."

"The police officers show an ETA of two minutes. If the men aren't approaching the house, no imminent danger. I need to clear the line."

"But what if they try to break in?"

"Our officers will be there any minute. Are you alone in the house?"

"Yes. My husband's out of town. My parents have my children for a few days."

"Take a deep breath. Stay calm."

Valorie breathed, looked around the living room. "All right. I'm trying." Not successfully.

"Thank you, ma'am." The dispatcher disconnected.

Looking at the phone, Valorie shook her head and headed to the kitchen, bumping into the sofa on the way. She opened the refrigerator, grasped a bottle of water, and dropped it.

She picked it up, fumbling again, but finally landing it on the counter. The top didn't budge.

Giving up, she tried to still her heart.

It didn't listen.

Instead, the beats pulsed against her eardrums.

Wild barking erupted through the back windows.

Bruce. What a name for their dog. Should've named him Brute.

Maybe she should let him in the house. No. He'd track dirt and grass all over the floor and leave hair and slobber everywhere. Besides, what if the men were out there at the fence? Better to keep Bruce outside—in case the men tried to come in through the back.

She peered around the cabinet at the security bolts on the back door. All in place. She breathed deep and wrapped trembling arms around herself.

Why did Mitch have to travel with his job? Couldn't they send someone else? She needed her husband at home to protect her and the kids.

Her thoughts shifted to that evil man in the van. Who was he? The suggestive tongue movements flashed through her brain. And those eyes. Such smoldering eyes. Nothing but emptiness. She shuddered.

"Get a grip, Valorie." She moved back toward the living room, bumping into the breakfast bar. "OW! That'll leave a bruise."

TICK. TICK. TICK.

BONG!

Valorie squealed, jumping back and crashing against the wall.

"The clock. The stupid grandfather clock." Shaking her head, she stifled a giggle. "Quit being silly. That man just wanted to mess with me. The van's probably not even out there now."

CREAK.

The empty house taunted her as she spun around, searching the darkening corners.

Nothing.

Of course, nothing. She grabbed a remote and switched on the TV, welcoming the chatter to fill the silence. She approached the window and pulled the curtain back only an inch, expecting an abandoned curb.

The white van. Still there. Empty.

With quivering hands, she pulled the curtain back a little farther, her gaze darting across the yard.

Nothing.

Where were the cops?

She looked around the room again. Shadows played against the walls.

Where did those men go? Were they hiding beside the house? In the backyard? Impossible. Bruce was back there. No one would dare mess with that beast.

But her feeble attempts to convince herself didn't calm Valorie. She turned on a table lamp, flooding the vastness of her living room with a soft glow.

Better.

At another creak, she looked up the stairs.

Too dark.

She raced up the steps, flipping light switches as she went. In every room, she turned on lights and checked every window lock. After pulling down shades and drawing curtains, she ended up in her bedroom, double checking the lock and alarm on the balcony door.

She scanned the street.

Van still there. Empty.

As she pulled the vertical blinds, the approaching police cruiser caught her attention.

Finally!

Valorie drew in a deep breath, closing her eyes and silently thanking the Lord while rushing downstairs. Several minutes passed before a ferocious bark made her jump and motion detectors triggered floodlights at the front of the house.

The doorbell rang, followed by a loud knock.

"Police."

She peered through the peephole. They looked like police. She pushed aside the stool, knocking it over.

Unlocking each bolt, she twisted the self-locking doorknob and opened the door a crack. "May I see your badges?"

One officer moved closer. The other looked upward, a slight head nod.

If she wasn't so frightened, his disrespect would make her mad. "Did you find those men?"

"Can we come in?"

"Yes, of course." She opened the door a little wider and motioned them inside before slamming the door behind them. The alarm beeped, insistent for attention. She turned and entered the code, her hand shaking as she shielded it from the men. She turned back toward the cops.

"Ma'am, we checked the van. It appears empty, secured. Not sure what you saw, but they apparently went into one of the neighborhood houses."

"But you can't see in the back. They could be there!"

"We knocked, looked through all the windows. I'm telling you, no one's in that van unless they melted into the side panels." A smirk played across his face.

Valorie's jaw tightened. "But you didn't see the way he looked at me. He followed me. I know it."

"I'm sure it seemed like he followed you. Nothing suspicious—only an empty van, parked for the night, maybe. Could be a handyman. We noticed a few paint cans in back and rang the doorbell at the house across the street. No one answered."

"What if they're hiding, waiting until you leave?"

The officer motioned at the locks. "Ma'am, you got more security here than most museums. Plus, you got the dog out back. We heard him. I'm sure he'll alert you to any potential intruders. With all that, you'll be fine."

Tears pushed against Valorie's eyelids. "I guess you're right. The way he looked at me, though. I don't care what you think. I swear he followed me home."

"Probably coincidence."

Her world blurred as the second officer pulled out a notepad, rattled off questions, and jotted notes.

When they finished, the officers unlocked and opened the door. "If they return and cause any problems, call again, but I doubt they'll be back."

"I hope not. I'm telling you, that man looked evil." A chill ran over her body. "Thank you, officers."

Valorie shut the door, her heartbeat ricocheting around her chest. She relocked everything, punched in the code, and pushed "at home."

Turning around, shivers slipped over her body. She tiptoed back to the kitchen and flipped the switch, soft lights flooding the room. She checked every door and window again, taking no chances.

Finally finished, she collapsed on a chaise lounge near the upstairs balcony.

Maybe the cops had a point. Mitch often accused her of paranoia. Her dad too.

Was she?

Something about that man, though—the look in his eyes. He had no good intentions toward her. She felt certain about that.

Inside. Safe. Locked away.

Her phone rang, and she jumped before checking the screen.

Mitch. She swiped to answer.

"Hi, babe. How's everything going?" His firm voice soothed her.

Valorie tried to control the spasms in her throat. "Mitch. I'm..." She paused. "I'm fine."

"You don't sound fine. What's going on?"

"Someone followed me from Mom and Dad's house. I thought I lost them, so I ran to the door just as the van came around the corner. They parked right across the street."

"Really? Someone you know?"

"No. An evil-looking man."

Concern drifted over the phone. "Is he still there?"

"No. The van is, but it looks empty. I called the police."

"Val. You can't call the cops every time you get scared when I'm out of town. Isn't that why we got Bruce?"

"Yes. But that man freaked me out." She fidgeted with a blanket.

"So, did the police come?"

"Yeah. Didn't find anything. Maybe I overreacted."

"You think?" Mitch chuckled. "Lock everything up and turn on the alarm. If they try anything, Bruce will let you know. We have the best locks. You know that."

"I know." She stilled herself and peered through the open bedroom door into the hallway. Nothing there. "How was your flight?"

"Uneventful. And I'm glad." Mitch yawned. "I need to get some sleep. Busy day tomorrow. I'll be back as soon as I can."

"Okay. I love you."

"I love you, too. Sleep well, and don't let fear keep you up all night."

She laughed. "You know me too well."

"Yes, I do. Take a hot bath and enjoy time without the kids. I'll see you soon."

Valorie went downstairs and placed the stool in front of the door—just in case. It made little sense, but somehow it made her feel safer. After pouring a small glass of wine, she turned off most of the lights, pausing at the lamp.

"I'll leave that one on."

She turned off the TV and dragged herself up the stairs. Maybe she should take a bath. But alone and naked?

No way.

Instead, she popped two melatonin pills, hoping with the wine they knocked her out until morning.

Chapter 2

A Dungeon?

Wrapping a robe around her body, Valorie shivered despite the warm summer day. She winced. Everything hurt, even the tips of her fingers, as if she fought for her life all night. In her dreams, she did. The comforter, half hanging off the bed, revealed a tangled mess of sheets.

Shudders trickled through her body, images replaying across her mind. Thoughts she didn't desire remained when she scrunched her eyes.

A dungeon.

Chains.

A naked man standing over her, beating her.

Doing unspeakable things.

Tears slipped from her eyelids, caressing cheeks as they slid to her chin. Just a dream—a nightmare she needed to forget.

Valorie crossed to the balcony door and peered between the shades at the empty street below. Did she dream the entire thing? Even the white van? She shook her head, opening the blinds, drinking in bright sunshine.

That part—not a dream.

The images returned and raged through her mind, a storm brewing beneath the surface. None of it could be real. She checked her phone. The day after Mitch left. If any of it happened, days, maybe a week, would be gone.

"Just a bad dream," she whispered to the silent house. No doubt the most realistic dream she ever experienced. Every inch of her body screamed, "It happened! All of it."

Paranoid?

Maybe her dad and Mitch knew her better than she wanted to admit.

Valorie tried to reason with herself. "It couldn't have happened. The tension from a nightmare has my muscles tight. That's all." But she couldn't shake the vivid reality of those images.

The Bible on her nightstand beckoned her. Maybe she should at least read a devotional. See if that helped. Sometimes it did. She perched on the edge of the bed and read for a few minutes. A bright thought for the day, but more often lately, these enthusiastic words of some writer did little to soothe her or draw her closer to God. If Mitch were there...

She let her mind drift. Mitch brought the Bible to life, always with the right verse to soothe her. As a child, she listened, pictured the stories as her parents and grandparents taught her. She lost that zeal—when that one date night stole her innocence and trust.

A horn blaring outside brought her back to the day before her. And with it, the return of images from her dream.

She gingerly descended the steps, checking the front door.

All locks in place.

What an imagination. Her fears did a number on her.

Shaking herself, she wandered into the kitchen, checking to make sure none of the back locks looked open.

"All good. See? You're being silly."

Valorie started a pot of coffee and paused as scratching at the back door caught her attention. Her eyes widened. She froze, listening.

A whimper.

"Oh, my stars. Bruce. Of course you're scratching. You're hungry."

She peeped out the window, making sure no one waited beyond the safety of her locks. Bruce sat beside the storm door, his tongue lolling to the side. Valorie chuckled. "Mitch and Dad are right. I'm too scared of nothing. Poor dog."

She pulled a treat out, and with the multiple locks undone, she swung open the door. Bruce jumped up, barking with a happy-to-see-you tone. Valorie stepped outside and filled his water bowl, then retrieved the other one for his food. Bruce raced around her, tail wagging.

"Sit, boy."

The dog obeyed—for a moment. He approached and backed off, attempting unsuccessful patience.

His mistress laughed and patted his head. "You're as impatient as I am paranoid. You know that?" She filled the bowl with food from an oversized tub, set it on the patio, and glanced around the yard. Nothing out of place.

While Bruce gobbled his food, she surveyed his soft coat. Smooth. Flat. Nothing alerting her of danger.

"There is no danger, Valorie." Why must she always assume the worst?

Finished eating, Bruce padded to her, begging for attention. His eyes latched onto hers, offering comfort and peace. She smiled to herself and embraced the dog's face—something she never did. He might want to give her a kiss. Not happening.

Still, the dog's tail wagged harder. She held up the treat.

"Sit."

Bruce obliged, waiting. "Good dog." Valorie tossed the treat, and he grabbed it mid-air.

"Good job." She petted him one more time, thankful for the moment of companionship.

Back inside, Valorie locked the door—all five bolts—and retreated to wash her hands before pouring a cup of coffee.

Suddenly, she stopped.

The alarm. Why didn't the alarm go off?

Valorie slowly turned around from the sink. In the eerie quietness, she looked around the kitchen.

She was outside for a good five to ten minutes. The alarm should be blaring. The phone ringing. Cops on the way.

Nothing.

She grabbed a butcher knife and tiptoed to the living room, glancing down the hallway and up the stairs.

No one in sight.

She looked at the door again, expecting a disengaged lock.

She checked the alarm panel.

Her breath caught in her throat.

No light.

No red.

No green.

Nothing.

Valorie whirled.

Her knees buckling, a gasp escaped as she grabbed the edge of the breakfast bar. The stool lay on its side.

Pictures whirled through her mind. The man. This time in her bedroom.

"No! It didn't happen! It couldn't have!"

She peered around the room, peeked down the hallway and up the stairs, then she grabbed the phone with quivering hands.

BRRRING.

Valorie fumbled the phone, catching it a second before it slipped from her hand.

She tried to calm her voice. "Hello?"

"Mrs. Ferguson?" A woman's soft voice broke through her jangled nerves.

"Who's calling?"

"This is Misti, from Ace Alarms."

"Seriously? I was about to call you."

"Really? Are you alright?"

"I... I... I think so."

"Our system shows an outage on your alarm. Do you have a power issue?"

"No. I just discovered my panel doesn't have any lights on it. Does that mean my alarm isn't working? For how long?"

Clicks came across the phone. "I'm trying to find that information, but my computer doesn't say for certain. When did you last check the alarm?"

"Last night. I double-checked it before going to bed around 9:00 p.m. It worked then."

"Hmmm. Could be something simple. Did you have a break-in?"

"No. I don't think so." Valorie hesitated. "I have multiple locks, and they all look secure."

"You know, we've had reports of kids in the area messing with systems. No robberies. Bored teenagers looking for an adrenaline rush. They don't think about the consequences of their pranks. My guess is they picked your house last night. Would you like me to send a technician to look at it?"

"Yes. Please." Valorie trembled. The woman's explanation did little to calm her. "Wait. How will I know he's your tech?"

"Once they assign the ticket, I can email a photo if you like—along with his name."

"Yes, please. Sorry if I sound paranoid. I had a rough night after someone followed me home."

"Oh goodness. Did you notify the police?"

"Yes. They came, but found nothing. Still... with my alarm not working..."

Dare she share the dream? No. The woman would think her crazy.

Misti's voice cut through her thoughts. "I can understand why you might feel uneasy. Check your email in about five minutes. I'm putting a rush on this for you."

"Thank you, Misti." Valorie choked back a moan.

"You're welcome. If you notice anything suspicious before our tech gets there, call 9-1-1."

"I will."

With the call disconnected, Valorie raced up the stairs to dress, still clutching the butcher knife.

She would *not* let some strange man catch her in a robe.

Chapter 3

Broken Alarm

UPSTAIRS IN THE CLOSET, Valorie laid the knife on a shelf. She stripped out of her nightgown and slipped on a pair of jeans. As she turned to choose a t-shirt, her reflection in the mirror stopped her.

Where did all those bruises come from?

She traced memories of the previous night.

The bar. Of course! She rammed into it. And the coffee table. And who knows what else she hit in her panic mode?

She surveyed the number of bruises on her body. She always had them—especially when Mitch left town. Twisting, she glanced at different places on her arms, legs, even her stomach. Did she hit all those spots? Against what?

She shook her head, bewildered by a body that looked as if someone beat her. Not possible.

Pictures from the dream flitted across her mind.

"No! I won't believe some stupid dream. None of it happened."

She pulled on her shirt. Red marks across her forearm screamed at her. Puzzled, she studied them. Maybe Bruce scratched her. His toenails needed a trim—always. That had to explain it, although they looked more like someone dragged a knife over her skin.

A scene from the dream took control of her thoughts.

A young woman with long, dark hair approaching. The glint of a knife. A few cuts before Valorie jerked her arm back.

"No! That was just a dream. I won't believe it happened. I can't."

The bong of the clock downstairs jerked her back to reality. Grabbing the knife, she headed to the office to check her email. She needed to feel secure when the tech arrived to look at the alarm. Enough of her insanity.

Was she losing her mind? Sometimes, she wondered.

Turning on the computer, a message from Ace Alarms appeared. She opened it without hesitating.

> ***The technician assigned to your case, Donny Temple, should arrive within the hour. Check his photo badge to verify his identity. Please see the attached picture. We are sorry for any inconvenience and promise to correct your issue as soon as possible. As always, thank you for your patronage. Your safety is our primary concern.***
>
> Misti

Valorie opened and studied every detail of the assigned technician. Looked nice enough. Clean cut, blond hair, and green eyes. No facial hair. Good. Certain she would recognize him, she gathered the knife and retreated to the kitchen. Staring at the blade in her hand in the stillness, she chuckled. If Mitch and her dad saw it, they'd both swear they needed to lock her up. Totally off her rocker.

Coffee. She needed coffee.

She poured a cup, breathing in the scent of spices and vanilla. Tension eased before she tasted the dark liquid. After a sip, she sighed.

Better.

Breakfast and wait for the tech. She'd be fine—as soon as he reconnected the alarm.

Breakfast finished and dishes washed, dried, and put away, Valorie blew out a breath.

Why hasn't that tech showed up yet?

The thought skipping through her mind, she refilled her coffee mug and headed to the living room. As she moved to the window, the thud of a car door caught her attention. Bruce barked. She never knew if that dog barked in warning or greeting. It sounded like he wanted to play with the guy more than he wanted to protect her.

She opened the drapes an inch. A blue and gold van with the Ace Alarms logo on the side sat in her driveway beside her Volvo. A clean-cut young man, holding a clipboard, approached the front door.

Valorie raced across the room as the doorbell chimed.

"Who is it?"

"Hello, Mrs. Ferguson. I'm Donny Temple. Here to check your alarm."

She peered through the peephole. "Can you hold up your badge?"

He complied, smiling. "I promise. It's me."

Her hands shook as she unlocked all the deadbolts. No choice but to trust him. He looked like the photo from the email. Her heart sped up when she opened the door. "I'm sorry. My husband and father tell me I'm paranoid. But I don't take chances."

"No, ma'am. You can never be too safe. Do you mind if I take a quick look at your panel?"

Running a hand over her mouth, Valorie hesitated for a second. "If you think that's necessary..."

"I find the issue there 90% of the time, so I always check it first. If you'd rather I not..."

"No. Of course. Come in." She looked across the street and down the road. No white vans. She closed the door, not locking it in case she needed to run.

Dang. She ought to have the keys in her pocket.

Donny tilted his head up after searching for the panel and crossed the few steps to it. For several minutes, he pushed buttons and looked over everything. Removing an instrument from his bag, the technician held it up. "Well, it appears you don't have any power coming to the panel. Did you check breakers?"

Valorie raised her eyebrows. "I... That's something Mitch, my husband, would do. I'm not sure..."

Donny chuckled. "No problem. Most of the time, they're in the garage. May I go through the house, or would you prefer to open it and let me go in from outside?"

"Oh, it's such a mess out there. We keep saying we're gonna clean it out. I remember seeing a gray panel out there, near the door from the garage to the house."

"That's it."

"Then you can get to it much easier from the kitchen."

"Excellent. This way?"

"Yes." Valorie locked the bottom deadbolt—just to be safe.

Donny sauntered around the breakfast bar and through the kitchen. Valorie followed, picking up the keys from the bowl on the bar and stuffing them into her pocket, hoping he didn't notice. Nonchalant, he opened the door, found a light switch, and flipped it.

"Yep. There's the breaker box, like we expected." He turned and flashed a grin at Valorie. "Hopefully, we'll find the culprit right here and be done." He opened the breaker box and checked for a thrown switch. "Well, darn. Apparently, this won't be a quick and easy fix." He shut the metal door and flipped off the light. "I don't suppose you know where the outside connection box is, do you?"

Valorie shook her head. "Probably on the side of the house. If it's in the back, I'll secure the dog."

"Yeah. They should put them in the back, but most of the time they get as close to the panel as they can. I'll check the garage side first."

Donny whistled as he danced back through the house. At the front door, he tried to open it. Glancing at the lock, he shrugged, unlocked the bottom bolt, and opened the door. "I'll be back. You can stay inside if you want."

She considered following him for a moment, but her cell phone pinged. "I'll get this call. If you find anything, go ahead, and fix it."

"Will do, and I'll let you know what I discover."

She grabbed her phone to check the text and reengaged the bottom lock.

Mitch.

Hi babe. Checking on you this morning. Everything ok?

No. The alarm's not working.

I saw that text you sent. Did you check the breakers?

The tech did.

Oh.

He's outside now, checking the connection box.

K. Let me know what he finds. Gotta run. Meeting's starting back up.

Valorie sighed, praying this trip got Mitch the promotion he wanted. At least then he'd be home more than working out-of-town. She sipped coffee, drumming fingers against the bar. To pass the time while Donny worked on the system, Valorie texted her mom to check on the kids. No answer, of course. More than likely, they went to the beach early. They spoiled her kids too much. After the beach, they'd go get burgers and fries, then ice cream. Same thing every time. At least they planned to keep the kids for most of the week, so Mom and Dad could deal with the sugar-rush fallout.

Before long, the doorbell chimed. Valorie peered through the peephole. Donny. She opened the door.

The young man held up a piece of wiring. "I found your problem."

Valorie leaned back, not sure what the wiring told her.

"Someone cut it. Shut down your entire system."

"What? Cut?" Valorie's heartbeat quickened. Tingles coursed through her body.

Donny shrugged. "Probably a bunch of kids. It isn't the first time I seen it in this area."

Valorie winced, the aches pushing to the surface. She knew better. The man in the van. Somehow, the dream didn't feel as surreal.

Could it have happened? No! Not possible.

Donny continued. "I replaced the wires, reconnecting the system. This time, I encased it, so for someone to cut it again, they'll have to work harder. Someday, they'll figure out a better way to connect everything so we don't have this problem. No one should be able to disarm your system from outside the house."

"No. They shouldn't." Valorie clutched the door frame, shallow breaths coming faster.

"You okay?"

She nodded and took a deep breath, held, and released it. "Yes. I didn't expect to hear that someone cut the wires."

"I know. Scary, eh? It won't happen again." The tech paused. "Um-mm... Can we check your panel now? Get you up and running again?"

"Yes, please."

He dropped his clipboard on the bar, went to the panel, and turned the system back on. Lights blinked, flickered, and went steady. "Green. All good to go."

"Thank you." Maybe she should ask him to check all the closets for her. Or not. He seemed okay, but... Not a good idea to invite a stranger into your bedrooms. She shivered.

Instead, she sent a text to Mitch while Donny finished the paperwork,

Someone cut the wires!

She tapped the phone, waiting for a response. After a minute, her phone pinged.

What?

Cut, Mitch. I swear that man in the van did it.

Nah. Couple of neighbors had the same thing happen. Kids. One guy saw them running away. Couldn't ID them.

I don't think so.

Val, you're paranoid.

She clenched her teeth. Counted to ten.

Sorry, babe. I should've encased it. The guys warned me.

Not OK.

I know. I'm sorry.

Valorie rolled her shoulders, taking and releasing another deep breath.

I forgive you. This time.

I'm wrapping up here early. Does that make it better?

Maybe.

LOL. You're tough.

You called me paranoid. Again.

Well...

Don't.

Maybe sometimes you get overanxious.

Maybe.

I'll be home soon. It'll be OK.

OK.

Gotta pay attention now. Getting funny looks.

OK.

Love you, babe.

Love you too. I miss you.

No response. She knew better than to interrupt meetings, but she wanted to tell Mitch about the dream. Or did she? He'd tell her that explained her super-hyped fear the next morning.

She didn't need his admonition. He'd remind her she needed to lighten up and quit letting fear take control. To trust God instead. She hated that one. Easy to say, but she didn't see God keeping intruders out of her house. Fear ruled her and had since high school. But she didn't have a clue how to quell it—make it leave her alone.

Her mind drifted back to high school. She didn't date much but that one time—with the local college football star. Every girl wanted to date him, and he picked her. She wished he hadn't. Big, strong. When he made a move on her, she couldn't fight him off. The pain—the shame as he stole her virginity. She never told anyone. Not even Mitch. Years of therapy helped her cope, but it never removed her fear of someone assaulting her again.

Donny shoved the clipboard in front of her, interrupting her thoughts. "All done. Please sign here."

Valorie sighed, disregarding the amount. She didn't care how much it cost. "Thank you, Donny. I appreciate you coming out this morning and taking care of everything."

"No problem, ma'am." He turned to the door and stopped. "By the way, if they call back to check my service, I'd 'preciate a positive review."

"Of course."

As Donny climbed into his van, Rita crossed the driveway. "Hey, Valorie. Are you alright?"

"Rita! Hi. Better now."

"Girl, this morning Tim told me he saw cops at your house last night. Now I see the alarm company. What's going on?"

Valorie hugged her next-door neighbor, thankful for their friendship. "Come on in. I'll fill you in over coffee." She locked every deadbolt behind Rita.

Rita shook her head. "Girl, when I'm here, I sure don't worry about being attacked."

"That's the point, my friend." Valorie bit her bottom lip. "Would you go with me to check all the closets? I just want to be sure everything's clear."

Rita raised her eyebrows. "Is that really necessary?"

"For me to feel safe—yes."

Rita grabbed the poker from beside the fireplace. The two drifted through the house, checking closets, beneath beds, and behind curtains. Nothing. More relaxed, Valorie led the way back to the kitchen, rolling her head and listening to tiny pops in her neck. Definitely better.

Armed with coffee and cookies, the women retreated to the living room, where Valorie detailed the previous night for Rita. As she shared the story, her hands quivered, sloshing coffee on herself. For thirty minutes, they chatted about the previous night.

Finally, Rita set down her coffee and placed a hand on Valorie's arm. "That sounds absolutely terrifying. I went to visit my sister and got home late. I'm sorry you went through it alone."

"Thank you." She rubbed her forehead. "I don't know, Rita. Sometimes, I think maybe Dad and Mitch are right. Maybe I'm too anxious—of things I shouldn't fear at all. I mean... It's not like they broke in. At least I don't think so."

"Wait. What do you mean you don't think so?"

"Well, that's the crazy part. In this vivid dream, the man from the van came into my bedroom, kidnapped me, and took me to a dungeon. There for days..." Valorie shuddered. "I don't want to describe all he did. Not only to me, but he had other women there. He used them to hurt us. One fed us poison, and he gave another a knife. She cut herself and grabbed my arm, slicing it several times. I jerked away. Then she cut the others, even attempting to kill one. In my dream, the evil man sauntered down the stairs, laughing. He acted like it was all one big game."

"Wow! How terrifying! But only a nightmare. Right?"

Valorie nodded. "Except..."

"Except what?"

"I told you how I kept bumping into things, so these bruises all over my body didn't surprise me. I'm such a klutz, anyway." She held out her arm. "But these thin, fresh marks. I can't explain those away."

Rita gasped. "Like in the dream."

"Yes. And to top it all off, I woke to no alarm and cut wires."

"That doesn't mean he did it. I mean, how would he re-bolt the door from outside?"

"I don't know." Valorie inhaled and swept a hand over her mouth before exhaling. "See that stool near the coffee table, lying on its side?"

"Yeah."

"Before I went to bed, I placed it in front of the door. If anyone came in, they might trip over it and wake me up. Despite two—maybe three—melatonin and a glass of wine."

"That makes sense." Rita reached back and rubbed the base of her neck. "But you didn't move it?"

"No. I found it there this morning."

The friend's eyes widened. "Maybe Bruce knocked it over."

"Are you kidding? You think I dared open that back door with prowlers on the loose? I left Bruce outside. And before you say it, remember the kids are at my parents' house."

Snapping her fingers, Rita twitched her mouth. "That's it. Your dad came by to check on you. He has keys, right?"

"Yes, of course."

"So after the neighborhood hooligans cut your wires, he came over, worried about you, and unlocked the door. Then he didn't trip, but he accidentally kicked the stool. He left and locked everything up behind himself, knowing if he didn't, you'd be terrified this morning."

"Maybe." Valorie chewed a nail. "I mean that would account for the stool. But why didn't I hear anything?"

"Girl—THREE melatonin with a glass of wine? If someone tried to kidnap you after that, he wouldn't even have to drug you. Get real."

Both ladies chuckled, although Valorie questioned the logic. Would her dad drive across town late at night instead of calling? And did she give him keys for all the locks? Maybe, but she didn't remember. She should ask.

Rita changed the subject, moving on to lighter topics to ease Valorie's stress. When her phone chimed, she looked at it. "Oh, my goodness. Where did the time go? I gotta get home and finish up the laundry. I'm glad you're safe." She rose and crossed to the door. "I'm home, so if anything else happens this afternoon or tonight, call me. I'll come over and kick that crazy man's butt."

Valorie laughed. "I bet you would, too."

One more hug and Rita crossed the lawn. As Valorie closed the door, a white panel van eased down the street, robbing her breath.

Chapter 4

Mitch

Valorie flipped on loud, upbeat music and busied herself with cleaning an already spotless home. Anything to ease the thoughts traipsing across her brain. She refused to let a white van passing her home send her into a panic attack. Instead, she took deep breaths and scrubbed counters, the refrigerator, floors, everything. Not stopping for lunch, she took a break around 2:00 p.m. and called her parents to check on the kids.

They didn't answer. Still at the beach?

So much for keeping with her rules about not having the children outside in the midday sun. Hopefully, they didn't forget sunscreen. For a moment, her brain drifted to frightening possibilities.

What if the van went back?

What if that wicked man took her children?

What if he killed them all?

And what if her nightmare came true? Did it already? Did she end up in a dungeon somehow?

Maybe she should go... No. If she showed up unannounced at her parents' house, both Dad and Mitch would call her more than paranoid. She swiped at tears, wondering when they escaped her eyes.

Keep cleaning. Just keep busy.

But pouring herself into household chores never cleared her mind. Her worst fears crept into her subconscious. Vivid images of herself in some putrid, dark cave flooded her brain, tugging at the edges of sanity. Trying to shake the scenes, she squeezed her eyes shut. Worse. The stench of rats and decay invaded her imagination. The breakfast and cookies in her stomach mingled with the coffee, swirling and rising, like an ocean surge about to crash through her throat and onto the floor.

She forced her eyes open and shook her head. "No."

Valorie scanned the room and rolled her shoulders. Ridiculous. Safe at home, no scents except lemon fragrances. No dungeon. No rats. No decaying anything.

With nothing left to clean, Valorie opted for cooking. Her stomach rumbled in agreement. After retrieving vegetables from the fridge, she grabbed a cutting board and a paring knife.

Make a salad. Focus on slicing and dicing.

With every cut, new images broke her concentration, mental images growing beyond her wildest fears.

Mitch's plane crashing, sending him to eternity without so much as a goodbye or one last, "I love you." He called around lunchtime, but nothing else about coming home early.

She wished.

The mind games continued their relentless pursuit, convincing her he got on a plane but would never make it home.

She breathed in deeply, slowly exhaling.

Again.

One more time.

Her heartbeat evened.

As she forced her thoughts back to the vegetables, a new scene emerged. Thoughts drifted to her parents' house. Expecting the normal peace, she opened the door to horror. Blood everywhere. Mom, Dad lying still, eyes staring without seeing. Running through the house, searching for her children. Screaming, crying.

The runaway-train heartbeat returned, pummeling her chest. So tight, she couldn't breathe.

Gotta go. Gotta get to them. Save them.

"No. Stop imagining these crazy things, Valorie. I'm not going." Her shout echoed off the cabinet doors.

"Not going where?"

Valorie spun, brandishing the knife. A half-sliced tomato launched toward the deep voice.

"Whoa!" Mitch caught the flying vegetable.

"Mitch! How dare you?" She backed to the counter, grabbing the edge.

"Sorry, baby. I thought you heard me come in. Then again, with the rock fest..." He chuckled and crossed the room.

"Not funny. You know better than to sneak up on me."

He laid the tomato on the cutting board and ran water over his hand. "I didn't mean to."

"You aren't even supposed to be here." Valorie glared at her husband. "And you sure aren't supposed to come up behind me without letting me know you're there. If I could throw straight, you'd have a knife sticking in you."

Mitch laughed and reached for her. "Guess it's good you can't throw knives, then."

Valorie shrugged away from him. "After last night and then finding the cut wires this morning..." She flipped around and returned to the vegetables. "You're so mean."

"Aw, baby. Don't be angry."

Her eyes stung as she blinked, willing herself not to cry. "It's not okay."

Mitch reached around Valorie and took the knife from her hand, turning and pulling her into his chest. "I didn't mean to scare you. Just wanted to surprise you."

They stood in the embrace for several minutes. He kissed the top of her head, rubbing her back. "I'm here. You're safe."

Sobs shook her body as the tension eased. She wanted the anger to stay, but in the safety of his arms, Valorie gave in to the warmth and comfort. After several minutes, she pulled away, grabbed the dish towel, wiped her eyes, and blew out a breath.

"I forgive you. But. Don't. Ever. Do that. Again."

"Especially when you have a sharp knife in your hand." His boyish grin broke her last resolve.

"Don't give me that innocent little boy grin. You look like your son." She smiled despite herself. "Why *are* you home so early? I'm glad, but I didn't expect you until tomorrow."

"When I talked to you earlier today, you didn't sound right. Something off. I wrapped up the meeting and headed out." He took her hand and pulled her toward the living room. "C'mon. Tell me what's going on."

They sat on the sofa, Valorie recounting the previous night's events. Her eyes widened and hands flailed like a frantic bird. Visions of the white van played with her brain, her heart fluttering the more she shared. Then she told him every vivid detail of her dream. The man breaking in, kidnapping, beating, and raping her. The dungeon with its spiders, snakes, and rats. Another woman cutting her arm... Details she didn't know she remembered.

Finished, she sat back, grabbing a tissue from a box on the coffee table.

"But it was all a dream," Mitch said.

"Yeah, I guess." Valorie held out her arm, showing him the thin, red lines, newly scabbed. "I can explain away the bruises all over me. I'm a klutz. I run into things. But I have no explanation for these marks. None."

Mitch shrugged. "Maybe you accidentally cut yourself but don't remember."

"How could I not remember cutting myself?"

"I don't know, baby. But there must be an explanation. Maybe Bruce scratched you. Wouldn't be the first time he got one of us."

"But the stool... I put it in front of the door last night."

"Why?"

"If someone gets past the locks and security system—or it gets disabled, like it did last night—they'd trip, and I'd hear the noise."

"Did you hear noises?"

"Well... no. And the stool ended up clear across the room on its side. How do you explain that?"

"Maybe you thought you put it there. But after the cops came, perhaps you didn't put it back. Maybe one of them accidentally kicked it over, and you didn't notice."

"What?"

"It's possible."

"I put it there." Valorie crossed her arms. "I know I did. Right before I went upstairs. Always do when you are out of town."

"Really? You're that terrified? With all the locks and security?" Mitch scrunched his eyebrows.

"Don't look at me that way. You don't understand."

"No, baby. I don't. Sorry, but I don't get why you're so terrified. All the time. About everything."

"I'm not scared of everything."

"Actually, yes you are. Look at the doors. Five deadbolts on top of a high-end alarm system? It's not normal. Right now, you're shaking because of a nightmare."

"Mitch, you weren't there. And I'm not sure it didn't happen."

"Val, listen to yourself. You can't believe that."

She jumped off the sofa. "Thanks for all the support. I'm going to finish my salad."

Mitch followed her to the kitchen. "I'm concerned about you, babe. Maybe you need to go back to counseling. You can't live in fear like this."

"It's worked so far."

"Has it?"

Valorie narrowed her eyes. How could her husband take all this so lightly?

He shrugged. "I don't know how to help you. But either you figure it out, or one day, God's gonna make you face the worst fears to heal you. And I don't want to see how that plays out."

With a final shake of his head, Mitch retreated.

"Don't you want some salad?"

"Not really. I lost my appetite."

Valorie picked up the knife and returned to slicing. In her mind, the vegetables became the unknown man from her dream. She stabbed a tomato, turning it into mush instead of evenly diced pieces. Tears fell, mingling with the mess before her.

Stab a man?

Never.

Too weak to protect herself. A victim, forever waiting for the next attack. Obviously, Mitch didn't take her concerns seriously, and although neither of them could explain the marks or cut wires, he didn't worry about her. No one did. Which meant she needed to take care of herself.

Counselor? Maybe she needed a self-defense trainer. Someone who could teach her to stand up for herself. Then she'd be less fearful.

Who was she kidding? How could she ever shake these fears? She didn't even understand them. Were they irrational? Not to her. No matter what anyone said. The counselor, Mom, Dad, friends... even Mitch.

"I'm hopeless. And now I'm talking to myself."

She sighed, finished the salad, and placed it in the fridge, her appetite gone, too.

Chapter 5

Morning Breath Mood

SUNLIGHT BURST THROUGH THE windows. Valorie's mood, as foul as morning breath, filled the bedroom. She stretched, looking toward the bathroom. The door stood wide open with no light or water running.

She looked at the clock on the nightstand. 8:00 a.m. "Mitch?"

After sliding out of bed, visiting the bathroom, and putting on a robe, she ventured downstairs. As she approached the kitchen, a pleasant aroma met her. Coffee. She sniffed. Cinnamon rolls? A note secured to the fridge caught her attention.

I'm sorry about yesterday, babe. The dream, real to you, left you rattled, and in my fatigue, I ignored your feelings. I shouldn't have dismissed your fear. You looked peaceful sleeping, so I didn't wake you. I found cinnamon rolls in the fridge and baked them along with leaving a full pot of coffee.

I need to go into the office for a brief meeting, but I'll be home early. Pack for a few days, and when I get back, we'll take a road trip—put everything out of mind for a while. Maybe it will help you relax and forget about the horrid dream that felt so real to you.

Oh, and I fed Bruce, too. Please ask Rita to look in on him until we get back.

I love you. Mitch.

Valorie inhaled, sucking in the flavorful scent. How could she stay mad at her husband when he left coffee and cinnamon rolls? A trip? She wondered where he planned to take her, but in the sweetness of her kitchen, she didn't care. With a fresh cup of coffee in hand, she grabbed a plate from the cabinet and placed a roll on it. She licked her fingers and opted for a fork.

Sitting at the table, she sent a text to her neighbor, asking her to feed and water the dog and watch out for anything unusual at their house.

While waiting for the reply, Valorie savored the treat, her mood soaring. Mitch had a point. She didn't like a sense of dread all the time. Why couldn't she be brave like her next-door neighbor or shrug things off like Mitch? Toying with an idea, she did a quick search for nearby self-defense classes. Maybe if she took one... Worth a try. Right?

The response came back from Rita.

No worries. Y'all taking a trip?

Yes. Mitch left me a note. Just me and him.

It'll do both of you good. He works too hard, and you worry too much. I got everything here. Don't worry about Bruce or your home. We'll look after both.

Thank you.

Valorie finished the roll, scooping the dripped icing up with her fork and licking her lips after devouring it. The plate washed and put away, she poured another cup of coffee and took it upstairs. Reclining in the chaise lounge, she read a quick devotional, half paying attention to the words. Her thoughts drifted to the trip. What should she pack? Mitch loved driving and surprises. Her? Not so much.

Road trip.

Valorie lunged from the chair, almost spilling her coffee. Road trips meant snacks. She needed a quick trip to the grocery store. Maybe surprise Mitch with a sumptuous picnic lunch. They could stop along the way—pretend they had no kids, no mortgage, no worries.

She bolted upstairs and set her mug on the dresser, pulled out a suitcase, and tossed clothes into it. Her spirit lifting, a song escaped as a hum, relaxing tense muscles and filling her with a modicum of hope.

If it didn't rain, they could have a wonderful few days. Maybe she should call her mother, make sure they could keep the kids longer. What if they couldn't? They might be tired of watching them, keeping up with such vivacious littles. Maybe they shouldn't ask so much of her parents. A cloud appeared over the joy she felt moments earlier.

As if reading her mind, the phone buzzed.

"Hey, Mom. I was just about to call you."

"Oh, good. Everything alright?"

"Yes. There?"

"Oh goodness, yes. The kids have been perfect angels, as usual. We're having so much fun with them. Michele helped make cookies yesterday afternoon, and of course, we go to the beach in the morning and late afternoon."

"Please tell me you put sunscreen on them."

"Of course, dear. That's also why we go in the morning and late afternoon. I know you don't want them out in the middle of the day when it's hottest. And I don't want them to get sunburns either."

"Thank you. I worry too much, but I'd never forgive myself if they ended up with skin cancer because I didn't protect them."

"I know." Her mother paused. "Listen, your father had a wonderful idea. He wants to take the kids over to Orange Beach for a day at Adventure Island. Plus, we already planned a zoo day, and little Mitchell really wants to go to the wildlife refuge. You know how much he loves animals."

Valorie chuckled. "He adores animals. I swear that boy will become a veterinarian when he grows up. But that's a lot. You don't have to do so much. They love just spending time with you and Dad."

"But we want to. I mean, we've got them now, and next month we have the cruise, and then before you know it, summer ends, and they're back in school. If we don't do it now, we might not get to it this summer."

"I don't want to wear you both out."

"Oh, we're fine. We make them take rest breaks every afternoon—bribe them with the afternoon beach trip." Her mother laughed. "Your dad and I might doze off, but the kids read or play quietly. They know to stay inside, and we put the upper locks on the doors, so they can't get out if they tried."

"That makes me feel better."

"Anyway, we can't do all we want in a day or two, so that's why I called. We want to keep them a few extra days."

"Really? Are you sure?"

"Absolutely."

Valorie glanced at the open suitcase. "Well... Mitch came home unexpectedly yesterday afternoon, and he went to the office today, but he's coming home early. He wants to take a short trip. I don't have any details, but..."

"That's perfect then. You need us to keep them a few extra days, and we want to keep them longer. I love it when God's plans come together without our help."

"Yeah." Valorie didn't concede God's hand in any of it, but it was nice when things worked out perfectly.

"I planned on buying the kids a few cute outfits anyway, so we'll go shopping this afternoon. Or I'll simply wash their clothes. They stay in their swimsuits most of the day anyhow." She laughed again. "Oops. I wasn't supposed to tell you that."

"I wouldn't let them, but you are grandparents, so..."

“Ha. Not that I needed your permission, but thank you, dear. Now you and Mitch have a wonderful getaway, and don’t worry about anything. The kids are fine, and I’m not letting them have sugar—well, not too much anyway.”

“Yeah, right.” Valorie smiled to herself. Her parents let the kids get away with far too much, but they watched them like hawks. Hopefully, she could let go of the what ifs. Relief washed over her, knowing the man in the van didn’t hurt them.

She considered asking her mother if she saw the van over there, but she didn’t want to get into that. Besides, she still needed to run to the grocery store. After finishing the call, she showered in ten minutes and threw on a summer dress she knew Mitch loved. Putting on a touch of makeup and pulling her hair into a ponytail, she grabbed her keys and headed to the grocery store, making sure she set the alarm.

Chapter 6

VALIDATION—MAYBE

VALORIE WANDERED THE AISLES, handpicking ingredients for the surprise picnic. In the fruit section, she looked up at a lovely young woman. Familiarity stared back at her. They gazed at each other, both glancing down at produce, then at each other. After a few minutes, the dark-haired woman approached and placed a hand on her arm. Valorie flinched and jerked her arm away. A tingle raced through her body, her vision blurring. She backed up, grasping the side of the apple bin.

"You're real," the woman said. "It wasn't a dream."

The sounds dimmed as Valorie studied the face. Why did she know her? Why did she want to run—far and fast? She drew in a sharp breath. Her mouth flew open. "My dream. Y... you... you were in the dungeon." Valorie swallowed. "Wait. You mean it happened? I'm not losing my mind?"

"I wondered about that myself, thinking I had a nightmare. But you're here. I'm here. It happened."

"How?" Valorie wobbled. "Wait. You... you're... you're the one who cut me."

"My name's Shamira. And yes, I did. I'm so sorry. Valorie, right?"

"Y... yes."

Shamira grasped Valorie's arm. "I am truly sorry. That dungeon played with our minds—all of us."

Distance. Put distance between them. Valorie looked at other shoppers. A head or two turned their way, but flipped back when she tried to lock eyes. She turned back to the woman—Shamira.

"But it can't be real. We spent days there—in my dream anyway—but no time passed. I woke up the next morning after I saw the white van..." Valorie covered her face. "It can't be real. I'm imagining this—imagining you."

"No, Valorie. I'm real. You're real. I can't explain any of it, how Drake did it, or why we woke up as if no time passed. As insane as it all sounds... it happened." Her eyes widened as she placed a hand over her chest.

Valorie shook her head. "No. I think not." She closed her eyes, forcing deep breaths before reopening them. "What are you doing here in Gulf Shores?"

"I didn't wait to see if Drake showed up at the restaurant where I worked. When I woke yesterday, I left a drunken boyfriend passed out, took money I hid from him, went to my job, quit, and got my paycheck. Then, in case it was a repeat of the day Drake enticed me, I got in my old truck and took off."

"He enticed you?" Valorie squinted.

"Yeah. Promised me a better life. Isn't that how he got you to the dungeon?"

"No." She rubbed her forehead, not wanting to remember. A picture filled her mind. "He... kidnapped me... out of my bed. At least I think, but... not. It didn't happen."

"If you dreamed it, I had the same one."

"And you came here? Why?"

"I'm passing through. I had no idea how to find you or any of the other women except Charissa. She's a nurse in a small-town hospital. I remembered that much, so I'm driving to Texas, looking for her."

"Charissa? Who's that?"

"She's the key—the reason Drake lured us all into his trap. Except for you, I guess. I didn't know he kidnapped you. That's horrible. He pitted us against each other and Charissa, trying to break her. But she rescued us. Her and Haniel—her friend. Don't you remember?"

"Not much. I thought... My husband and neighbor both convinced me it wasn't real. And I won't think about it. I don't like the parts I can't unsee."

"You got the worst of it. I hate all you endured. And I am so sorry I cut your arm."

"I didn't dream it?" She held out her arm. "You left these on me?"

Shamira nodded, casting her eyes to the floor. When she looked up, her chin trembled, wetness flooding her eyes. She placed fingers on the lines. "I did, and I'm ashamed. It's one thing if I do it to myself, but I had no right to cut you. Please forgive me."

A man reached around them. "Excuse me. Some of us want an apple."

Rude. Valorie stepped forward and nodded, swallowing a knot. "OK." She didn't trust herself to say more.

Shamira sighed. "I gotta find Charissa—at least try. Come with me."

"Are you crazy? I don't know you. My family's here. My husband and kids—my parents. Even if I wanted to, I can't run off to Texas. If you're right and all that stuff happened..." She shuddered. "Texas has nothing for me. Go, and I hope you find what you need. I'm good right here, safe with my husband, doors bolted, and an alarm to keep me safe."

Shamira moved toward Valorie, reaching for her, then stopped. "I understand. But don't let your guard down. I think Drake still has plans for all of us. Keep your eyes open and your spirit listening. Stand firm in faith."

"Faith hasn't gotten me all that far in life. But I'll be more cautious than ever."

"Good. Don't let fear paralyze you, though. If you do, that evil man wins at his game. Don't give him that pleasure."

Easy for her to say. Valorie didn't know how she could fight back against the evil she sensed despite the holes in the memories of her dream. She shivered again, rubbing her bare arms.

The nightmare somehow happened. How?

Shamira pulled out her phone. "Give me your phone number. I'll let you know when I find Charissa."

Valorie hesitated. Did she dare? What if this woman was part of the evil man's plan to take her again? She locked eyes with Shamira, weighing what she saw and felt. She pulled out her phone, knowing she could always block and delete the number.

"Alright."

After exchanging numbers, Shamira gave her a brief hug. Valorie didn't return or encourage it. The women finished choosing fruit and parted ways with a promise to stay in touch. Valorie trembled, still trying to grasp a reality that couldn't be true.

Finished with shopping, she pushed her cart to the door and stopped. Her gaze darted around the parking lot, searching for anything unordinary. She checked beneath cars, scanning for a body, arm, foot. Anything. Quivering, she clutched her keys and hurried to the car. As she loaded groceries, she kept looking up, searching for a white panel van.

If Shamira existed, and the dungeon existed, so did Drake.

Was he waiting to grab her again?

She headed home, constantly checking the rearview mirror. Nothing.

Valerie pulled into the driveway and stared into the distance. How could she explain meeting Shamira in the grocery store? Mitch wouldn't believe it.

That meant she'd never tell him. With car doors still locked, she pulled out her phone and looked up the self-defense course. She punched in the number and hit send.

Chapter 7

A Plot

DAGON LEANED BACK ON the sofa in Drake's office, sipping a Black Russian. "Too bad about Smitty's accident."

"Whatever. Morons should never play with guns." Drake's coal-black eyes drilled into his soul.

Dagon controlled a shiver, although he knew better than to cross his boss. He'd never admit knowing the truth about what happened between Drake and Smitty. No taking chances of having a similar 'accident.'

"What we do now, boss?"

"Haven't you lost that Russian accent yet?"

Dagon shrugged. "Sorry, boss. I try."

Drake rolled his eyes. "Why take them captive again? I had all six women under my power. Thanks to you imbeciles, they got away. And Charissa... She's stronger than before. I lost her. Forever. She's closer to my sworn enemy than she ever dreamed of becoming. And her new relationship with the doctor? He encourages and leads her to maintain faith."

So dramatic. Dagon bit his upper lip then took another sip. "But you have plan, da?"

"I lost Charissa, and of course, the power-hungry wench, but the others... They're weaklings. I might win their allegiance—if I can break them down before they figure out what happened."

"Impressive plan. Who you want I pursue first?"

Drake ran his fingernails through his beard. "The terrified one. Easy target. I think they forced her to run rather than her deciding to leave. She didn't have the guts. I could have kept her for the rest of her life—if not for the others. Simple task. She fears everything. I already made her face the worst fear by taking her from where she felt safe."

Dagon licked his upper lip, intrigued. "Nice."

"Not. Nothing pleasurable about it. I fueled her fear, and that was my plan. I suspect she won't recover easily, even if she believes the entire incident wasn't real."

Dagon leaned forward. "What now? Repeat?"

"No, you idiot. Find out what else she fears and make those terrors realities."

"She run to you, da?"

"Yes. Because when she reaches her lowest, perhaps I'll step in, charming her back to my lair."

"I like. We make happen now?"

"You can't rush something like this. While you watch Valorie, I'll send others to spy on the rest of the women."

Dagon downed the rest of his drink. "I understand. No rush. I watch."

"Watch and learn."

"Da, boss." He stood, ready to leave.

Drake's voiced hardened. "And Dagon—check in with me but do nothing until I say move. Above all, make sure she has no contact with any of the other women. The plan all falls apart if they see each other. They'll know the dungeon happened, and that cannot be the case. They must believe it was all a horrible nightmare."

"Got it, boss. Watch, wait, report back. I do job well. You see. I no moron."

As he turned, Dagon smiled to himself, determined to show his boss. And with all the women back in the dungeon, he'd take out Drake—and enjoy them himself.

Chapter 8

Marine Buddies

Chad Tyler stepped off the airplane and strolled through the jetway. A light traveler out of habit, he shifted his duffel bag, thankful he didn't need to wait for luggage at a carousel.

A man headed straight toward him, paying more attention to his phone than the surroundings. Chad started to sidestep, avoiding a collision, but something familiar about the man stopped him. He squinted, possibilities racing through his thoughts.

As he looked up, the phone man drew back his head. "Tyler? Chad Tyler?"

"Ha. It is you. Captain Mitch Ferguson." Chad saluted. "Technically, it's Major Tyler—at least until a few days ago. Now, just Chad."

"What?" Mitch grinned, saluted back, and grasped Chad's arm. "You finally left the Marines?"

"After 20 years, seemed like the right time."

"Two-and-a-half times longer than I wanted, brother." Mitch lifted an eyebrow. "So, what are you doing here in Florida?"

Chad pulled Mitch to the side as passengers hurried past them. "I could ask the same of you. Don't you live in Gulf Shores?"

"Yeah. Returning from a business trip—the final. Maybe a few random later."

"Last time we talked, you mentioned traveling a lot. New job?"

"Sorta. They finally promoted me. Now I get to send other people on trips while I run things from the office. My wife couldn't be happier."

"I bet."

A flight announcement came over the PA, stopping the conversation for a moment.

"So, Major Tyler retired?" Mitch scratched his chin. "Why are you here?"

As a Marine trudged past, glancing up at gate numbers, Chad saluted him, then looked down at his jeans and T-shirt before shrugging and flashing a smile. "Well, I planned to rent a car and drive to Gulf Shores, looking for you."

"No way. Why?"

Chad looked down, heat consuming his face. "I'm lost, Captain. Don't know what comes next. All this time, I never forgot you."

"Hey—just Mitch, brother. I walked away from the rank long ago."

"Yes sir. You put your degree to use, unlike those of us who re-upped. You saved more than my life back then. Your faith set standards. I went through the years determined to model the same for my men. You always knew what to say or do, when, and how—to calm my troubled soul and lead me."

"I did all that?"

"Yes. For me and dozens who knew and respected you."

Mitch shrugged. "If I believed in coincidences, I'd be amazed we ended up bumping into each other at the airport."

"Almost literally. You should look up instead of at your phone while maneuvering a busy airport."

They both laughed. Mitch said, "I know. Valorie always wants to know when I land. She's terrified my plane will crash. Honestly, she's terrified about everything."

"Good thing your traveling days are ending."

Mitch ran a hand over his face. "Hey, I have an idea. I'm parked at the terminal. Let's get my car, grab some lunch, drive back to Gulf Shores, and catch up. I'll call Valorie and tell her to expect a guest for dinner. I can always take you to a hotel or something later."

"Man, I don't want to impose."

"No imposition. I should have kept in touch with you better. The few letters—not enough. I can't wait to hear why you resigned."

"Retired, buddy. Retired—with the emphasis on tired."

"Gotcha." Mitch headed to an exit. "You got bags."

"The one on my shoulder."

"Me too. Some habits don't die. Light and quick, huh?"

"Exactly."

"Let's go."

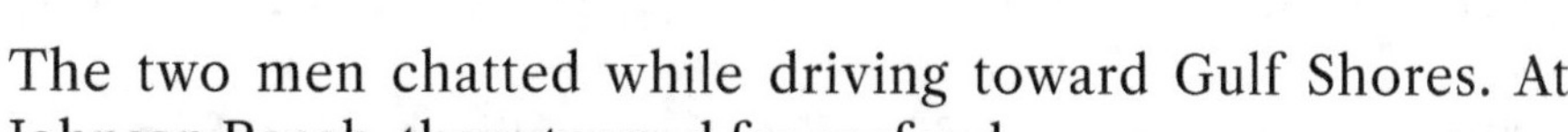

The two men chatted while driving toward Gulf Shores. At Johnson Beach, they stopped for seafood.

Settled with drinks and orders placed, Mitch ventured to deeper subjects. "Why did you decide to retire? I expected you to stay in until you reached General."

"Hardly. I didn't really want Major, but I enjoyed the instructor side of it, and the pay increases didn't hurt. The thought of staying in another four years, maybe reaching Lieutenant Colonel... I couldn't—too much."

"Too much what?"

"Too much politics, too much immorality, and too much loss. One too many wars, and they'll never end. Watching widows with children cry—bad enough. But powerful men dropping to their knees—weeping over a lost wife? No kids should grow up without a daddy, but babies growing up without Mama? I couldn't stand it anymore."

"Wow. Never thought of all that. Two tours gave me more conflicts than I wanted."

Chad sipped his drink and paused while the young waitress placed plates before them and winked at him.

He rolled his eyes. "These women flirting with me, even out of uniform. Crazy. Enough about me. What about your family?"

Mitch chuckled. "We met soon after my discharge, dated for a few years before I proposed. After a year of wedding plans, we finally got married. Neither wanted to hurry into parenthood. For the first five years, we both worked, traveled a lot on weekends, and enjoyed amazing trips. Then Mitchell Jr. surprised us about eight years ago, followed by Michele two years later. Kids change everything. We moved to Gulf Shores so Valorie's parents could help with the kids. I settled into building my career."

"Sounds like a fantastic life."

"Mostly." Mitch's eyes clouded.

The waitress returned and refilled their glasses, looking straight at Chad. "Anything else, sugar?"

"No thank you." Chad forced a smile. She sashayed from the table, and he looked back at Mitch. "Mostly fantastic, but?"

"No but."

"God don't like liars."

Mitchell laughed. "That ain't fair—turning my words on me."

"Something bothering you, brother. See it in your eyes."

"It... I... Valorie gets so paranoid. Not a little anxious, but full-on terrified for no reason."

"Unhealthy level?"

"You know how some of our buddies ended up with PTSD? Like that level. Something triggers her, and she shuts down completely. We have five deadbolt locks on both the front and back doors, a special bolt on our balcony door, and a quality alarm system. She barely goes out these days."

"Did something happen to her?"

"Not that I can put my finger on. They lived through a hurricane during her childhood—lost everything. But that doesn't account for these unrealistic fears."

"Fear stems back to a traumatic event. Maybe she doesn't remember or simply refuses to revisit it. Or she doesn't want to tell anyone what happened."

"Maybe. She went to counseling, and it helped. At least, I thought it did. But a month ago, I came home from a trip, and she almost stabbed me. Threw a tomato instead of the knife." Mitch licked his lips and filled his fork. "Thank God for the tomato in her hand."

Chad laughed. "I'm glad she didn't throw the knife. Did you figure out what caused it?"

"Not really. She said a van followed her home. She called the cops, but they found nothing. I'm not sure they took her seriously. She has a habit of hearing people trying to break in anytime I go out of town. When I came home, she shared this bizarre dream and swore it happened."

"Could it?"

"Nah. In her dream, she spent days in a dungeon. After a couple nights away, I came back early because she sounded so distraught."

"Hmmm. Maybe she needs more counseling."

"Thank you. Exactly what I said. Talk about a pissed wife. Made it up to her with an out-of-town getaway. She seemed almost like the old Valorie I met and fell in love with. Until we got back home. Instead of making an appointment with her counselor, she signed up for a self-defense class."

"That sounds like a plan. Maybe if she feels capable of defending herself, she can let go of some fears."

"Maybe. But she obsessed over these classes, signing up for more. Sometimes, I ring the doorbell, so she knows I'm home. I sure don't want her decking me when I walk in the front door."

CRASH!

Chad jumped, moving his right hand to his hip. He shook his head and released a breath. Poor server—whole tray down.

Mitch raised his eyebrows. "Nervous?"

"Sorry buddy. Are you sure I should come home with you?"

"Not if you jump at every loud sound." He grinned. "But yeah. She's not crazy all the time, and I want you to meet her and the kids. If anything ever happened to me, I'm sure you'd watch out for them. I trust you more than anyone I know."

"Of course. But don't go dying on me, man. I ain't ready to take on a crazy widow and two kids."

They both laughed and finished their meals with lighter conversation. After paying the bill, Mitch called Valorie and told her about running into Chad.

Finished with the call, he said, "All set. She's delighted and already planning what to make for dinner. We might need to make a quick stop by the grocery store. And she said not to think about going to a hotel. She won't have my long-lost Marine brother staying anywhere besides with us."

"We'll see about that. I prefer privacy these days."

"Copy that."

The friends strolled to the door, Chad ready for a less talkative, short drive to the Ferguson home. Less certain about his decision to look up Mitch, given the situation with the wife. He couldn't help wondering why he felt compelled.

As they stepped into the bright sunlight, Mitch looked at a text on his phone. "Valorie with her 'short' grocery list."

He stepped to the curb, keyed the reply, and looked up.

Chad smiled and flipped a gum wrapper into a nearby trashcan. When he looked back, the world distorted into slow motion. He reached out. "Mitch!"

A sickening thud reverberated against his ears, a white panel van rolling over his buddy and speeding away.

Pounding blood rushed through his ears, his eyes trying to comprehend the scene playing before him. "Nooo!"

He bolted to Mitch's side. "Stay with me, brother. Stay with me."

Mitch reached up a hand, blood oozing from his mouth and ears. "Chad... I... Don't... forget. Val... kids... Protect them."

"I got 'em, Captain. Don't worry. I got them. Just stay with me." He refused to accept defeat. "You'll be OK. Hang on." A crowd gathered. Chad looked up. "Call 9-1-1."

A woman nodded, already talking into her phone.

A hand grasped Chad's shirt. "Remember."

The hand fell, eyes glazing over as a last breath sputtered from Mitch's body.

Chapter 9

Police at the Door

Valorie looked at her phone again. Mitch's last text—1:29 p.m. She glanced at her watch again, the pot roast filling the kitchen with a savory aroma. Much longer and it wouldn't be fit to eat. Mitch promised to drop by the store, but when he didn't make it home by 3:30, she packed up the kids and went herself, leaving him a voicemail.

She dialed his number for the tenth time. Still no answer.

JR strolled into the kitchen, the back of his hand against his forehead. "When's dinner, Mom? I'm famished."

"So dramatic. I am impressed with the big word, though."

He threw her a wide grin. "Really? I been reading—lots."

Valorie ruffled his hair.

"But seriously, Mom, the smell in here keeps distracting me from playing."

Michele joined them. "Me, too. I'm hungry."

"We're waiting for Daddy to get home. He ran into an old friend who's coming with him."

"But where are they?" Michele's whining didn't help Valorie's nerves.

"I'm sure they'll be here any minute." She looked at the clock again. 6:52. "Go wash up while I make your plates. I'll call Daddy again—can't imagine why they aren't home."

But Valorie could imagine. In her mind, Mitch's blood lay splattered on the highway, the victim of a tragic auto accident.

Not that she wanted to voice it, but as she picked two plates off the table, her hands twitched.

After dialing his number again, she placed food on the plates for her kids. “Not fair to make the kids wait because Daddy and his friend stopped off for a drink or something.” Her nostrils flared as heat rushed over her body. “He could’ve at least called.”

Both kids stormed into the dining room. “Who could’ve called?” JR fixed his gaze on her.

“No one, honey. Mommy’s a little frustrated with Daddy.”

“Aren’t you gonna eat with us?” Michele smiled, easing a bit of tension.

“I should wait for Daddy, since he’s bringing a friend. But you two go ahead. I know you’re both *famished*.” She forced a smile and checked her phone.

No calls or texts.

Thirty minutes later, Michele and JR picked at each other, only half their food eaten.

Valorie slammed her phone on the table. “Enough. Both of you. Get upstairs and put on your pajamas. I’ll be up to help you brush teeth and get into bed.”

“But Mom...” JR furrowed his brows.

“No buts. You both had a long day with your grandparents.

“But we didn’t take a bath.” Michele poked out her bottom lip.

Valorie gritted her teeth. “I said enough. No buts. Get upstairs.”

“Yes, ma’am.” Both children scooted back from the table, still poking each other and squealing.

Rubbing her forehead, Valorie took their plates to the sink, scraping the leftovers down the disposal. She rinsed them off, tapping her foot, and tossed them into the dishwasher. She didn’t care if they broke or whether they got clean.

Finished, she wiped the counter, retrieved her phone, and then tossed it back on the table before heading up the stairs.

With the kids finally asleep, Valorie tiptoed back downstairs, expecting to find Mitch and his friend lounging in the den. The stillness unnerved her as she glared at the front door, willing the two men to walk through. As usual, her thoughts did little good. She checked her phone again, hoping Mitch called or sent a text.

Still nothing. She tried calling him yet again, but his phone went straight to voicemail.

With a quick retreat to the dining room, she picked up her plate, ventured to the kitchen, and filled it with food. Although she kept it warming in the oven, she didn't look forward to ingesting dry food. Her stomach growled, demanding she eat, regardless of her less-than-enthusiastic appetite. After a few bites, she took the half-filled plate and dumped the remains of dinner into the garbage disposal.

She rubbed her neck, pacing around the kitchen. When Mitch called, he promised to be home within the hour. Seven hours later, no sign of the men and no answer to her repeated calls.

What happened?

Valorie chewed a thumbnail, pushing images to the back of her mind. If he had an accident, someone would call. Right?

As minutes clicked away, she meandered through the house—to the den, back to the living room, retreating to the kitchen again as if Mitch sneaked in while she paced. She looked out the back window, wondering whether they might be outside on the patio.

Nothing except Bruce lying on his cushion, his head resting on his paws.

She picked up the phone, preparing to call Mitch again, and jumped when the doorbell rang.

"Finally."

Valorie rushed to the living room, disarmed the alarm, and looked through the peephole. To her surprise, two uniformed police officers stood at the door instead of her husband.

Chills dropped into her belly, her entire body filling with tremors. She unlocked the deadbolts and slowly opened the door.

"Yes?"

"Are you Mrs. Mitch Ferguson?"

Valorie nodded, her breath catching.

"May we come in?"

She tried to speak, but nothing came out. Clearing her throat, she tried again. "Yes. Please."

The female officer glanced around the room. "Are you alone, ma'am?"

"My kids are upstairs asleep. What's this about?"

"Please, come over here to the sofa."

Valorie shook her head. "No! Tell me!" Tears flooded her eyes, spilling down her cheeks. "It's my husband, isn't it?"

The officer cleared her throat, eyes glistening as she peered at her partner.

He said, "We have some bad news, Mrs. Ferguson. A hit-and-run vehicle struck Mitchell Ferguson around 1:30 this afternoon. Because of the ongoing investigation, we couldn't notify you before now. The paramedics did all they could, but he died at the scene."

Knees buckling, Valorie collapsed, a loud wail escaping. "Nooooo! No. It can't be true. I talked to him. At 1:29. No. He's not dead."

"I'm sorry," the female crouched beside her. "Let me help you up."

Valorie jerked away from the officer. "Go away. I know Mitch's on his way home. He'll be here any minute. He and his friend stopped somewhere. That's all."

The officers both shook their heads, staring at her.

"What? I know he's alive. I..." She crumbled, pressing hands over her ears, not wanting to hear anything else.

The male officer joined his partner, crouching beside Valorie, gently pulling her hands down. "I am sorry, ma'am. Can we call someone for you?"

Valorie sobbed. "My dad. I need my daddy."

Chapter 10

Reality

A TALL MARINE STOOD before Valorie. White gloves, crisp uniform, no emotion in his face—except the glistening in his eyes. Did he know Mitch? He placed the folded American flag in Valorie's hands. She cringed, grateful Mitch's parents didn't insist on a 21-gun salute.

Flanked by her son and daughter, she tried not to look at Mitch's mom. Tears rushed down her cheeks as his father leaned toward his wife. While he kept tears hidden, the puffiness surrounding his eyes told her he shed many before they got to the cemetery.

She glanced at the never-ending line. Where had all the people in uniform come from? They filed past, leaning down and offering condolences. Each spoke of Mitch's honor and impact. That should make her proud of him. Staring at his casket, their words only made her angry.

How dare he leave her alone with two kids to raise? She cared less how much he influenced all these men. Who would influence their son and daughter?

Her father placed a hand on her shoulder, steadying her as he always did. As another stranger approached, Valorie dabbed at wet spots beneath her eyes, fighting the rude words inching closer to the surface.

Two young women squatted before her, each reaching for a hand.

She blinked and shook her head. "Shamira?"

"Yes, honey. We're here."

"But how... I don't understand."

Shamira squeezed Valorie's hand. "A woman called. Rita, I think. When she told me what happened, I begged Charissa to come with me. We can only stay a few days, but we wanted to be here for you."

Valorie looked at the other woman. "So... Charissa? The dungeon I dreamed about."

A soft smile covered Charissa's face. "Yes. I can't explain it either. We both thought we dreamed about the dungeon, but when Shamira showed up..." She shrugged. "No explanation. How else do we know each other?"

Thoughts scrambled, Valorie attempting to make sense of these two women showing up at Mitch's graveside service.

Her father patted her shoulder, indicating a long line of people lingering to console her.

She looked back at the two women. "Can you come by the house later? I'm sorry. So many people loved Mitch."

"Of course. We'll wait over there."

They walked past a row of markers to the road.

Valorie looked up at the next stranger and reapplied what she hoped resembled a stoic face.

As the line melted away, the flag Marine kneeled on one knee before her. "Valorie, I'm sorry we didn't meet before this. I came by the night of..." He cleared his throat. "I'm Chad, Mitch's friend."

"You were with him."

"Yes."

Heat rushed through her body as she stared into honey-brown eyes, tensing as she drew in steady breaths. "Why didn't you do something?"

Chad hung his head. "It happened too fast. He stepped off the curb and... I couldn't do anything." He blinked several times and inhaled. "I owed Mitch my life—literally. If I could take his place, I would in a heartbeat."

Valorie softened. "It's not your fault. I'm sorry." She searched his eyes again. "You're hurting too."

He nodded. “I still have his car. Your dad told me to use it, but I’ll bring it by the house.”

“No rush. I never drive Mitch’s car, and I sure couldn’t now.” Tears escaped then, unstoppable grief washing over her.

Chad wrapped arms around her and let her weep into his shoulder.

She pulled away and wiped at the wetness. “Please come by the house. We have too much food. I just need one more minute here with the kids.” Her children appeared by her side with red-rimmed eyes and runny noses. JR swiped at the nastiness with the sleeve of his suit.

Chad stood and ruffled the little boy’s hair. “I’ll wait over there in case you need me.”

As he walked toward Shamira and Charissa, Valorie stood, legs wobbling. Her dad reached out and grabbed her arm, his strength increasing hers. Steadied, she reached down and took Michele’s and JR’s hands. “Let’s say goodbye to Daddy one last time.”

After more tears and hugs, a few more times of touching the casket, her dad finally pulled her away. “It’s time to go, Valorie.” His voice quivered, but he stood beside her, the rock he’d always been.

She nodded, wiped her cheeks, drew in a wavering breath, and turned toward the groups of people waiting.

So many people.

Lord, how could she get through the rest of the day?

“Daddy, I can’t bear it. Please. Must I endure more ‘I’m sorry’?”

“For a bit. We’ll be there, though. These people hurt, too. They loved Mitch. Can you hold on a little longer?”

“No.” Then she nodded. “Maybe if you’re there. Thank you.”

The world around her blurred as she approached the small group near her dad’s car. She still didn’t know what to make of Charissa, Shamira, and even Chad, yet their presence drew her.

All three faced her, concern shimmering in the afternoon sunlight.

Valorie turned to the kids. "Go with PawPaw and Mimi. I'll be there soon."

Mitch's parents took their hands. "We'll take them home so they can play. No rush. We'll be there to greet family and close friends."

"Thank you." Valorie's breath quivered. "They've had enough of all these people."

Mr. Ferguson nodded. "Not just them." He side-hugged her and took off.

"Wait!" Valorie moved toward them.

Poppa turned around, scowling, while JR and Michele tugged at their hands. "What?"

"Please keep them inside until I get there. I won't be long."

"Sure." The older image of Mitch turned back and hurried the kids to their car.

With an uneasy feeling, Valorie turned back to Chad and her dungeon friends, biting her upper lip. "I have so many questions."

"I know." Charissa gently touched her shoulder. "Shamira and I talked nonstop when she first found me, and she told me about running into you at the store."

"I don't know what to think anymore. The last few days... a blur. I can't focus on anything."

Chad shook his head. "Me too. I can't imagine how you feel."

Valorie puffed out air, an inner chill brushing against her bare arms. "But this place... I don't want to talk here. Follow us to the house. We'll change clothes, greet people, eat. Later, when it quiets down, we can sit and talk."

They nodded in agreement.

As Valorie turned to the car, she stopped and gasped. Across the street, a dark-suited man stared at her, then cackled as he flashed a broad smile. He gave her a two-finger salute and climbed into the back seat of a Mercedes.

By her side, Chad touched her elbow. "Do you know him?"

Wide-eyed, she stared at the vehicle.

Charissa and Shamira stood behind her. "Was that...?"

"Couldn't be." Valorie tensed. "Could it?"

Shamira drew back as the car zoomed past, tinted windows hiding the occupants. "If not, Drake has a twin."

Chad stepped forward. "Who's Drake?"

Valorie shuddered. "That's a conversation for later."

Chapter 11

The Funeral

CHAD FOLLOWED, WONDERING ABOUT the man in the Mercedes. The apparent stranger rattled Valorie and the other women. They must know him, and from their responses, not in a good way.

And that laugh? Rude at a funeral. Goosebumps trickled across his arms. Something evil about that man.

He shook off the feelings. Maybe he should talk to someone. Watching Mitch die messed him up. He hadn't slept well since. No wonder his senses tingled at everything. Chad sighed, trying to pay attention to the traffic surrounding him, dreading the interaction with his buddy's family. But he needed to be there—to make sure Valorie and the kids didn't need him.

He wished Mitch told him more about his wife. Distraught, yes. He expected that, but she seemed normal enough. Surrounded by family and friends, he toyed with the idea of his buddy over-dramatizing the fear issue. It didn't matter.

"I promised, Captain, and I won't let you down."

As they approached the house, Chad surveyed the area. So many cars. It didn't surprise him. Everyone loved Mitch. Parking down the street, he eyed every vehicle. No black Mercedes. After cracking his neck, he walked, keeping an eye open for anything that looked like trouble. Satisfied with his surveillance, he crossed the yard at the same time as Charissa and Shamira. Should he question them about the man?

Before he approached them, Valorie exited the family car, wringing a handkerchief. He moved toward her instead. The two women did the same. They obviously intended to protect her, too. For the moment, he could be alright with that. At least until he knew more about them.

Inside, he kept his distance, observing, listening, and trying to figure out all the dynamics. One thing he knew for certain. With so many people in the house, he wouldn't talk with Valorie alone for hours. He could wait.

Dishes clean, leftover food tucked away in the refrigerator and freezer, Chad dried his hands. At least he did something helpful. Uncertain how to approach Valorie, he sauntered into the living room. Shamira ushered the last visitor out of the door while Valorie leaned back in the recliner and closed her eyes.

Her mom came around the corner with a plate and two cups. "Chad, thank you for all the help. Not sure how these made it upstairs, but I think it's the last of all the dishes. I'll clean these up."

He crossed to her, hand outstretched. "Please. Let me take them, Mrs. Daniels."

She waved him away. "You've done plenty. Go relax. I got this."

Chad shrugged, grinned, and trekked across the room to an empty chair near the sofa. Shamira and Charissa slumped on opposite ends. Valorie's dad came from the back of the house and ventured to the second recliner. He gently placed a hand on his daughter's arm.

"Valorie."

Her eyes popped open. "Oh, hi Dad."

"You look exhausted, baby girl."

"All those people."

"They all love you, honey."

"I know. It's just... Too much."

As her eyes filled, Chad looked away, refusing to see the tears come again.

Her dad spoke again. "You did fine." He patted her shoulder. "I fed Bruce and locked up the back door for you. Your mom got the kids bathed and in bed, but they want you to tell them good night."

Valorie nodded. "I'll go." She shuffled across the room and dragged herself upward.

Mrs. Daniels appeared from the kitchen. "Does anyone need anything else?"

The two women and Chad all shook their heads.

Mr. Daniels rose and threw his arm around his wife. "Maybe a good night's sleep now that we're past the funeral."

Chad stood. "Have you both been here since..." He swallowed.

They nodded.

"If you want to go home, I'll stay. I can sleep right here on the sofa—keep an eye on Valorie and the kids. Make sure everyone's safe."

Charissa said, "We planned to get a hotel room, but Valorie insisted we stay here. We'll be in the guest room."

Shamira nodded. "I think you two should go home tonight. Valorie will need you more after we go home. You can get a good night's sleep and take your time coming back."

Mr. Daniels rubbed his lower lip. "It sure would be nice to sleep in my bed. And I didn't have a chance to check mail or anything." He turned to his wife. "What do you think?"

"Are you three sure? I mean..."

"Don't give it another thought." Chad moved closer to the couple. "Shamira's right. I'll be around for a while, but you could use a night off. Let us take over for you here."

Mrs. Daniels blinked her eyes. "My daughter has good friends." She grabbed a notepad from the bar and wrote a phone number. "Here's our number if you need us to come back."

"Thank you, ma'am." Chad accepted the paper from her. "I don't think that will happen, but it's good to have your number in case. It'll take time before Valorie's anywhere close to normal."

A silent affirmation filled the room.

After a minute, Mr. Daniels cleared his throat. "I'll go up and tell Valorie and then get our bags." He turned to Mrs. Daniels again. "You alright down here?"

"I'll come up and say goodnight, too. Besides, I do not trust you to get all my stuff."

"Hmpf." Mr. Daniels put on an indignant face, but the twinkle in his eyes belied any offense.

The older couple ascended the stairs, and Chad turned to the two ladies in the room. "While we're alone, what do you two know about the man in the Mercedes?"

"Drake?" Charissa shook her head. "Wait until Valorie's parents leave, and we'll talk." She glanced up the staircase. "He's bad news. And the story the three of us ladies share sounds far-fetched. We don't talk about it—not sure we believe it ourselves."

"I'm intrigued." He ran his hand over the stubble on his chin. "I need to pull Mitch's car into the driveway. Parked way down the street. Do you ladies need me to move your car? Help with bags?"

Charissa answered. "No, we did that earlier. But thanks." She sank back into the sofa. "By the way, how do you know Valorie?"

"I didn't until today—at least not in person. Mitch and I served in the Marines together. I flew into Pensacola and ran across him at the airport. He insisted I come with him and meet Valorie and the kids. We stopped for lunch. Neither of us had eaten." Chad clenched his teeth.

Shamira's eyes flew wide. "The day of the accident?"

He nodded, swallowing a massive knot growing in his throat. He tried to ignore the pictures flashing in his brain. The van heading straight for Mitch. Never swerving or slowing. As memories toyed with his mind, a thought popped. Did the driver maintain his speed or accelerate?

Chad shook his head.

Charissa stood and moved toward him. "Chad, are you alright?"

He forced a smile. "Tired. As I'm sure you are. I'll be right back."

As he turned and surveyed the multiple locks on the door, he wondered. Was Valorie paranoid, or did she have a reason for the fear?

As Chad approached the front door, bags in hand, Valorie's parents stepped from the porch. Mrs. Daniels embraced him—again. "Are you sure about staying? You look worn out."

"And you don't?"

"Point taken. I'm sure I look pitiful."

"Not at all. But you can't hide those dark circles or the drooping eyes." He smiled. "Yet somehow, you're still beautiful."

"Hey, don't be hitting on my wife." Mr. Daniels chuckled. "I'm glad you're here, Chad. We'll sleep better knowing our daughter doesn't have to go through tonight alone. She still obsesses over that nightmare."

"Maybe God warned her of coming doom. Happened a lot in combat."

Mrs. Daniels patted his hand. "Maybe so. Thank you, anyway. And please try to get some sleep. We'll get over here as early as we can, although I doubt we can beat those two little ones."

Chad held up a hand. "Don't. You both sleep as late as possible and take your time coming back. Not sure when Valorie's friends plan to leave. I doubt she'll want me here when they go. She'll need you more then."

Mrs. Daniels smiled. "Thank you again. You're a good man—like our Mitch."

Heat rushed through his body even as a grin sneaked from his lips. His mom died many years earlier, and he missed her. He couldn't dare think of Mrs. Daniels as a mother, but he wanted to.

He waved as they climbed into the car and drove into the settling evening.

Chad scanned the neighborhood, turned, and walked through the door. Valorie sat on the sofa between her friends, eyes half-closed. She bounced up, heading toward him. "I'm glad you're back inside. Need to lock up and set the alarm."

"I got it. Relax." He crinkled his nose. "Well, I got the locks. You'll have to take care of the alarm. I don't know the code."

Despite the weariness, a warm smile crossed her face. A few bits of makeup remained, most of it washed away from tears. Still, she looked beautiful. Crazy or not, he understood why Mitch stayed with this woman. The unrealistic fear troubled him. On the day Mitch died, he brought up the excessive security. They added it when they moved into the house. Not new. Nothing to do with the Drake character or her dream.

Valorie returned to the sofa, and Chad took a chair near the women. He wanted to ask, get a feel for whether a threat existed, but eying Valorie he refrained. One night on high alert. Never hurt him before, and perhaps she'd sleep late and give him a chance to talk more with the other two women.

For the next hour, the four of them chatted, Valorie sharing fond memories laced with tears, the others listening. Chad choked back his emotions and told a few humorous stories, trying to get a laugh from Valorie. He succeeded for a moment or two before tears flowed again.

Finally, she edged off the sofa. "It's late. Perhaps we should all try to sleep. Knowing my children, they will wake us all at first light."

Charissa and Shamira nodded, both women stifling yawns.

Valorie moved toward the stairs, pausing. "Oh, no. I forgot to get sheets for you, Chad. Are you sure you want to sleep on the sofa? It's not that comfortable."

"No worries. I've slept in far worse conditions. I'll be fine with that throw."

She shrugged. "OK." Trudging up the stairs, her shoulders stooped as if they held the entire universe on them.

He took a shaky breath, turned off lights, and stretched out as soft "good nights" filtered down the steps.

Chad's eyes flew open, searching in the darkness.

Noise.

What?

He rolled and crouched beside the sofa.

Blinking. Demanding adjustment to the darkened room. A squeak on the stairs bolted him to his feet, vision clearing. "Who goes there?"

"It's me, Chad. Valorie."

His hands flew to his face, covering his eyes and rubbing. "Sorry, Valorie. You scared me."

She giggled, peeking around the wall. "I scared you? Usually, I'm the one scared of everything."

He shook his head, fumbling with the lamp switch. Soft light dispersed the darkness. He scanned the room again, making sure no one hid in shadowed corners. "Guess I slept hard." He glanced at his watch—0213 hours.

"I should be so lucky. Sorry I woke you. Came down to get a cup of tea, hoping it might relax me."

"No problem. Let me get it for you."

"No. Go back to sleep. I'll try not to make much noise." She moved toward the kitchen, paused, and turned around. "Unless you want to join me."

"I'm awake now. Not much of a hot tea fan. But I wouldn't mind a beer if you have one."

"Done." She disappeared into the kitchen and returned minutes later, a cup in one hand and a beer bottle in the other.

"Thanks." Chad motioned to the sofa. "You want to talk? Or would you rather go back to bed?"

Valorie shrugged. "I can't sleep. Keep thinking about that night. When the two of you didn't show up, I got so angry. After cooking all afternoon, the kids and I waited." She paused, looking at the dining table. "Finally broke down and fed the kids, but I fumed instead of eating. Figured you stopped off for a beer or something. Not that Mitch drank much, but he didn't always call if he was late. I ended up going to the store, angrier by the minute, because he didn't come home early enough to get what I needed for dinner." Red rimmed her eyes. "It didn't occur to me until much later that something went wrong. I put the kids to bed and came back down, wondering whether to call Mitch for the hundredth time, and swaying between worry and anger."

Chad looked at the door, imagining how worried she grew as the day drifted into night. "I should have called you. The cops took Mitch's phone, though, so I didn't know your number. And then they kept asking me questions—took me to the station for a statement. I can't imagine the horror you endured. The not knowing. Wondering why he didn't come home or call." He blew out a breath. "I came by the next morning. Your dad said you were sleeping, but I should use Mitch's car. I hope you didn't mind."

"I didn't know. Guess I've operated in a fog for days. It all seems like a dream. He'll come busting through the door any minute. Won't he?"

"I wish, Valorie. He saved my life, you know?"

She shook her head.

"In more ways than one." Chad took a sip of his drink. "Literally pushed me to the ground. Shoved me down while a hailstorm of bullets flew above us. Afterward, I realized how close I came to death. Later, I think he sensed how much it shook me. We talked for hours." Chad ran a finger around the top of his beer and set it on the coffee table. "Mitch told me about his relationship with Jesus, then invited me to pray with him. It changed me. Don't get me wrong—I loved being a Marine, despite all the death and wounds I saw." Chad leaned back. "Obviously." He grinned.

"I stayed in until retirement. But I never feared death again. He shared his faith with me, and I tried to live it the way he did."

"Mitch had strong faith. Much stronger than mine."

"You're a believer, though. Right?"

"Yes. But this fear thing won't let go. I try to trust, believe, pray. All that. After all this, I don't know if I can believe. The things I fear most—they're happening."

"Like what?"

Valorie scrunched up on the sofa, biting her lip and scratching her nose. Finally, she took a deep breath. "I always feared someone coming into my home, taking me somewhere, and raping me."

Chad's breath caught. "That happened?"

She ran fingers over her lips. "I think so."

He tilted his head. "You think? Don't you know?"

"That's just it. A couple of months ago, Mitch took a trip. My parents begged to take the kids for a couple of days—not that I relished being alone. But with them, the kids, and Mitch insisting, I dropped JR and Michele at my parents' house." She peeked around the room, pulled her knees into her chest, and continued. "This evil-looking man followed me home in a white panel van. I called the police, but they found nothing. The next morning, I woke after the most horrifying dream you can imagine. Days in a dungeon, and yes, the man raped me there—at least in my dream. My entire body ached."

Chad stirred when she paused, then leaned forward, wanting to hear the rest.

Valorie shivered and continued. "I had bruises everywhere, but I dismissed them. Everything in the house reaches up and hits me when I least expect it. Then I noticed cuts on my arm, and they matched what I remembered from my dream of someone cutting me. A woman."

The air kicked on. Both jerked.

"Geez. Even the AC scares me." Valorie chuckled. "Anyway, a day or two later, at the grocery store, I ran into Shamira and realized she was a woman from my dream—the one who cut my arm."

The hair on Chad's neck came to full attention, chills encompassing his body. "No way."

"Yes. And she experienced something similar. Seeing each other assured us both. Somehow, it all happened. It made no sense, aside from a supernatural occurrence. But neither of us knew each other before that. She lived in Tennessee and never came near Gulf Shores. We have no explanation. She showed up now, for Mitch's funeral, with Charissa, which we knew only from the dream we both had."

"I don't know what to say, Valorie." He leaned back again. "It sounds unbelievable, but..."

She cocked her head. "But?"

"My years in the Marines took me many places, and I saw things no one could explain. If I believe in angels, which I do, I can't discount demons and otherworldly experiences. Seen too many."

Valorie sighed. "You believe me?"

"Let's say I don't disbelieve you."

"That's more than Mitch gave me." Tears slid down her cheeks.

Chad paused, wanting to comfort her, yet hesitant. He retrieved his beer and took a slug. "Was that your worst fear?"

"One. Mitch traveled so much I always feared him dying in a plane crash. Well, his plane didn't crash, but he died all the same." She rubbed her arms as if trying to warm herself. "And then Drake showed up at the cemetery."

"Drake? The Mercedes guy?"

She nodded. "I don't know why or how he even knew to be there."

"Wait. Who is Drake?"

"The man who followed me home from my parents' house. The man who somehow took us all to the dungeon. And the man I believe wants to destroy my life."

Pictures flashed through Chad's mind. Standing at the curb, checking messages while a van barreled toward Captain Ferguson.

A white van.

A white panel van.

Chapter 12

Surreal

VALORIE STARED ACROSS THE yard as JR and Michele raced, Bruce nipping at their heels with an occasional bark. Wisps of white clouds against a blue sky beat against her reasoning.

How could the sun shine when she saw nothing but gray?

Only two days earlier, they buried Mitch—saw that wretched man at the cemetery.

Drake.

At least, that's what Charissa and Shamira called him.

But it couldn't be real. None of it could be real. If only she could wake from this horrible nightmare, Mitch would come bounding through the door, assuring her she dreamed it all.

Wake up! Just... Wake... Up!

But she saw the man at the cemetery. She couldn't deny it. The two women she knew only from the dungeon dream still offered her comfort, slept in her guest room. And Chad? Where did he come from?

Clueless.

Maybe she was losing her mind. Maybe her brain held her captive in one place—this reality—while Mitch and the kids watched her slip into a semi-comatose state in true life.

A tray filled with glasses and iced tea plunked against the patio table, bringing Valorie out of her stupor. Shamira plopped into the chair across from her while Charissa poured tea.

"We thought you might like something to drink." Charissa placed a glass in front of her.

Valorie blinked.

If this was a dream, it screamed reality.

The kids skipped to the deck, both shouting. "Iced tea!"

Michele wrinkled her nose. "Is it sweet?"

Shamira giggled. "Is there any other kind?"

JR frowned. "Grams doesn't put sugar in her tea. She likes it straight up. Whatever that means. But she makes two pitchers when we're there." He scrunched his nose. "Her sweet doesn't taste like Mom's, but Gramps sneaks his from our pitcher."

Valorie smiled at the kids. Maybe not a dream. But that meant Mitch died, and the thought overwhelmed her. She took a sip of the cold liquid, forcing it past a knot lodged in her throat.

Charissa took the seat beside her. "You okay? Sorry. Stupid question. Of course you're not okay."

Valorie shrugged. "It's all surreal, like I escaped from the dungeon, but never woke up. And all this? A nightmare." She leaned her head back, begging the tears to stay put. Failing. "Why can't I wake up?"

Charissa placed a hand over Valorie's. "Because you aren't asleep, hon. I wish you were, and then I could shake you and take all this horror away. But I can't."

Both kids came around the table, eyes rimmed with red, and hugged Valorie.

"It'll be okay. I'll protect you now." Sweet JR, such a little man, suddenly growing up.

She patted his back. "I know. You always watch out for me when Dad's away. I need time to get used to the idea of him never coming home." Tears welled—again. She swiped at her eyes, willing herself not to cry in front of the kids. "Look. Bruce has a squirrel to chase. Why don't you go help him?"

Everyone turned toward the dog. His butt in the air, Bruce almost touched his nose to the ground, toying with the squirrel that sat atop the wooden trashcan holder. The squirrel moved. Bruce countered, barked, waited. The squirrel moved again, and the dog followed. Finally, the little guy scurried up the fence and jumped into a nearby tree. Bruce went wild, barking, circling. He rose and placed paws on the trunk, searching among branches, looking over at his family. He sniffed the air, circling, and lumbering back to the same spot. The squirrel peeked around a leaf and chittered.

"Silly, Bruce. You can't climb that tree." Michele patted his head. The squirrel jumped onto the fence and scampered into the neighbor's yard. Bruce rushed the fence, banged his head against the boards, and bounced back. He whimpered, shook, and then sat on his haunches and cocked his head.

The air filled with laughter as JR and his sister threw their arms around their pet.

Valorie looked around the table at her friends. Yes, friends. Bruce tried to jump up the tree again, and she couldn't stop herself from joining in the laughter.

Silly dog indeed.

Oh, the day Mitch brought him home—the tiny bundle of fur. She didn't want a dog, but how could she say no to the children? Especially the overgrown man child?

Mitch.

Her laughter stopped as she faded back to the grayness of her soul.

Shamira leaned forward. "It's okay to laugh. Even in your grief, you can find funny moments to get through it."

Valorie nodded, wiping away a wayward tear.

Charissa's phone chimed. "Hello? No, I'm still in Alabama. I took bereavement time, plus my regular days off." She shook her head and sighed. "I'll be back by then." She ended the call and rubbed her head. "I swear they won't let me miss a day. Even on my regular days off, my boss calls and asks me to cover for some twit with a hangover."

She looked at Valorie. "I don't want to leave, Valorie."

"You can't stay forever. Go home to your job. I'm fine."

The screen door slammed, launching Valorie to a standing position, searching for her children. Her heart reverberated in her ears until she spotted them playing beside the giant oak. She glanced at the gate into the alley. Thick padlock in place. No alarm, but no one went back there except for utilities.

Charissa laid a hand on her arm, easing her back into the chair. "You don't seem fine. You seem lost, scared."

"Agreed." Shamira leaned back and took a long drink.

"Maybe. But that's not so different from before. Well, the numbness—that might be new. If I'm numb, could be I'm not as scared. Maybe?"

Chad sat beside Valorie. "Yeah. Tell yourself that. The shock wears off, and emotions flood you."

When did he appear?

Oh yeah. The slamming door.

Charissa turned to Chad, a glint flashing from her eyes. "My boss called. Shamira and I have to head out tomorrow morning."

"You have a life. I'm figuring out next steps. Looking at a nearby place to rent."

Valorie sat straighter. "You don't have to do that."

"I promised Mitch, and Marines don't break promises. I'll watch over you and the kids. Until you don't need me." He scratched his nose, poured a glass of tea for himself, and sighed. "It's as much for me as for you."

"With that settled, I feel better about leaving." Charissa sat back, crossed one leg over the other, and bounced her foot. After a minute of silence, she continued. "Valorie, before I leave, we gotta talk about the dungeon and your fears."

Arms crossed, Valorie shook her head. "Not going there."

"Valorie, we must." Charissa pulled at her bottom lip. "How much do you remember?"

Chad leaned forward, intent on the women. "I want to hear this."

After looking up at the sky, Valorie said. "I want to block out what happened there—if it happened at all."

Shamira leaned forward. "It did, Valorie. You know it. We're here. We all saw Drake. Isn't that enough proof for you?"

Valorie shrugged. “I could be dreaming you guys for all I know. Some people think I’m crazy. Maybe I am.”

“Huh. I know it sounds insane. The timeline doesn’t work. I don’t know how to explain that. Something supernatural?” Charissa took a sip of tea, glanced at the children playing on the swing set. “You aren’t crazy. Shamira’s right. Whether we want to believe or remember, it happened. For Chad’s benefit, I’ll share the escape. No need to go through the rest of it.”

Valorie took a deep breath, but she kept her arms crossed. “Fine.”

Chapter 13

Yes, a Dungeon

Valorie eyed Charissa, chills creeping up her spine.

Why was she dragging this up? Especially then.

With a deep breath, Charissa closed her eyes for a moment and then leveled her gaze at Valorie. "You remember the chains?"

"Of course. They covered my body, kept me captive with spiders, snakes, and rats surrounding me. It terrified me. I still smell the muskiness. Feel the chill in the damp air. How I remember that and not much else—I don't know. Even when Mitch came home, I couldn't sleep without a night light on in the bathroom and the bedroom door locked."

"I'm truly sorry, Valorie." Charissa placed a hand over her heart. "You should have never been in that dungeon. You didn't choose to go, and Drake will one day answer for that. The rest of us made a choice and joined him there—not knowing he deceived us. But toward the end, Drake moved you upstairs out of the dungeon. I didn't understand why, and I didn't care. After I figured out how to break the chains, God compelled me to go back, help you all break free, and lead you to safety. Of course, Haniel urged me along and went back to help."

"I don't remember breaking any chains."

"You didn't much. With Drake discovering the escape, we found you and practically carried you over a balcony."

A memory played at the edges of Valorie's mind. "A powerful man with kind eyes?"

"Yes. You remember Haniel?"

"Yeah. He threw me over his shoulder and climbed down with me. I thought for sure he'd drop me and break my neck. Later, he made me jump over a cliff, or he'd leave me for Drake to recapture."

"Exactly. See? It happened just like that." Charissa licked her lips. "The key to freedom—breaking the chains."

"How?"

"The past. Dwelling on it, letting it feed our anger, fear, whatever negative emotions in us, made the chains grow."

"That's ridiculous." Valorie dropped her hands to the chair arms and scooted back.

Shamira leaned back. "Sounds ridiculous, but that's what I remember. When I prayed for forgiveness, those chains on me fell to the ground." Her eyes sparkled. "It changed me, Valorie. Forever."

"Well, not me. I have more fear now than ever before. And the worst ones are happening." Valorie crossed her arms again with a giant huff.

"Don't you see?" Charissa's eyes pleaded for Valorie to understand. "Because you didn't choose freedom, you still wear most of your bonds. You alone can release them. We can pray with you, but ultimately, it must come from your heart."

A low, soft whistle came from Chad's direction. "A supernatural thing. I've been all over the world. So much you can't explain without spiritual eyes."

"Um hmm. It took me a while to see it, but when I did... I didn't stop for a second to find a way out of that stinking place." Charissa leaned forward.

Across the table, Shamira rubbed her arms despite the warm day. "When I realized Charissa got out, I wanted to break free, find her, and slit her throat. As I had those thoughts, the chains thickened and tightened around me. But then she came back." She put her hand over her mouth for a second. "I still wanted to cut her. But she crossed the room and told me the secret to freedom.

Impossible. I did it anyway, and when the chains broke, I hugged her. Then we went to rescue everyone else."

Charissa nodded. "Except that one power-hungry witch. She wandered around upstairs with Drake, no visible chains. In the end, she betrayed us—gave away our location." A quivering breath stopped her for a second. "I'm still working through that one. Might have a few layers of shackles to break."

Not sure what to think, Valorie looked over at Chad, who stared at her with intense honey-brown eyes. So much like Mitch. She shook her head. Not Mitch. Her voice quivered. "What would you have me do?"

Charissa shrugged. "That's something you have to ask God about. He'll tell you who you need to forgive, what caused your overwhelming fear, and how to break free. I don't have all the answers, and even though I may have a clue, He won't release me to tell you. It won't be as powerful if it doesn't come from Him."

"Well, I'm not inclined to talk much with God at this moment. He took Mitch from me—my second greatest fear. I won't let my children out of my sight, because I'm not letting anything happen to them. He will not make that fear a reality." Valorie stood. "JR, Michele. Time to go inside and clean up for dinner."

"Aw, mom. We're having fun."

"Your fun time is over. You need baths and food, and with all that's gone on, you haven't gotten a decent night's sleep for days. C'mon now."

"Yes, ma'am." The chorus of two drifted across the patio.

She turned back to the table. "I appreciate your concerns—all of you. Maybe later. Right now, I can't deal with anything else."

Charissa got up and moved to Valorie. "I get it. But I don't know when I'll see or talk to you again, so I had to say my piece. Drake still wants to destroy you, but even if he didn't, we have a deadly enemy who roams around seeking someone to devour."

"Don't throw Bible verses at me, Charissa. Just don't. Not now. Never. I got enough of that from my late husband."

Chad rose, knocking the chair backward. "Whoa. Valorie, I know you're hurting, but don't you dare badmouth Mitch. I get it. Sometimes he drove me crazy with all the verses he knew, but he was always right. And you know it. And Charissa has a point. You may not have physical chains, but the way you act, you might as well be trapped in a dungeon."

His eyes flamed with the same fire she saw often in Mitch's eyes. Not menacing, but just as frightening, because Chad spoke the truth. Tears gathered at the corners of her eyes, threatening to burst into a flood. That fire came from a strong faith in God. She believed in Him, but she never saw such a fire in her mirror image.

Why couldn't she have that strength? Did she want it?

She bit her upper lip, pushing down emotions. "You're right. But I can't. Not now." She turned toward the children. "Kids. Inside."

They disappeared through the door, and Valorie followed, sensing those honey-brown eyes drilling a hole into the back of her head.

Why did she care? She barely knew the man. Having him around comforted her. She told him things even Mitch didn't know. Her mind drifted back to the night of Mitch's funeral, to Chad's rugged cologne, his gentle touch.

Her mind snapped back to reality. What was she thinking? That man could be rude despite his attractive points. Still, with her husband in the ground less than 72 hours, why would she feel anything for his Marine buddy?

Ludicrous.

She must be losing her mind.

No matter what anyone said, she couldn't imagine any other explanation.

Chapter 14

On the Run

Early the next morning, Chad woke to the sweet aroma of coffee brewing. A slow smile spread across his face, broken without warning by memories from the previous evening. He needed to apologize to Valorie. Calling her out on badmouthing Mitch—not wrong. The timing sucked.

He cracked one eye. No one around.

Slipping from under the covers, he grabbed a nearby t-shirt and tiptoed to the bathroom, searching for the fellow early riser.

Valorie perched on a stool at the breakfast bar, sipping from a cup. "Morning, Chad."

He took a few steps closer. "Valorie. How did you sleep?"

"I didn't."

"That's too bad." He swallowed a small knot in his throat. "Listen, I'm sorry about last night."

She scrunched her nose. "What?"

"I came down on you for what you said about Mitch. Maybe a little too harshly—stupid timing."

"It stung." She shrugged a shoulder. "But you're right. Mitch had faith stronger than anyone, and you have that same glint in your eyes when you defend your faith."

"Aren't you a believer?"

"In God and Jesus? Sure. The rest of it..." She took another sip. "Not enough, apparently. Mitch used to say if I had stronger faith, I wouldn't let fear control me. Charissa's accusations... too much. I overreacted."

"Understandable, considering everything."

She rolled her eyes and wiggled her head. "You must be Mitch's hidden brother."

"What?"

"You're just like him—sound like him, act like him, patronize me. Why can't you just tell me I overreacted?"

A grin sneaked up on Chad, accompanied by a chuckle. "Thanks. I'm no Mitch. He modeled an authentic, godly man. But you're right. No slack, even if your heart aches like never before. I mean, why should I give you room to grieve?"

At that, Valorie chuckled. "Touché. I should be grateful for your understanding. And I am. You don't have to be here with this crazy recent widow, but you came—and stayed. Forgive me for lashing out." She stared at her empty hands and blinked. "I don't know what to do, how to feel, what to think."

"I know. It may never get better, but it will get different. In time, you will get past this."

She rubbed her eyes and stood. "Let me get you some coffee."

"Maybe in a bit. I'm gonna fold up the covers and go for a quick jog. Feeling sluggish after all that amazing food and no exercise. And I need to clear my head—grieve my way."

Valorie nodded. "I'll lock up behind you. Just let me know when you get back. I hope the kids sleep late today, and I don't want to wake the girls too early. They have a long drive home."

"Gotcha."

Chad retreated to the den, folded sheets and blankets and put on his running shoes.

When he stepped into the bright sunshine, Chad stretched. He breathed in the fresh air, letting it fill his entire body and shake off the sorrow from inside the house.

His mind snapped to full alert.

Hairs on his arm bristled.

His right hand twitched. Moved to an empty hip.

He gazed around the neighborhood. Who was watching him? Houses stared back. Empty. No pulled aside curtains. No curious neighbors.

Nothing.

Unoccupied cars in driveways.

No suspicious vehicles.

Except...

Two houses down on the opposite side of the street, a Honda Accord hugged the curb, windows down. A dark-haired, burly man held a phone to his ear.

Chad snickered.

Dude, get a grip. Not in a war zone anymore. No terrorists here.

Or were there? He couldn't explain it even to himself, but something about that man...

At a slow jog, he tried to convince himself of an overactive imagination.

He didn't succeed.

Chad kept his run short, trying to clear his head. But the Accord and driver haunted his thoughts. Overreacting? Maybe, but he didn't want to stay away for too long. After one trip around the block, the car remained parked. Although he no longer saw the driver, the windows remained down. Foreboding niggled Chad's mind. He stared at the car, rubbed his neck, and then cracked it.

"Now who's paranoid, old man?"

He knocked on Valorie's door. Bruce crashed against the fence. Low in his throat, a growl rose. He barked.

Chad jumped. "Hush, Bruce. You'll wake everyone in the house."

The bark shifted. Bruce's growl changed to a whimper.

Chad laughed. "You crazy dog. You 'bout scared me out of my shoes."

Valorie opened the door, looking around him, wildness where pupils belonged. She grabbed his arm and pulled him inside, slamming the door behind him.

"What's up?"

Her breath shuddered. "Thank God you're back." Rapid breaths shook her body, visible shudders consuming her.

Chad placed his hands on her shoulders. "Calm down. Tell me what happened." His mind raced back to the car and its empty driver's seat.

Valorie collapsed against him, quivering. "A call."

"A call?"

She nodded.

Chad stroked her hair. "Shhh. It's okay. I'm here. I got you."

Her breaths slowed, shallower, as she clung to him.

He licked his lips. "Tell me about the call."

"Nothing. Probably some bored kid. Just silence. Eerie silence."

"When did this happen?"

"A minute after you left. Then again, maybe five minutes ago."

Icy fingers worked their way down Chad's spine. He drew Valorie closer. "I'm sure you're right. Probably a kid being stupid."

She looked up at him, lips pressed together. "Yeah. I'm sorry. About everything..."

"No worries." If only he could convince himself, despite the stinking gut feeling.

Valorie nodded and pulled back from his embrace. "How about that coffee now?"

"Sounds good."

Color returned to Valorie's cheeks, but he didn't dare head to the shower yet. Her trembling hands told him she wanted to distract herself from the fear, but the slumped shoulders and furtive eyes told him she still wore it like a bodysuit.

They both jumped when her phone rang.

Chapter 15

Donuts and Coffee

Chad stood, his arms crossed, while Valorie picked up the phone.

Her hands and voice quivering, she answered. "H-hello. Morning, Dad. I'm fine." She listened. "No, I just had a couple of silent-breather calls this morning. Freaked me a little." She chuckled. "I know, Dad."

Chad headed into the kitchen for coffee, then thought better of it. He turned back to Valorie and pantomimed a shower. She nodded.

Ten minutes later, he returned to the kitchen. With Valorie on the phone and more relaxed, he smiled and filled a mug.

Valorie ended the call. "Mom and Dad insisted on bringing breakfast, which, knowing them, will include an assortment of donuts and sausage rolls." A smile played with her lips. "Thank you for calming me down earlier."

"No problem. I'm glad your dad called. You seem better now."

"I'm still his baby girl, you know. He has a way of soothing me—better even than Mitch could. I don't know what I'd do without him. Even if he insists I'm paranoid."

"Paranoid or not, silent phone calls freak out most people—especially with nerves already in overdrive."

JR wandered into the kitchen. "I'm hungry. What's for breakfast?"

"I dunno. Grams and Gramps offered to bring it today." Valorie gave him a hug.

JR's eyes grew wide while a goofy grin spread from his lips up his cheekbones. "Yay! Donuts."

Valorie shook her head. "Why don't you go put some clothes on while you wait for them to get here?"

"Awww." He pouted. "Do I gotta?"

"You have to get dressed, and brush teeth..."

"And make my bed, and all that junk." He turned to go back up the stairs, then glanced back at his mom. "Could we go to the beach today?"

"Not today. It might storm."

"Bummer." Halfway up the stairs, JR met Michele, rubbing her eyes. "Hey, Chele. You might as well go back up and get dressed, brush teeth, and make your bed."

"You're not my boss." The little girl placed both hands on her hips, every bit a miniature Valorie—except for the fear factor.

"Fine. I'll get donuts first when Grams and Gramps get here." He pushed past her and ran up the stairs.

"Slow down, JR. And Michele, your brother is right. You need to get dressed."

"Yes ma'am. Gramps really bringing donuts?"

"Probably. They know what you two like most."

"Yay!" Michele eyed Chad, scratched her nose, and narrowed her eyes before turning and racing upstairs. She almost tripped over Charissa at the landing.

"Whoa. Careful." Charissa patted Michele's head before coming downstairs, Shamira following her. "What was that all about?"

Valorie sighed. "Super excited. Mom and Dad insist on bringing breakfast. For them, that usually means donuts and sausage rolls."

Shamira grinned. "Sounds good, but... Do I smell coffee?"

Chad retrieved two mugs from the cabinet. "Just brewed another pot."

"Another?" Charissa scrunched her shoulders. "How long have you two been awake?"

"Hours." Chad smiled at the ladies. "Already been out for a morning jog, slew a few dragons, and got a shower in." He held up his mug. "On about my twelfth. Joking. Only my second. But who's counting?"

Charissa laughed. "Why didn't y'all wake us?"

"And deprive you of beauty sleep?" Chad backtracked. "Not that you need more." Heat rose from his belly to his face. "I mean... You know what I mean."

All three women laughed at him, relishing his moment of embarrassment.

When the doorbell rang, he didn't bother excusing himself, but raced to answer it. He took boxes and bags from Mrs. Daniels, holding the door open for her and then putting everything on the breakfast bar. "Where's Mr. Daniels?"

"He's getting a few groceries from the car."

"Mom! I have more food than I can use now. Why did you get more groceries?"

"Oh, honey. You know your dad. He's making sure you stay stocked up without worrying about maneuvering through the store." She shrugged. "He—okay, we—figured you had enough on your mind without wondering if you needed milk."

She moved aside so Chad could help with the groceries. As he waited for Mr. Daniels to load him up, he glanced down the street. Behind the wheel of the Accord, the driver glanced down, a phone in his hand.

Who was that man? Why did he sit there, watching, waiting?

Chad shivered despite the sultry breezes.

Chapter 16

Goodbyes

For once, Valorie gawked at the food her parents pulled from containers. Besides the normal overkill of fresh donuts, they brought healthier options. Breakfast burritos, miniature smoked sausages, and a variety of cheese and fruit trays. Valorie went to the cabinet to pull out plates and silverware.

Her mom placed a hand on her arm. “I know you don’t like the paper plates and plastic ware, but I didn’t want you stuck in the kitchen after everyone leaves. If you want, we’ll take the kids for a while so you can have time alone.”

“Thanks, Mom. I’m not sure I want to be alone with my thoughts yet.” She sighed. “Then again, I need to sort a few things in my head, and a nap might be super after while. I didn’t sleep much last night.”

Her mother caressed her cheek. “I could tell from the dark circles, honey.”

Valorie hugged her mom, demanding the tears stay behind her eyelids. She didn’t like the idea of yet another round of crying. Pulling back, she forced a smile. “I’ll be okay, Mom. Just gotta get past the shock of everything.”

“I know. We’ll help you through it.”

“Of course.”

Surrounded by people, they finished setting out the feast.

After more than an hour of eating, talking, and consuming multiple pots of coffee, Valorie retreated to the den where she sank into an overstuffed chair. She eyed her Bible and devotional guide, untouched for almost a week. The morning after Mitch's death, she tried reading it, but her brain shut out the words. Would it be different in the wake of devastating days of sorrow? She doubted it. Tempted to try reading a bit, a sound at the door forced her head up.

Charissa waited at the threshold. "I hate to interrupt, but we gotta get going. I intended to leave early. So much for my plans." She giggled. "I enjoyed the time with your mom and dad, though. And I hope one day to have kids as sweet as yours."

"Thank you, Charissa." Valorie waved her over. "So strange. When you showed up, I didn't know you. Yet, I did."

"I know. I felt the same way when Shamira showed up at the hospital where I work. Then she told me she bumped into you by accident on her way to Texas. We still have a difficult time grasping how the dungeon can be real."

Valorie nodded. "Yeah." She snickered. "I almost didn't let y'all stay with me. Since I ran into Shamira that day, I wondered if maybe Drake sent her. How else would she know where to find me, you know?"

"Exactly." Charissa rubbed her arms. "I think we can chalk it up to divine intervention. I have no other explanation. And the whole dungeon thing reeks of supernatural mystery. Did you tell Mitch before he died?"

"Yes, but he didn't believe me. He insisted I dreamed it all—even seeing Shamira." She curled up in the chair. "You're single, right? Did you tell anyone?"

"I am, although a certain doctor asked me out soon after the dungeon ordeal. I couldn't bring myself to tell him about it. Then Shamira showed up, and after two or three weeks of prodding, I finally told him. He wouldn't take no for an answer, concerned about how well I knew her."

"Did he believe you?"

"Not at first, but later, he said Holy Spirit convinced him. He had a dream, and one day he saw a man outside the hospital that looked a lot like my description of Drake."

"No way. Was it him?"

"Not sure. We looked at video camera footage—he can ask for it from security as a doctor. Overall, it looked like Drake, but too fuzzy to confirm the face."

"That would drive me inside with locked doors forever."

"I understand, but I can't live in fear, Valorie. And I don't want to see you do that either."

Valorie swallowed and cupped a hand over her mouth.

Charissa reached out and took her other hand. "I don't mean to upset you. Drake may be finished with us all. He wanted me, but I stood firm against him, and he fled. Just like Peter said he does. 'Rebuke the devil, and he will flee.' You aren't ready—not with all this trauma going on. But someday, you must face him down and get past the fear."

"Do you really believe I still have all those chains around me? Trapping me?"

Charissa gazed at Valorie, then looked up. Her eyes darted back and forth as if searching. She nodded and returned her gaze. "Yes. In my mind, I see more than before. He may see you as someone he can recapture and control. When you're ready, call me. Together, we'll break them."

Valorie jumped at the sound of a throat clearing. Shamira stood in the doorway. "Sorry to interrupt. It's time to go. Chad already loaded our luggage for us."

Charissa and Valorie stood and embraced. Shamira crossed the room and joined them in a three-way hug.

Valorie's vision blurred. Drops trickled down the other women's cheeks. She glanced away and rubbed an eye with one finger.

Outside, saying a last goodbye with one more hug, Valorie caught Chad staring down the street. A car fired up its engine and inched away from the curve, the dark-headed driver rolling up the window as he drove past.

Was that someone she knew? No one from the neighborhood. The back of Valorie's neck prickled.

Chapter 17

The Call

As the Accord drove past, Chad's heartbeat increased. He snapped a quick photo of the license plate, needing to know who it belonged to—in case something happened. Gut feeling or whatever, he wouldn't take a chance on the stranger.

Inside, Chad pushed down the emotions raging through him.

Michele and JR pleaded with Valorie. "Pleeeeese. Let Grams and Gramps take us to the beach. We'll be good. We promise."

"I don't know, kids." Valorie hesitated, and Chad wondered if she saw the Accord.

As they argued, his mind drifted to the last vacation he remembered with his family. Dad surprised them that December by coming home on leave without warning. After an entire month waiting, Mom signed them out of school and got assignments. They drove for hours to reach a somewhat warm beach. Every day felt like Heaven with his dad beside him instead of off fighting wars. The strongest man Chad knew, until he met Mitch, his dad left in January and came home in a pine box.

JR brushed against Chad as he raced Michele to the stairs.

"No running inside. And don't forget to grab towels and the sunscreen," Valorie shouted after them, collapsing onto the sofa.

"They'll be fine." Mr. Daniels patted Valorie's hand. "You worry too much."

"They're all I got left."

"You still have us, honey." Mrs. Daniels lounged beside her daughter.

Chad crossed the room and plopped into the chair beside Mr. Daniels. Assured her mom had Valorie in a conversation, he shielded his mouth with his hand, leaning toward her father.

"Did you notice that Honda Accord earlier?"

"No. Why?"

"It's been a couple of houses down all morning. Call it a gut feeling, but it didn't feel right."

"Reason for concern?"

Chad shrugged, eying Valorie who continued talking with her mom. "Could be. I got the license plate and a buddy who works for the local PD. I'll check it out."

Mr. Daniels nodded. "I'll keep my eyes open."

"Good." Chad inhaled, calming himself. "I may be off base. Lack of sleep. Emotions high after all this."

"No harm in caution."

"Yeah. My thoughts exactly."

Mr. Daniels locked eyes with Chad. "I'm glad you're here for Valorie. But don't let her paranoia infect you. She sees darkness in the brightest sunlight."

"Gotcha. But something about that guy—creepy." Chad looked over at the women, Valorie's eyes boring into him. Crap. How much did she hear?

The kids reappeared, donned in swimsuits and weighed down with life jackets, towels and an assortment of other items. Valorie sighed and retrieved a beach bag from the coat closet. "Here. Let's make things easier, huh?"

Grabbing their grandparents' hands, the two pulled them to the door. Valorie unlocked it and held it open as they hugged her and scooted out.

Michele turned to Chad. "Goodbye. I'm sure you will be long gone by the time we get back." She stuck out her tongue and ran through the open door.

"Michele!" Valorie stared after her daughter with a wide-open mouth. She shook her head, closed, and locked the door, and turned to Chad. "Chad, I'm so sorry. I don't know what got into her. Michele doesn't usually act that way."

"She was a daddy's girl, wasn't she?"

"Yes. But that's no excuse. I'll deal with her this evening."

"No need. I want to stay here, keep an eye on things for you. But I can get a hotel around the corner or maybe find a BNB down the street. Close, but not in the house to remind Michele of what she lost."

Valorie looked out the window, the curtains open to reveal blue skies. She walked over and glanced both ways down the street. "I'm still spooked by those calls. And I saw that car with the dark-headed driver. Then I heard you saying something to Daddy. You saw it too, didn't you?"

Chad's mind raced, considering how he could downplay the situation.

Valorie raised her eyebrows. "Well?"

"Yeah. I saw it. Several times today—starting with my morning run."

"What? Early this morning?"

"Yes. I didn't think anything about it, but when I loaded bags for the girls, I noticed it again." He purposely left out the other times coursing through his brain. No need to frighten Valorie more. "But then, he drove off. Hey, I'm still learning to live as a civilian again, not looking for terrorists around every corner." He chuckled, trying to sound convincing.

Valorie plopped into a chair, not looking amused by his confession or buying it. "Look, Chad. I know it may seem awkward, and if you want to stay somewhere else, I understand." She stared out the window for a few seconds in silence. "Honestly, I don't want to be alone—even with the kids here. Especially with the kids here. That creep left me with tingles. He might be harmless, but something about him... And then the hang-up calls. It could have been him. Right?" She crossed her arms, hugging her shoulders. "I'll deal with Michele, but if you could stay just a few days, I'd appreciate it."

"I have nowhere to be, Valorie. As long as you want me here, and I don't cause too much of a problem with Michele, I'll stay."

"Well, Michele may not be your biggest fan, but JR loves you. Mitch traveled so much, but when he came back from a trip, JR took every step he made. He needs a good male role model—someone who pays attention to him and doesn't mind throwing a ball around once in a while."

"He's a good kid." Chad relaxed into his chair, content with silence, while Valorie retreated to hidden thoughts.

She catapulted out of her chair. "Oh my gosh! I forgot to feed and water Bruce!"

Chad stood and touched her arm. "I'll check on him. You relax. Maybe go up and take a long, hot bubble bath and a nap. I'm here. Nothing's getting past me."

Tears pooled in her eyes as she pinched her lips together. "Thanks."

Chad slipped outside while she mounted the stairs. "Hey, Bruce." He embraced the dog's face with both hands. "Hungry?" He looked over at the empty water bowl. "Definitely thirsty."

Bruce answered with pants and licking his lips.

Chad peered through the window while filling the water bowl. No Valorie. He pulled out his phone, located a contact, and punched send. "Detective Davis, please. I'll hold."

While waiting, he filled Bruce's bowl with food, then took a seat in the patio chair. Leaning back, he glanced back through the window. Still no Valorie. Good.

"Detective Davis. How can I help you?"

"Hey Davis. Chad Tyler here. I need a favor."

"Chad. Good to hear from you. Where are you?"

"Gulf Shores."

"Still? I heard you were with Ferguson when he died. How you holding up?"

"I'm good. Watching out for his widow and kids."

"Ha. I should've known. You old softy."

"Yeah. Whatever. I promised Mitch. Have they found out anything about the driver or van?"

"No. Witnesses said the van didn't have plates. Do you know how many white panel vans we have in this area? Hundreds. Don't know that we'll ever find the guy. It was a guy, right?"

"From what I remember, yes." Chad patted Bruce, who appeared with a slobbery ball in his mouth. Chad threw it. "So that favor?"

"Sure. If I can."

"I'm staying at the Ferguson house. Saw a Honda Accord several times today. Dark-haired man driving—gave me the creeps. Something feels off."

"Are you sure you aren't still overseas in your head? Facing down the enemy."

He laughed. "Maybe. I keep asking myself that."

"Cops around here know the Ferguson woman. They call her Loons. I can't share how many attempted break-ins she has on file."

"I know. Mitch called her paranoid."

"Is she?"

Bruce dropped the ball in Chad's lap. He threw it again. "A little. Lots of locks on the doors. And she uses them. Even with a full house and a muscled Marine on site."

Davis laughed. "I knew it!"

"She's not all bad. Something spooked her—a long time ago, I think. But she can't shake the fear."

"Poor thing. Now her husband's gone. Gotta be devastating for her."

"Yeah." Chad peeked back at the window. "Anyway, I snapped a photo of that car's plate. Can you run it?"

"Sure."

Chad sent a text with the photo attached. "I sent a text."

"Okay. Hold tight."

Clicks came over the phone. Chad waited, leaning forward in the chair. Bruce panted back to the shade and dropped to the ground at Chad's feet. He stroked the dog.

"I got it. Hmmm."

"What?" Chad stiffened.

"It's registered to a low-life rental company. I'll do a bit of digging, but odds are the guy paid cash and used a fake name. I'll get back to you."

"Thanks, Davis. Just send a text. I'm alone right now, but I don't want to spook Valorie."

"No more than usual, you mean?"

"You're ruthless, woman."

"Yes, and that's why I'm the best detective you'll ever know."

"I know you as a soldier. But I won't argue with you."

Chad ended the call, patted Bruce a few more times, and sauntered back inside. He filled a glass with ice and water before heading to the den. He needed peace, a break from the storm brewing in his gut.

Leaning his head back, he opened one eye when his phone pinged a few minutes later.

Davis.

> I was right. Rented to Joe Blow. Original. Address doesn't exist. Phone number bogus. Sorry.

Eyes wide opened, Chad wondered. Why would someone watch Mitch's widow? What did his friend get into?

And how the blazes would he get himself out?

Chapter 18

Who's That Man?

The man jogged past his car. Dagon snatched his phone and pulled up a map's app, doing his best to fake searching for a location.

No looking up.

No eye contact.

And above all, no exchange with the man.

He risked a glance as the Marine jogged down the street. Couldn't help but wonder. Could he take him? A slow, cocked smile spread across his mouth and cheeks. Not yet. Later. A twinge in his lower back made Dagon long for an intense workout, but tasked with always keeping eyes on the woman, he didn't have that luxury. Perhaps when they settled in for the night, he'd sneak in a run and 100 push-ups.

Why not make a move now? Take Valorie already? Seething rage mounted, his fingers twitched against the steering wheel. Stupid Drake. Wait until he got rid of the boss and took over. Suppressing an urge to scream, he grasped the wheel and shook it.

That evening, Dagon's phone beeped out the ring tone reserved for Drake.

He breathed in, calming his voice. "Da, boss."

"Where are you?"

"Still in car down road from your pet project."

"Please tell me you moved so they don't suspect anything."

Dagon rolled his eyes, glad not to see Drake this time. "Of course. I drive around block to little store. Get drink and piss."

Following a slew of curses, the sound of glass shattering left Dagon sucking in a breath. "I used the outside bathroom when someone came out. Got the drink from a vending machine away from cameras. You think I stupid?"

"Well—yes. I do. Did you at least park in a different place?"

"A little farther back, but if I go too far, they no think I visit the same house. Then, they be suspicious."

More curses came through the phone, followed by a sharp inhale. "In exactly two hours, go to the park at the end of the main road. I will bring an unfamiliar car. You will take it and park in the other direction and farther from the house. I'll give you binoculars to use, but they cannot see them or you. Capiche?"

"Boss, why we not rent house—or take from owner? Either way suits me. Then I hide, and they never see me."

Drake cursed again, Dagon imagining the boss's spit hitting the phone. "If I want your moronic ideas, I'll ask. I don't plan for you to watch them that long. The Marine will pack up and leave or move in permanently. I'm betting on the former."

"Why you think he leave?"

"He knows war and military. You think he wants to stick around with a grieving woman?"

Dagon's muscles tightened. He tried popping his neck. Didn't work. "Sorry, boss. Just trying help."

"Trying to help, moron."

"I forget. Sorry."

"Two hours. And don't do anything stupid in the meantime."

Dagon disconnected the call, noted the time, and slumped down in his seat. His jaw clenched. He curled hands into fists. Why not kill Drake tonight? Then come back, take on Marine, and snatch woman for himself. With Drake gone, he could assume ownership of the castle and dungeon to keep playthings. The thought chilled his blood, shivers running through his entire body.

“Teach him to call me moron. I show him who real boss.”

Dagon stopped the Honda near the park restroom one hour and 55 minutes later and killed the engine. He didn’t remember the last time he peed without worrying about someone seeing him. He sneaked into the men’s side, relieved himself, and raced back to the car. As he started the engine, a black SUV with tinted windows rolled up.

“Crap. Cops. Maybe FBI.”

He looked over the area, seeing no one else.

While Dagon considered backing and peeling out, a tall, bulky man stepped from the passenger side. He held a Browning across his chest, a glint of warning in both eyes.

Not cop. Not FBI.

Drake.

True to form, 30 seconds later, another bulky man came around and opened the rear passenger door. Drake slipped out, his lips curled in a permanent scowl. He crossed his arms. “Just had to do something extra, didn’t you?”

“Had to piss.” Dagon pushed down the heat rising rapidly through his body.

“Yeah, yeah. Quit drinking.”

“Gotta do something while watching prey.”

“It best not be that cheap vodka you consume.”

“Only water.”

“Well, cut back, idiot. What if someone saw you?”

“No one here this time of night.”

“Except cops. The park closes at dusk.” Drake jerked his head up at the driver. “Toss him the keys and let’s get out of here.”

Dagon caught the key ring. “Keys in ignition of Honda.”

Drake stepped toward the car while the driver opened the rear door, and the bodyguard glanced around before taking long strides to the passenger side.

"Go do your job, idiot. And no more drinking tonight."

Dagon half-nodded, watching the Honda taillights disappear. For a second, he considered pulling his gun and putting a bullet through the brake light. Priceless idea. At least a traffic stop. Then he remembered the Browning. Yeah. Not best idea.

"I not idiot."

He climbed into the SUV. Nice choice. He could pose as FBI.

After turning the key, Dagon picked up his phone. He found Valorie's number and pushed send.

When the woman answered, he took slow, even breaths.

She gasped.

He sped up the breathing, enjoying several moments of her panicked voice. "Who is this? What do you want?"

He tried a maniacal laugh and growled. "Mine."

Disconnecting the call, he raced from the parking lot, wishing Drake had included lights to mount on the dash. Tomorrow might be more fun.

Chapter 19

Appearances

CHAD VENTURED DOWN THE stairs, hoping to get in an early run.

As he passed the den, JR looked up, his eyes brightening. "Chad!"

"Hey buddy. Why are you up so early?"

JR shrugged. "I dunno. Just woke up." He grinned. "Wanna watch *Wild Kratz* with me?"

"Wild what?"

The little boy rolled his eyes. "Couple of guys who go exploring and become animated. Pretty cool. I learn about stuff."

"Interesting. Your mom OK with that?"

JR giggled. "Yeah. One of the few she lets me watch."

Chad sat next to JR and ruffled his hair. "She wants you to grow up well."

"I know." He sighed. "But sometimes..."

"What?"

"Promise not to tell?"

"Sure."

"She treats me like a baby."

A chuckle slipped out. "You are HER baby."

"I'm not. Eight is NOT a baby."

"Maybe. Wanna know a secret?"

JR's eyes widened, and he leaned into Chad. "Yeah."

"My mom still thinks I'm her baby."

"She does?" JR's mouth hung open. "But you're a grown-up."

"Um-hum. I know."

"SOOO... what happens when she calls you 'baby'?"

"She's my mama." Chad laughed. "She may be little, but she still scares the h... haystack outta me."

JR shook his head. "Nuh-uh. I don't buy it."

"True. I promise."

JR's gaze turned back toward the TV, and he furrowed his brows. A smile played across Chad's lips. Teachable moment?

Little fingers drummed the boy's lips. "Promise?"

Chad nodded. "Yeah man. Respect yo mama, little dude."

"K." JR slumped down, getting more comfortable to finish his show.

Catching movement in the hallway, Chad scooted to the edge of the sofa.

Michele stood in the doorway, arms crossed and virtual daggers shooting from her eyes. "You still here? Why? Just go home. We don't need you."

"Chele, that's rude." JR glared across the room.

"I don't care. You shouldn't be in my daddy's place. He sits there on Saturdays." She stormed from the doorway, tiny feet pounding up the stairs.

JR shook his head. "Sorry, Chad. She shouldn't be so mean to you."

"I don't blame her. She's hurting, bud. Doesn't know what to do with the pain. Maybe she's right."

"Who's right?" Valorie's soft voice broke into the conversation.

"Mom. Chele was rude to Chad."

"She's just upset, honey. I'll talk to her, then we can make pancakes."

JR's eyes widened as a grin erased the scowl. "Peanut butter ones?"

"Is there any other?"

Surprisingly absorbed into the senseless world of a kids' show, Chad snapped to attention when the doorbell rang. Unsure whether Valorie came back down from comforting her daughter, he crossed the room, stopping near the hallway at the sound of locks sliding, followed by her voice.

"Hey, Rita. C'mon in."

"Hi neighbor. I brought over a ham."

The sound of locks echoed through the stillness.

"You didn't need to do that. I have so many leftovers already."

"Well, that's the beauty of a ham. You can use it for a sandwich when you get tired of all the heavy stuff."

"Thank you. I'm sorry we haven't had a minute to talk."

"I understand. Your company gone?"

"Mostly. Chad's still here. Although they chose a nearby hotel, Mitch's parents may stay forever."

Both ladies laughed.

Valorie lowered her voice. "I'm not sorry they don't like my house."

"Not your favorite people, if I remember right."

"They're not so bad. But Mitch's mom creeps me out sometimes, like she's trying to catch me doing something wrong. And his dad... He goes in-and-out constantly, talking on the phone or something. And he never locks a door behind him. Never!"

"That must drive you crazy."

Chad started to step back from the doorway, guilt engulfing him for eavesdropping.

Then the neighbor's voice lowered in volume, stopping him. "Look, Valorie, I didn't want to say anything."

"But?"

"It's just... Well... A couple of neighbors are talking."

"The ones that always talk behind my back?"

"Yeah. Those. So maybe it doesn't matter."

"Rita, what are they saying?"

"They mentioned the Marine guy."

"Chad? He's a good man. At least I think so. And you know I suspect everyone."

"I know. He seems fine. I'm glad he's here to watch out for you, Valorie. Really. But it looks a little strange—him practically moving in right after Mitch's death."

"Oh, girl..."

The voices receded. But Chad didn't need to hear more. His thoughts warred while he rejoined JR on the sofa and slumped against the cushions.

Rita had a point. Appearances. If the neighbors were talking...

Maybe he should leave. Go home. But where was home? He hadn't known such a place since his grandparents died. Neither of his parents ever wanted him.

He shook his head, trying to clear his thoughts. They burrowed deeper, relentless in their pursuit of honor. He couldn't stay—not risking Valorie's reputation.

His promise to Mitch pounced through his memories. He couldn't leave the widow and children without protection. More a gut feeling than anything solid, a sense of danger chased him. Pulling out his phone, Chad did a quick search.

Bingo.

Two doors down on the opposite side of the street. A small bungalow for rent. Perfect. He completed a booking for one month. If things didn't settle down by then, he could always extend his stay.

JR switched off the TV. "Do you smell that?"

Chad looked up and sniffed. "Something."

"It's peanut butter pancakes." He hopped up and grabbed Chad's hand. "Let's go. I'm STARVING."

Not resisting, Chad followed the little boy.

In the kitchen, Rita leaned over the cabinet, watching Valorie flip pancakes and sausages, a human robot going through the motions.

Rita glanced over at them. "Well, good morning, guys."

Chad dipped his head. “Morning, Rita. Valorie, you need any help?”

She turned from the griddle. “Not here, but Bruce would appreciate food and water. If you don’t mind.”

“Not at all.” He headed toward the door, then turned back to JR. “Wanna help, buddy?”

“Sure.” JR scurried across the room, turning off the alarm and throwing back locks.

Too efficient. Did he share Valorie’s fear, or had the kid grown so accustomed to the way of life he didn’t think twice about her routine? Maybe he could help her overcome whatever frightened her so much. If not, maybe he’d at least keep her safe and teach the kids they didn’t have to fear everything.

Yep. A bungalow down the road sounded like a perfect plan.

Chapter 20

Neighbors

AFTER REFILLING RITA'S MUG again, Valorie rinsed plates and plopped them in the dishwasher. As she worked, her neighbor's voice droned—something about a new neighbor, then how she believed old man Smothers might have a lady friend.

"You know, he inherited his mother's estate, and then when his first wife died, I hear she had a massive life-insurance policy. I'm sure that little gold digger hanging around wants his money. I tried warning him, but he doesn't want to hear it."

"Hmmm." Valorie didn't care, but Rita's comment captured her thoughts. Mitch took care of all the financial part of their lives, and she always had plenty of money for whatever they wanted. But now? No income. Did that mean she needed to find a job? What if she couldn't make enough to support herself and the children?

Imagination kicking into high gear, she pictured herself packed into the mini-van with both kids, dirty, hungry, nowhere to go. How would she ever pay the mortgage? Even with a teaching degree, she never used it. Who'd hire her without experience?

"Valorie?" Rita stood beside her.

When did that happen?

"What? Sorry I didn't hear you."

"You looked a million miles from here."

"Guess I was."

"What were you thinking about?"

Valorie added detergent to the dishwasher, closed the door, and pushed the start button. "A lot." She shrugged. "Do you keep up with paying bills—stuff like that?"

"Are you kidding? Tim makes the money, but if I left bill paying up to him, we'd eat out every meal and forget about all the people we owe. He never handled money well, so he turned it over to me at the beginning of our marriage." Her eyes widened. "Do you pay the bills? Or was that all on Mitch?"

"I haven't paid a bill since..." Valorie crossed to the table and sank into a chair. "Oh, Rita. I never paid bills. Even after college, I went back home and lived with Mom and Dad until I met Mitch. They bought my car. Dad paid cash for it and gave me a credit card for the gas."

"Didn't you work?"

"For a while. But I saved a little and spent most of what I earned. No need to pay bills. When we married, I tried, but it made me anxious, so Mitch took over. We created a budget, so I knew how much to spend on groceries and such. We always had enough to travel, even after the kids came."

"That's when you quit working, isn't it?"

"Yes." Valorie stood and paced. "I saw the bank statements, and we always had a decent balance, so I didn't worry. I have no idea about any of it."

Rita moved to Valorie's side. "I'm sure Mitch had everything in order. But you probably should look at finances sooner than later."

Valorie moved to the window and looked out at Bruce napping on the patio. "Yes. I suppose so. What if...?" She turned to Rita. "I don't want to know."

"Know what?"

"We could be broke, but Mitch didn't tell me. What if we have no money?"

"Do you hear yourself, hon? Mitch wouldn't do that. He made good money, and you never overspent."

Valorie went back to pacing. "Maybe I did. I loved shopping—too much. And we both had new cars, this house..."

Her throat tightened, and her stomach clenched. "I haven't worked in over eight years. What am I gonna do? No one will hire a crazy, grieving widow."

Placing an arm around her, Rita guided her to the living room. "Valorie, sit down and relax. It'll be all right. I'm sure Mitch had everything under control. You have time before deciding anything."

"Maybe." Valorie rubbed her face. "I'm afraid to even look, but I have to."

"Again. Not today." Rita patted her hand. "Besides, Mitch had life insurance, right?"

Valorie brightened. "Yes. We did that when I got pregnant with JR. Neither of us wanted to leave a child without money for the future."

"Well, there you go."

"Plus, I think his job covered him, too. Especially with him traveling all the time." Valorie leaned back against the sofa. "Not a huge amount, but maybe I can get past the next few months."

"Did you file on the insurance for his funeral expenses?"

Valorie searched her mind. "I don't remember. That's all a blur. Dad will know. He went with me to handle all that stuff while Mom stayed with the kids."

"Maybe he already took care of making those calls, then."

"I'll ask him." She paused for a moment. "I should have done a better job keeping up with things. I don't know if I can sit at Mitch's desk or look through anything. His domain, you know?"

"I understand, but you have to eventually. How else will you know?" Rita stood. "You can do this, girl. You're stronger than you think."

Sudden exhaustion swept over Valorie, leaving her wanting to curl up in a ball and fall back asleep. "I feel about as strong as a snail—and with about as much energy as one."

"A snail?" Rita grinned. "Never heard that metaphor."

"Yeah. I'm creative when I don't try." She almost chuckled.

"Well, snails may not look all that strong, but they certainly persist."

"Until they run across some salt."

"Ooohhh." Rita grimaced. "That's sick."

"It is, isn't it?"

"Yep." Rita shook her head once. "Do you need anything before I head home—other than for me to hide the salt shaker?"

At that, Valorie couldn't deny a slight laugh. "No. I'm fine. The Fergusons called. They'll drop by soon, loaded with containers to package and freeze the millions of casseroles in my fridge. At least we won't starve."

"Good."

Valorie stood to walk her friend to the door. "I'm glad you're next door, Rita. I need a close friend right now. And thank you for what you said about Chad. It feels safer with him standing guard. But I didn't think about how it looks."

"Hey, I know there's nothing going on. But you know how our neighbors love a bit of gossip."

"Yeah. And I sure don't want to be the one who fuels it."

"Me either." Rita unlocked and opened the door. "Oh, look. Your favorite people—with far more than containers. Have fun."

Valorie peeked outside. Her mother-in-law headed their way with a box of donuts in her hands. Great. Just what her children didn't need more of. She sighed and forced a smile, wishing her heart felt it.

Chapter 21

Chad's New Home

SWEAT DRENCHED CHAD AS he rounded the corner, satisfied with a morning run to clear his mind and activate a sluggish body. Best run since he landed at the airport. In the driveway of the bungalow he booked, a woman opened her car trunk and pushed a sign into it.

Chad approached, waving at her. "Hey. I just rented this house online for a month. You the Realtor?"

She licked her lips as her gaze roved over him. "Could be. I'm Marta. The owner wants to sell, but with no prospects, he agreed to the idea of long-term renters. Let's step inside, get some water for you, and I'll show you around."

Chad glanced down the street at the Ferguson home. Nothing out of place. "Sounds good."

He followed Marta inside.

After touring the bungalow, Chad jogged the last bit to the Ferguson home, arriving as Mitch's parents exited their car. Loaded with boxes of donuts and bags of groceries, Chad thought of the day after Mitch's funeral. Poor Valorie. Two sets of parents overloading her and the kids with more than they needed.

He shrugged. People dealt with grief in different ways.

Mr. Ferguson waved. "Hey, Chad."

"Morning. Need a hand?"

"Sure."

Mrs. Ferguson's upper lip curled on one side. "You're still here? Staying at the house?"

"I plan on leaving today." He glanced up the street, searching for the Honda he'd seen earlier. In the middle of the block, an SUV with tinted windows sat on their side of the street, pointed the opposite direction.

The driver ducked his head. Could be the same guy. Not sure.

He turned back to the couple. "Don't want to get in the way. Just monitoring things."

"Of course. Feed the woman's fears—like she needs any fuel." She flung her handbag over her shoulder and stomped toward the house, not bothering to carry anything other than a box of donuts.

"Sorry, man." Mr. Ferguson sighed. "She doesn't let emotion show."

"Oh, I sensed exactly what she felt. Well."

"You're not doing anything wrong, Chad."

"I know. Appearances. Right?"

"Yeah, I guess."

The two men gathered the groceries and reached the door in sync with Rita's exit. "I would offer to help, but looks like you two have it under control. If Valorie needs anything, call me." She pseudo waved.

"Gotcha." Chad shook his head as she walked away.

"Good friend?" Mr. Ferguson asked. "Or neighborhood gossip?"

"Bit of both."

They chuckled and ventured inside.

By the time Chad showered and dressed, JR waited in the guest room, pushing toy cars beside the bed.

"What'cha doing?" The little boy pointed at the duffel bag on the bed. "It looks like you're leaving."

Chad sat on the floor beside JR. "Yeah."

"I don't want you to go."

"I know, bud. But... I should."

"Why? It's 'cause of Chele, isn't it?"

"No. Not at all."

"She just don't know she needs you here. But she does—I do."

Chad looked around the room, the softness and feminine touches foreign. He sighed. "I know you miss your dad. And you like having another guy around."

"You make us safe. I heard Mama say so."

"I'm not going far, bud. You won't see me every day, but I'll keep watch."

"Promise?"

"Of course."

"You sure it isn't because my sister talked so mean to you? 'Cause I can pummel her—if Mama's not watching."

"No. You cannot pummel your sister. Ever. Good men don't hit women, bud."

"Yeah. I know. Dad always said that, too."

Michele's soft voice drifted from the doorway. "You better listen to him. You're not supposed to hit me."

Chad turned toward her. "Hey, Michele. You can come in."

She pouted, then took two steps forward. "You really leaving?"

"Yes. It's time."

"I didn't mean to be so nasty." Red ringed her tiny eyes. "I'm sorry. You don't have to leave 'cause of me."

"Oh, honey. I'm not. Really." Chad reached out to both children, who scooted into his arms. "Your mom needs time alone. Too many people for her to think. But I'll stay close. K? And I'll check in. Make sure no one bothers you. Sound good?"

JR and Michele nodded. Then, without warning, Michele threw her arms around his neck, squeezed, and abruptly yanked herself away. Glints shooting from her eyes, the little girl stood and pushed her fists against tiny hips.

"Just don't try taking my daddy's place. He'll be home soon." A deep scowl slipped across her mouth. She whirled, rushed out the door and into her room, slamming the door behind her.

"Yes, ma'am." He cocked his eyebrows at JR. "She's a tough one. Daddy's girl to the core."

JR snickered, then grew solemn. "She's wrong. I know Daddy's not coming home. Ever."

Chad pushed down the wad of nothing blocking his throat and patted the little boy's back. "No, he's not, bud. I'm sorry."

JR wiped his eyes with the back of his hand. "I'm the man of the house now. And it'll be alright."

He got up, straightened his shoulders, and headed to the doorway. Before leaving the room, he turned. "But if you want, you can be my wingman."

"Sure. I got your back, little brother."

Chapter 22

Reporting In

DAGON SIPPED FROM THE soda can. Should've remembered Stoli to add spice. Drake wouldn't like it, but endless sitting, watching... Too much.

The military guy left the house, this time carrying a duffel bag.

Leaving? This could be the break he and Drake wanted. Without the man, Valorie had no protection. The security and extra locks—deterrent. Not as easy to disarm after the tech encased wires, but doable. He liked challenges.

He waited, expecting the man to get into one of the many cars parked in the driveway. Instead, he hoisted the bag and headed down the street toward the tropical bungalow—the one he suggested taking over. Drake never listened to his ideas.

At a nonchalant pace, the man crossed the street and entered the driveway of the vacant house. Dagon's nostrils flared as the man pulled something from his pocket.

Keys?

No. Not possible.

"You idiot. You supposed to stay with widow—guilt and all that. Or just leave. Go home. Not move down street." Dagon pounded the steering wheel. He dreaded the next conversation with Drake.

On cue, his phone beeped. "Crap." He swiped to answer. "Da, boss."

"Any update?"

"Well..." Dagon looked around. Did Drake have eyes on him? "I about to call."

"Really? Why do I doubt that?"

Dagon ignored the dig. "Yes. Just happened. Marine left."

"Excellent. We can move forward, then."

"No."

"No? How dare you tell me no?"

"He left—but only two doors down."

"Son of a... How could he move two doors down?"

"Empty house—one I say take over." Dagon watched the bungalow, the Marine no longer in sight.

"You said nothing about an empty house." A strain of expletives came over the phone.

Dagon flinched. "What now?"

"Keep him away from the widow."

"How I do that without showing our hand?"

"I. Don't. Care. Just do it!"

Call ended, Dagon glared into the distance. The parents' car remained in the driveway, but when they left, he'd take the woman. Easy enough. If he took her that night, no Marine. The kids... who cared?

Another beep from his phone. Dagon hesitated, breathing deeply before answering. "Da."

"I have a better idea. Let the widow stew in her grief, get comfortable."

"How that help?"

"She'll let down her guard. Then we strike."

"Finally, we take her."

"Not quite." Ice clinked in the background.

Dagon squeezed the phone, picturing the boss's throat in his hands. "When?"

"A few weeks, maybe a couple of months. The reward will be sweeter. Find an empty place—one where you can see both houses."

"What?" Heat rose, flashing through his body, teeth clenching. He glanced over at the widow's place. No movement. "Empty house."

"Moron. Of course. You can't keep sitting in the car. The Marine sees you, he gets suspicious, never leaves. In a house, they won't notice."

Dagon rubbed his mouth, choking down what he wanted to say.

"You there?"

"Da, boss. I take house. If anyone home..."

"Why do I care? Just don't leave a mess for me to clean later."

"Got it."

"I'm a genius. Should've thought of this sooner."

Dagon disconnected the call, not waiting for Drake's prattle about his amazing idea. Moron, huh? He grabbed the can, crushing it between his thumb and middle finger. Fists balled, he tamped down his temper and looked around the neighborhood. Which house? Didn't matter. Anything was better than a stupid SUV.

Once he had a base, he'd make a plan—one Drake didn't expect. Boss said no rush. Good. Time to think, watch, wait. And when he struck, he'd target more than the widow.

Chapter 23

ONE MONTH GONE

WEEKS PASSED AS VALORIE maneuvered life without Mitch. Sometimes, she pretended he went away for yet another business trip. It got her through most days, but around 6 p.m., reality hit hard. No call to ask about their day or share his. No complaining about the newest sniveling coworker or demanding customer. No 'I love you. See you soon.'

And no assurance of her safety.

Over a month since that fateful night, the memory burned hot. She rifled through the stack of bills on the breakfast bar. Sooner than later, she needed to deal with them. How? No clue.

A past due stamp caught her attention. Mitch never let a bill go past due. Never. She fidgeted with the envelopes, flipping through them a second time. She crumpled against the granite countertop. How could she be so careless? "Oh, Mitch. I miss you for so many reasons."

Venturing toward the stairs, she glanced into the den. JR and Michele lounged on the sofa, the TV blaring, and both laser focused on the screen. How long had they been watching? And what?

Her son looked up. "Hey, Mom."

"Hi honey. What're y'all watching?"

"Cartoons. Grams helped us find the channel."

Valorie sat beside Michele. "Sweet. Those are the old ones I watched as a kid." She caressed her daughter's hair.

Michele snuggled closer. “Daddy will love them. I can’t wait ’til he gets home.”

“Baby, you know Daddy’s not coming home, right?”

Michele pulled away. “Of course he is. Don’t say that.”

“Michele, he lives in Heav...”

“No! He does not!” The little girl jumped off the sofa. “He’s coming back.” She stormed from the room.

“Michele!”

JR reached out his small hand. “Mom. Let her go. She knows. She’s just in denial.”

"Where did you hear that?"

He shrugged. "I dunno. Something on TV maybe."

A deep sigh rose in Valorie, but she didn’t give in to the usual tears. Instead, she put an arm around the little boy. “Oh, my son, how did you get so smart?”

“I listen. A lot.”

Valorie hugged him, squeezing extra hard. She didn’t want him to grow up too fast, but he didn’t have much choice. Not without a dad. She swallowed a golf-ball sized lump. “I wish you didn’t have to be so big all the sudden.”

“Are you kidding? I’m the man of the house now. I kinda like that. Chele doesn’t. Which makes it even better.”

“Yeah? Don’t get too big for your britches little man. Remember, I’m still the mom here.”

“I know.” He flashed a disarming smile, looking so much like his dad the tears toyed with her eyes again.

Valorie forced herself off the sofa. “I need to work on paying bills. If you need me, I’ll be upstairs.”

“OK, Mom. Can I watch this cartoon longer?”

“Sure. A little. But then you should do something to use your mind. School’s starting soon, and you don’t want a mushy brain.”

“I’m good. No mush here.” He tapped his head and grinned.

Valorie ventured out of the den and up the stairs, her legs growing heavier with each step.

Approaching Mitch's desk, she sighed. Where to start? Overwhelmed, she pulled out the chair, sank into it, and dropped her head. "Oh, Mitch. Why? If you were here, you'd explain it. Say it's part of God's plan. But it can't be. How can God leave me to raise the kids alone without a clue even how to pay the bills? Or where you left the checkbook."

She crossed her arms on the desk and let her forehead fall. Tension and aches traveled down her neck, flowing over her body. No tears left for crying. She remained there for what seemed like hours, pushing away the room's stillness.

Why didn't she spend more time in there with Mitch?

Why didn't she know where he kept anything?

A beep on her phone forced her head up. A text from Chad.

Checking on you.

I'm fine. Thanks.

Need anything?

Yeah. Someone to tell me how to do all this financial crap. At least where Mitch kept the stinking checkbook. Can't tell Chad that though.

She hesitated a minute before replying.

No. We're good. Paying bills. Watching cartoons.

I'm getting pizza. Want some?

The kids love pizza.

Who doesn't love pizza?

We have all these leftovers. I shouldn't.

In the freezer. Right?

Well, yeah.

ᵒᵒᵒK. They'll keep. I'm sure the kids want pizza.

Of course they do. Always.

Settled. Be over in about an hour.

Valorie checked her watch. How did it get to 5 p.m.? She texted back.

Thank you.

She tossed the phone on the desk. At least she wouldn't have to cook. But if she didn't find the checkbook, they might end up eating by candlelight another night.

Where would Mitch keep it? The middle drawer enticed her. Maybe. She pulled it open. Pens, paper clips, notepads. No checkbook. One side of the desk served as a file cabinet of sorts. The other side held small, medium, and large drawers. She tried the top, small one.

Locked. Hmmm.

She opened the other two. They held a variety of items, but nothing helpful. Next, she tugged on the file drawer. Locked? Weird. That must be where he kept the important papers and checkbook. Made sense.

Where would Mitch put the key? Certainly not on his key ring. Would he?

A manila envelope laid on the desk—the effects they released from the morgue. She shuddered. Didn't want to look inside.

Placing a hand on it, she suddenly remembered. The keys! On a tie rack in the closet. During a trip, he needed information and told her where to find the key.

Full of hope, she bolted from the office and into the bedroom. She glanced at the undisturbed bed—hadn't slept there since Mitch's death. Instead, she stayed in Michele or JR's room, pretending to fall asleep. If she did, the effort to move... Too much.

Holding her breath, she looked at the untouched bed and ran a hand over the quilt he bought for her during that last getaway. Extravagant. She chided him for spending so much money, but he insisted on paying for the workmanship.

The air kicked on, yanking her back to the task at hand. In the closet, she found the ring with several tiny keys and headed back to the office. The first one she tried fit the top drawer, where a checkbook stared up at her. A deep sigh escaped. Another of the keys fit the lock on the file drawer. She opened it and rifled through the folders.

Organized Mitch. One folder tab stole her breath.

In Case of Death.

When did he do that? Hands shaking, she lifted the folder out of the drawer, laid it on the desk, and opened it. On the top, a single sheet of paper listed everything she needed to know. Companies with contact names and numbers, account numbers, passwords and pins, details she never considered. And beneath the cover page, smaller folders held documents, starting with both his and her wills. She gazed at it for several minutes, trying to make sense of anything.

She slipped the file back into place, determined to revisit it later. Another label revealed a folder for bills. The one she most needed. Inside, she found a few items, not as many as she thought. Perhaps he arranged automatic payments for the mortgage and cars, insurance. The most important things. That could cause problems with no money going into the account.

Her throat tightened. She couldn't deal with the bills. Not yet.

Tomorrow. First thing tomorrow.

When her phone rang, she jumped. "Hello."

Silence. Then breathing. Deep, prolonged breathing.

"Who is this?"

More silence. Another breath.

"Stop it. Stop calling me!"

Valorie slammed her finger against the end button and swiped, then tossed the phone in the chair beside the desk. Hands shook as she replaced the checkbook and file and fumbled with the keys. They dropped. "Dang it!" She bent and scooped them up. After several failed attempts, she finally got the right keys in the correct drawers and relocked both.

Instead of returning the ring to the closet, she pocketed it when the doorbell chimed, followed by the phone ringing again. Same number. She swiped decline and bolted down the stairs.

Peering through the peephole, Valorie whimpered.

Chad. Thank God.

"Valorie? It's Chad."

"I know. Just a second." She disarmed the alarm, unlocked all the deadbolts, and opened the door, peeking around him. "Did you see anyone out there?"

"No. Should I?"

"No." She slammed the door, relocked everything, and keyed in the security code on the panel.

"Whoa. What's going on?"

"Another breather call."

"Wait. Another?" He tossed pizza boxes onto the breakfast bar.

"Yes."

"I knew about one—weeks ago. You got others?"

"Yes." Valorie stumbled to the front window and looked outside before closing the blinds. "Nothing. At least, not that I see."

Chad grabbed her shoulders and spun her around. "How many calls?"

She shrugged. "A few. At first. This week, every day. Sometimes several a day."

"Why didn't you say something?"

"What good would it do? No one can do anything."

"You should've told me. Next time, I answer."

"You can't be here all the time, Chad." Her knees wobbled, nausea filling her stomach.

Chad pulled her close. "It's OK. I'm here now."

Valorie melted into his embrace, letting his warmth and strength soothe her.

"Let my mama go!" Michele's squeaky voice broke the moment—right before she kicked Chad in the shin.

Chapter 24

Michele

"MICHELE!" VALORIE BACKED AWAY from Chad and stared at her daughter. "How dare you kick our friend!"

Chad touched her arm. "I'm fine. Let it go."

"I most certainly will not. Young lady, explain yourself."

Michele crossed her arms and stuck out her tongue at Chad. "You can't hold Mama. That's for Daddy."

Valorie's muscles tensed as she moved toward Michele, who didn't back down. "You cannot kick people. Especially not someone who brought pizza for you."

Chad stepped between the two, wincing. "Calm down you two."

"You're not my daddy."

Valorie nudged Chad out of the way. "He is our guest. And you will show respect."

JR ran into the room. "Chad! I heard the doorbell, but I was pooping."

Everything stopped. Valorie gasped and covered her mouth. Leave it to JR. Master of inappropriateness at the perfect time to diffuse a situation.

Chad laughed. "Little brother, TMI."

Valorie tried to stifle her own laughter but failed. After a few seconds, she shook her head. "JR, that isn't something you announce. But thanks for letting us all know." She sighed and turned to Michele. "You need to apologize, Michele."

The little girl's bottom lip protruded, quivering. "No."

"I didn't ask." Valorie stooped to Michele's level, purposely moving closer. "You will apologize. Or you'll go to bed without dinner."

"Valorie." Chad touched her arm.

She shook her head and grasped Michele's shoulders while the girl's tiny nostrils flared. "Now, Chele."

Michele huffed out air. "What kind of pizza?"

Chad grinned. "Cheese, Canadian Bacon with Pineapple, and one loaded with everything."

Michele scrunched her nose. "Not fair. You know I like Hawaiian pizza."

"Yeah, I remembered."

"Fine. Sorry."

Valorie looked around the living room, trying to squash anger and embarrassment. "Like you mean it, little girl."

Michele let out a dramatic sigh. "OK." She faked a big smile. "I'm sorry I kicked you."

"You're forgiven." Chad held out a hand, offering a truce-shake. "But you shouldn't kick—unless it's an evil man trying to hurt you, or your mama or brother."

Michele ignored the hand and turned toward the kitchen. "Where's the pizza?"

Valorie opened her mouth, but Chad's gentle hand on her shoulder stopped her.

He shook his head. "Don't fight this one, Val."

She swallowed. Only Mitch called her Val. For a moment, his presence flooded the room, keeping the peace between her and the daughter who so often tried their patience. Unexpected tears played behind her eyes, begging for release. She denied them and cleared her throat, motioning for Chad to move to the kitchen.

"After you."

"I insist. You're my guest, and after being kicked, you should go first."

He chuckled. "That little kick? No biggie." He limped to the kitchen. "I brought soda, too." He whispered to Valorie, "and a six-pack. Gotta have the right drinks for pizza."

"You know, a beer sounds pretty good right now. Maybe I will."

JR already had plates on the table and glasses with ice for the drinks. So grown up. Had he planned his grand entrance because he heard the argument? Her little man couldn't forget how to be a child. But she treasured his peacemaker style. So much like his father it pierced her heart like a knife.

With the pizza consumed, kids bathed and in bed, Valorie returned to the kitchen where Chad finished cleaning. He popped the tops off two more beers and handed her one.

"I shouldn't. I already had one."

"So. Two won't kill ya. Not like you're driving."

"I know." She accepted the cold bottle. "Thanks."

"You're welcome."

"Not just the pizza and beer." She glanced around the kitchen and closed the curtains. "You showed up at the perfect time to calm me. And honestly, I don't normally spank the kids, but I sure wanted to put a belt to my daughter's behind tonight. She doesn't act that way. I don't get it."

"I do."

Valorie squinted. "Care to share?"

"She walked in. Saw my arms around you."

"So? My dad does that all the time."

"Yeah. He's your dad. I'm... a stranger."

"But you weren't hurting me."

"No. But I'm not her daddy. Not trying to be. She doesn't know that."

"She thinks you're trying to take his place or something?"

"Maybe."

Valorie ambled to the living room, sipping her beer, and slumped into a chair. "That's crazy."

"Deep inside, she knows he's dead. But denial's easier than truth."

Valorie nodded. "She sometimes talks as if Mitch went on a business trip and hasn't come home yet."

"He did."

Valorie covered her mouth. "You're right. To a four-year-old... He's just on a trip."

"She can't reason, you know."

"But I told her he died. That he isn't coming home again. Daddy told her Mitch lives in Heaven now."

"Maybe she doesn't understand death." He sat on the sofa near Valorie. "When she sees cartoons, a character dies. But he gets up and goes again. Or the same character appears in another episode. Death isn't final for her."

"I didn't let them see Mitch in the casket. Didn't think they should."

"I get it. Agreed. My father died when I was five, and they made me look in the casket. Traumatized me. Nightmares for months. Still plague me occasionally." He took a deep draw of his beer. "But it made his death real—not that my dad spent much time with me before that. Too busy."

"That's horrible, Chad."

"Huh. Made me tough. But Michele... She didn't see Mitch dead. In her young mind, he's still off on that trip, and he's coming home. She's protecting him and your marriage without knowing it."

"Wow. You should be a child psychologist. I didn't think any of this."

Chad shrugged and leaned back against the sofa. "Cut her slack."

"Some. But I won't let her kick you again. Not acceptable." Valorie leaned back in the chair and took another drink. "And I'm glad you insisted on coming tonight. I needed this."

"Yeah. Me too." He finished his beer. "And if you get more calls, let me know."

She studied his face. Something, but she couldn't place what. Concern? Did he know something?

She chided herself. Quit being paranoid.

But the old fear took hold, and she doubted even two beers would help her sleep.

Chapter 25

ANOTHER MONTH DOWN

VALORIE'S DAD REMOVED HIS glasses and leaned back in Mitch's office chair. "Well, sweetheart, we need to take care of a couple of bills today. And we need to make some phone calls. Do you have death certificates?"

"Yes. They're in the stack of mail downstairs." She sank into the armchair. "How bad is it?"

"Not bad. Mitch planned well for you and the kids. You already have his life insurance filed from his job. HR took care of it when I notified them of his death. Did you get that payment?"

"I... I'm not sure."

Her dad sighed. "We'll check the bank account again. It's been weeks since we looked at it."

"I never was good with money. Mitch always took care of it, so I didn't need to worry about anything other than making sure I didn't overspend."

"Sorry, but now you'll have to take care of finances." Dad steepled his fingers. "But you don't have to worry."

"But I am. What if I can't find a job? What if I run out of money before I do? What if..."

"Stop. Unless you do something stupid, you'll be fine."

Her dad held up a document. "This is a $500,000 life-insurance policy. That alone will take care of you for years. We'll talk with a financial adviser I trust."

He turned that face down and picked up two more documents. "Credit life clauses on the vehicle loans and mortgage. Do you understand what that means?"

She shook her head.

"The cars and house will be paid off. We need to notify the banks. When you're ready, we can sell Mitch's car."

"No. I can't sell his car."

"Will you drive it?"

She stood and moved to the window. "Of course not. He loved that car, but it only works for two people."

Her dad beside her, she leaned in, his arm embracing her shoulders. "It isn't good for a car to sit in a garage. Let it go, baby."

"It's too much, Dad. Where do I start? I can't possibly remember all I need to do. I barely remember to feed the kids."

"Or yourself, I think."

She shrugged. "Maybe. I'm not hungry most of the time."

"I know you're grieving. We'll get through this, and your mom and I will help." He moved back to the desk. "Let's make a list. As we take care of each task, you can mark it off. Maybe that will help with feeling overwhelmed."

Valorie nodded. "K."

But she didn't feel okay. Why couldn't Dad just do it all for her? A knot grew in her stomach as raindrops pelted the window, the gray skies matching her mood. Turning to her father, she sighed. "I'll do my best, Dad, but you have to help me. I can't do this alone."

"I know. Come log me into the bank account so we can check funds and pay these past-due bills."

As summer moved toward the end, Valorie caved to her children's incessant pleas to play in the backyard. With the checkbook and bills in hand, she sat on the patio, using the opportunity to pay everything like her dad taught her. She uttered a prayer of thanksgiving for him, knowing the past two months would have ruined her. He handled most of the phone calls to creditors, filing insurance and paperwork to pay off the cars and house.

Signing the last check for the month and sealing the envelope, she blew out a stream of air. The alarm on the gate chirped. She bolted from the chair while Bruce ran to the gate, barking. No one used the gate unless she invited people over, but that knowledge didn't slow down her pulse.

As she stepped off the patio, JR zipped past. "Chad! Can we toss the football?"

Valorie put a hand on her chest, willing her heart to calm.

Michele sauntered over to her mother. "I don't like football. Can I have more tea?"

"Sure honey. It's on the table."

Chad rounded the corner of the house, Bruce bouncing at his feet and JR tossing the football into the air and catching it. "Hey, everyone. Give me a second, little bro. At least let me say hello." He walked toward Valorie. "Sorry about the intrusion. I rang the front bell but didn't get an answer. When I heard the kids, I came in the back gate."

Valorie's gaze darted around the yard. "It was unlocked?"

"Yeah. Probably from Michele's birthday party last week."

"I thought we locked it afterward."

"Me too, but so much craziness with people coming and going. Someone probably slipped out after we locked it."

"I hope so. I don't like the idea of anyone coming into the backyard without me knowing it."

Bruce bounded up and pushed against Chad's hand, begging for attention. "With Bruce back here, you shouldn't worry." He squatted down and ruffled the dog's face. "Good boy. You won't let any evil person in, will you?" The dog woofed and licked Chad's face. "Ooh. No slobbers please."

Valorie laughed. "Now you know why I don't get in his face." She turned back toward the table. "You locked the gate now, though?"

"Of course."

"Thanks." She picked up her glass. "Want some tea?"

"Naw. I'm good. Gotta throw around a football." He winked and joined JR in the yard.

A soft voice came from the table. "Yeah. Go do the guy thing." Michele looked away, as if she didn't say anything.

Valorie sat beside her daughter. "Why do you dislike Chad so much?"

The little girl shrugged. "I dunno. He comes around all the time."

"I'm glad he watches out for us."

"Yeah, I guess. But he should go home."

"He does."

"No. I mean his *real* home. You know, where his family lives."

"Not sure he has much family, baby. Not like we do anyway." A noise in the alley made Valorie sit up straighter. "What's that?"

"A 'lectric-guy truck."

"How do you know that?"

"I watch 'em from my window. You never let us play outside."

"It's been too hot. And I don't always have time to sit out here."

"We got a fence. No one can steal us."

Valorie shook her head. "Honey, you're barely six. You don't know what could happen if I don't watch you closely."

"My friends play in their yards without mamas. They don't disappear."

"Sorry, honey. I don't want to risk it. I don't know what I'd do if anything happened to you or JR." She placed a hand on Michele's back. "But speaking of playing, maybe run a little more before we have to go inside."

Michele downed the rest of her tea and wiped her mouth with the back of her hand. "K. But I'm not playing with the boys." She rolled her eyes and scampered off toward the playhouse, where dolls and stuffed animals waited for their young mistress. Bruce followed her, hoping she might let him in her tiny pink house. She stopped at the door. "No, Bruce. You drag in too much yuck."

"Wonder where she got that from?" Valorie smiled at herself. She seldom let Bruce in with his entourage of dirt and grass. But hearing her daughter scold the dog, she considered lightening up a little.

Or not.

In the alley, a utility bucket rose to the power transformer. A muscled man bent over the side.

Odd. What was he looking at?

Chills trickled up Valorie's arms. He had no reason to look in the yard. She glared up at the man. Her hands trembled. He looked her direction and backed away from the side. Did she know him?

With knees like rubber, Valorie side-stepped to the gate, checking to make sure Chad locked it. The bolt in place, she sighed, but the weakness in her knees spread through her body. "Kids, let's get inside and clean up for dinner."

"Moooommm."

"It's time to get inside. Now." She looked back at the bucket, still suspended above her back fence. "Chad, you're welcome to stay for dinner."

He trotted toward her. "You okay?"

She forced a smile. "I don't like workmen staring at my kids."

Chad looked around. "Where?"

Valorie jerked her head up once. "There."

"The guy in the bucket?" He shrugged. "Probably checking to make sure his partner cleared the fence."

She swallowed hard. "Maybe. Just something about him. Unnerving."

"Oh, Valorie. You worry too much. I'm sure it's nothing."

"To you." She turned back to the kids, still running around the yard. "I said it's time to go inside. C'mon."

"Yes, ma'am." The chorus of obedience eased her mind a little. Until the man's head bobbed back into view. He stretched his neck, looking again at her family. She didn't like it.

Herding the kids and Chad through the back door, Valorie thrust every deadbolt into place and armed the alarm.

As the kids raced off to wash hands, Chad shook his head. "Valorie, someday you gotta control that unrealistic fear of yours."

She glared. "You sound like Mitch."

"Well, he was right. You're too scared of nothing."

Gritting her teeth, she turned to the refrigerator. She bit back words fighting to explode, not daring to drive Chad off with a strange man stalking her and the children. "I'm sorry. I try."

A soft touch on her shoulder elicited a tiny jump. "Sorry. Didn't mean to spook you."

She turned, resisting an urge to grab Chad. After a deep breath, she sighed again. "I made chicken salad for dinner. I hope that's okay with you."

"It's fine." His eyes searched hers. "I know you're still scared after what happened to Mitch. Only been a couple of months. But please. For the kids. Get a grip."

She nodded, not trusting her voice.

Chapter 26

An Opportune Moment

Dagon waited in the utility bucket, listening to chattering of children in the yard mingled with the mother's warnings. Did she never let them out of sight?

"Just go in house. Two minutes."

His thoughts didn't make it to the woman's mind. He peered through binoculars, careful to keep his head low. Sitting at the table with a book, she glanced up every minute.

She didn't cooperate with plans. "Why you so scared?"

He snickered. Well, she should fear him. But how did she know that? He'd been careful not to show himself since the last time she saw him in the bucket. Didn't want her too frightened. But she never left the kids alone. Not for a second.

Movement outside the front gate caught his attention. The neighbor's voice drifted through the air.

"Valorie. It's Rita. I made cookies. Let me in the gate."

He glanced at the table. Mother cocked her head and laid the book on the table. "Hey, Rita. Give me a second."

Dagon didn't breathe as she moved toward the gate and pressed in the code.

Just go out. For one minute.

Instead, Valorie opened the gate, let the neighbor inside, and relocked it. Not enough time for his plan. The women chatted, kids rushing over to grab cookies before returning to whatever game they played. Endless moments passed, his neck tensing as he hoped for a break. Just one.

This entire game bored him. Drake insisted they wait. What did he know? Sitting in a bucket, always waiting—hoping for one minute alone with kids.

If he didn't get it soon...

Maybe he should go back to Russia.

Finally, the women moved back to the gate. On the other side, a man read the water meter. The dog barked, running to Valorie.

"Bruce. Quiet."

The dog stopped barking but stared at the front yard.

Dagon looked down at his partner. "Be ready, Guy."

Valorie punched in the code, and a buzz gave Dagon hope. When the gate opened, the dog charged, barking fiercely at the strange man on the other side of the fence.

The woman grabbed for the animal, missing him while the meter man dove into the truck, his partner pulling away from the curb. The dog shot into the street, following the strangers.

The women stepped away from the gate. Valorie glanced back at the children. "Stay here."

"K Mama."

The lock clicked as the woman shut it.

Now. I go.

Dagon jumped from the bucket, bending knees to soften the landing. He grabbed a bolt cutter from the truck, snapped the padlock, and pushed open the gate. The boy kicked a ball nearby, but the girl was too far away. He'd have to lure them closer. He looked back at Guy and motioned him forward with his head.

He waved. "Hi kids. Having fun?"

The boy stiffened. "Hey, mister. What are you doing in our yard? You gotta leave."

"Just being friendly—working on lines out here. I tire of bucket."

The little boy squinted his eyes. "It looks kinda cool. I mean the riding up and down."

"It can be fun. Wanna try?"

The child looked at the closed front gate. "I shouldn't. Mama said stay here. She won't like it."

"I not tell." Dagon flashed a smile.

The little girl approached, hands on hips. "JR, you better not."

"Aww, c'mon Chele. Just a quick ride. It'll be fun."

"No. We can't do that. We gotta stay in the yard."

"It take only a minute. Mom never know." He motioned for the children to follow him.

"I don't know..." The boy hesitated.

Dagon looked toward the front. "Enough. We go." He grabbed the girl first, his partner pushing through the gate with duct tape, which he slapped across her mouth.

The boy pounded him. "Let her go."

Dagon laughed. "A flea hitting me. Oh, no."

He slapped the boy's face, knocking him down, and thrust the girl into Guy's arms. No hesitation, the other man charged back out the gate with her in tow.

JR jumped to his feet as Dagon reached to pick him up and shoved tape over his mouth. As the boy squirmed and kicked in his grasp, he pushed through to the alley. "Stop fighting. I kill sister."

The boy's eyes widened. He shook his head violently.

"You be good, I hurt neither. You struggle, I kill both. Girl first while you watch."

Dagon closed the gate behind him, leaving the padlock on the ground.

He shifted the load, drawing a fob from his pocket. Fifty feet away, a car's trunk popped open. He lifted it and both men tossed children in. Slamming the trunk lid, they catapulted around to the doors and jumped inside.

Without a backward glance, Dagon started the car and raced to the end of the alley.

Not stopping, he turned away from the neighborhood.

Banging filled the car from the back.

Guy glanced back. "Geez. We gotta quieten those kids. If someone hears them..."

After checking the rearview mirror, Dagon shouted, "Stop it! You want to die? I come back there, you die now."

The noise ceased, replaced with muffled whimpers.

"You'd really kill them?"

"Maybe."

At a red light, he pulled out his phone. "Boss. I got kids. Where I take them?"

"Anyone see you?"

"Of course not." Dagon checked all mirrors, holding his breath. "No one following."

The light turned green, and he drove through the intersection.

As the deep voice came over the phone, he sighed. "Well, well. Perhaps you did something right. Finally. Drive around for about 30 minutes. Then take them to the other house."

"The one on..."

"Don't say where, idiot. Just go there. Take me off speaker."

Dagon clicked a button and held the phone to his ear. "Da, boss?"

"Guy with you?"

"Da. He helped."

"Once you get the little brats inside, lose him."

"Lose?"

"Yes, imbecile. I don't need more than one moron out there potentially spreading gossip. He drinks. He'll talk—brag. Make sure that doesn't happen."

"Understood." Dagon disconnected and continued driving.

The man looked over. "What else did he say? Do I get my money now?"

"Yeah. We drive a while, deliver brats to house, and then you paid."

The other man rubbed his hands together. "Excellent."

Drake didn't like loose ends. He had a point. Guy talked big, always bragging about his crimes while he downed cheap booze. Like he wanted to impress all the idiots around him. No room for a heavy drinker who could ID them.

Dagon eased up on the gas pedal when a patrol car passed him. He didn't want to end up in prison. Or worse. If he messed this up, the boss might end him, too. Might anyway.

But Dagon didn't survive so long without thinking and planning. The boss? He could turn on him. Consider him another loose end. Not if he had a plan, though. He'd practice on Guy, then make a move on Drake. Who was an imbecile? Not him.

The big man let a smile play on his lips.

Chapter 27

Not Supposed to Happen

JR dribbled his soccer ball around the yard. His sister never wanted to play with him. Just as well. She didn't know or care much about soccer. But he wanted to get better. He missed the evenings and weekends when Daddy played with him. His breath shuddered as he shrugged off the sadness.

Couldn't let Mama see him crying. It'd make her sad all over again.

Just then, Rita showed up—with cookies. Nice. He ran over to the table and grabbed two, gobbling them in seconds before returning to his solitary ball game.

"Hey, Chele. Wanna play soccer?"

"No. I'm eating cookies."

"I'll wait."

"No way. I don't like soccer. Besides, I'm having a tea party with my dolls—in my little house." She stomped across the grass. "And don't ask. No boys allowed."

"Fine. I don't wanna be in your stupid house, anyway."

Bruce's wild barking interrupted him.

What was up with that crazy dog? He never barked like that.

JR looked toward the front gate. Bruce rushed through it, and JR froze.

His mama looked at them. "Stay here!"

"K, Mama." Where else would they go? He didn't want to chase the dog.

His sister poked her head out the playhouse door, shrugged, and started to head back inside.

Without warning, the back gate opened, and a strange man eased through.

Chele stopped, staring at the stranger as if she wanted to scream.

"Hey kids. Having fun?"

JR stiffened, studying the man with a weird accent. "What are you doing in our yard?" He took a step toward the intruder. "You gotta leave. NOW."

The man shrugged. "Just friendly—working on electric lines. I tire of bucket."

The boy squinted, looking up. He always wondered what it would be like, seeing the neighborhood from so high. "Kinda cool. I mean the riding up and down."

"Can be fun." The man cupped his hand over his mouth. "Wanna try?"

JR glanced back toward the front of their yard. No mom. No Rita. Gate still closed. "I shouldn't. Mama won't like it."

"I not tell." The odd man flashed a smile.

Uncertain, JR glanced at the bucket again. Maybe a quick up and down...

Michele stepped beside him, hands on her hips. "JR, you better not."

So much like Mama. He didn't need two fraidy-cats under one roof. "Aww, c'mon Chele. Just one ride. It'll be fun."

"No." She stamped her foot. "We can't. We gotta stay in the yard. Mama said."

The man waved them toward the bucket. "It take only minute. Mom not know."

His gut churning, JR wanted to follow, but he hesitated. Something about the man. How did he get through the gate? Wasn't it always locked? "I don't know..." Did he dare?

Michele moved toward where he last saw his mother. "Maaammma!"

The man swooped past him to his sister. "Enough! We go!"

With horror, JR witnessed the man seize Chele and swiftly retreat to the back gate. A different man appeared, holding something gray. JR pounded against the first man's back. "Let her go!"

The man's laugh sent bumps flitting down JR's arms. "A flea hitting me. Oh, no." From nowhere, an over-sized hand connected with his face, knocking him down.

JR looked up as the second man scooted out the gate, his sister tucked under his arm.

He jumped to his feet, but massive arms encased him. A hand slapped something over his mouth.

Tape?

JR wanted to scream. But it came out muffled. He hit and kicked. He squirmed. The man pushed through and shut the gate. JR kept fighting, screaming against the tape.

"Stop fighting. I kill sister."

JR froze. He shook his head hard and stilled himself.

"You be good, I hurt neither. You struggle; I kill both. Girl first while you watch."

This couldn't be real. He had to be dreaming.

Wake up! Wake up, JR!

A chirp sounded. The man tossed him against a hard surface. Carpet. A tire.

The back of a car? No!

Chele stared at him, terror filling her wide eyes.

He grabbed her hands as the lid closed and everything went dark.

Yanking the tape from his mouth, he whispered to his sister. "Kick, Chele. Kick harder than ever in your life. We gotta make noise."

Both kicked and pounded on the trunk lid. He panted, sweat covering his face. Chele did her part, kicking and breathing like she ran a race.

A booming, muffled voice spoke with a harshness JR didn't like. "Stop it! You want to die? I come back there, you die now."

Out of breath and exhausted, JR stopped kicking. One more pound on the lid before he gave up. Chele curled up closer to him, shaking and sobbing.

"It's okay, Chele. I got you." He peeled the tape from her mouth.

"Ouch."

"I'm sorry." He stroked her cheek.

His breath quivered as he tried not to shake. But his body didn't listen.

Chapter 28

Gone

Valorie stepped away from the gate, hesitant to go too far. "Bruce. Come back." She turned to Rita. "Stay here while I go after that stupid dog."

"No one will get past me. Go get him."

By the time Valorie reached the front of the house, the dog had chased the truck down the street. "Bruce!"

The dog turned, his tongue lolling to the side. He ran toward her, emitting a single "woof." Midway down the block, he stopped, sniffing the ground.

"Don't you do it, dog. Not in someone else's yard."

Bruce continued sniffing for a few seconds and stopped.

Valorie threw a hand over her mouth. "Bruce. Don't you dare."

He lifted his head, looking at her, then returned to sniffing.

Valorie glanced back. Rita stood near the front of the house. She motioned her back toward the gate and rushed toward the dog, intent on grabbing his collar before he left a mess she didn't want to scoop. As she neared the dog, he hiked his leg, a stream of yellow flowing on the neighbor's rose bush. Better than him squatting. Three more steps, and she'd have the dog. He turned and sprinted across the street.

"Stop. Bruce! Come here!"

He playfully darted around the yard, looking back at her every few seconds.

Valorie blew out a breath. Chasing him wasn't working. Instead, she squatted down. "Bruce. C'mon sweet dog. Let's go find the kids. Where's JR? Where's Michele?" She tried pulling out a calm tone instead of the one bubbling inside. "C'mon, dog. I'm gonna beat you to death if you don't." With the smile and sweet tone, she wondered. Did he understand what she said?

Bruce continued running around the yard, enjoying his freedom.

Valorie tried a different tactic. She whistled.

Nothing.

Again. She whistled twice moving closer to the dog. "C'mon buddy. Let's go home and get a treat. Wanna treat? C'mon."

He stopped, his ears perking. In no hurry, he strolled to the street, paused, and then crossed as if he had all day.

Wait. Just wait.

Valorie convinced herself not to lunge and renew the dog's insistence on running wild.

Finally, he reached her side of the street before stopping to sniff yet again. She edged toward the dog, but when his head came up, she paused. He moved closer, keeping a few feet between them. Without taking her eyes from him, Valorie moved a few squatted steps closer, her thighs aching.

She needed more exercise. A main crossroad lay a few feet from them, passing traffic buzzing by. No wonder her legs hurt. Her house stood a long block away. On some streets, it'd be two blocks.

Bruce moved another few steps in her direction. She lunged then, grabbing his collar before he reacted. The dog barked—she swore with a smile across his mischievous face. His tongue lapped at her, hitting his mark before she could pull back.

"Ooh, Bruce. Disgusting. Stop that." Despite her revulsion, she laughed. It shifted from her throat to her belly. "Okay. Okay. Can we please go home now?" Valorie wiped away the slobbers, still clinging to his collar.

Standing, she tugged at the dog. He still wanted to sniff the ground. "Better get you home before you leave something that gets us both in trouble."

He tried to draw her off course, but Valorie kept him moving to their house. A sudden thud in her stomach stole her breath. Where did that come from? She shook her head.

Rita stood by the gate, opening it as the pair approached.

"Thank you. I don't know what got into this crazy dog. He never bolts like that."

"Maybe he didn't like the meter guy."

"Maybe." Valorie looked around the backyard.

Where were the kids?

Everything looked in order. The back gate closed. But no JR. No Michele.

"Kids! JR! Michele!"

She turned to Rita. "Do you see them?"

Rita shook her head. "Are they in the playhouse?" She moved across the yard and peeked into the small opening. "Nope. Not here."

Valorie's throat closed.

Rapid breaths seized her.

She ran to the back door and flung it open. "KIDS!"

Nothing.

Rita joined her, racing through the house.

They called both names, anxious for a response.

Getting none.

Terror laced Valorie's voice, her heart pummeling against her ribs. "Where are they?"

Rita shrugged. "Maybe we missed them outside. They love playing hide-and-seek."

Valorie scanned the room and headed to the garage. "Let me check the garage."

"Ok. I'll go back outside and look again. They're here somewhere."

The garage stood in silence, mocking Valorie's fear.

She stooped, checking beneath the cars. Her breath caught at the sight of the chest-style freezer.

They wouldn't dare get in it. Would they?

Valorie opened the lid. Nothing out of place.

She blew out air and headed back into the kitchen.

At the bottom of the stairs, she placed hands on her hips. "Kids, this isn't funny. Come out at once."

No answer.

"I mean it! If you don't come down right now, you won't get to watch TV tonight. Not a minute of it!"

The house echoed back an eerie silence.

Tears gathered. She had to get a grip. Valorie whipped around at the sound of the back screen opening.

Rita stood in the doorway, her face pale.

"What is it?"

Shaking, Rita motioned outside. "You should see this."

The two women hurried out the door, Rita leading the way to the back gate.

Valorie stared in disbelief.

The locked chain.

Cut.

Lying powerless on the ground.

As her knees met the grass, Valorie trembled. The world tilted. A whoosh filled her ears. Breath wouldn't descend to her lungs.

What had she done?

"I should never have left them alone."

Rita kneeled beside her, a hand reaching out to steady Valorie's tremors. "I'll call the police. We'll find them."

Valorie looked up, her friend's face blurring. She wanted to hope it was all a bad dream, but she knew better.

Chapter 29

Police

Detective Davis caught the case.

Two kids missing. Distraught mother.

Not a typical day on the job. Not a call she wanted.

Most of the time, missing kids showed up at a neighbor's or friend's house. But when children disappeared, no one ignored it. She flipped the switch for lights and siren and raced to the home, hoping this case ended before starting.

At the scene, Davis approached the responding officer. "What you got?"

"The mom says the kids were in the backyard. Dog got lose. She chased after him. When she came back, no kids." He shrugged. "We checked the yard, house, and alley."

"Any sign of struggle?"

"Nope. Gate to the alley was closed but not locked."

The detective followed him through the front gate, noting the alarm. "Did she have the gate alarm activated?"

"I… no… not sure." The officer scratched his head. "Probably not if she had to chase the dog. I'm not sure why she disarmed it and opened the gate. Name's Valorie Ferguson."

Davis jotted a note on her pad. Wait. She knew that name. The woman Tyler mentioned.

She shivered. "Any neighbors see or hear anything?"

"No. The woman next door was here, visiting, and said it was only a few minutes. She stayed by the gate while the mom chased the dog but heard nothing."

"And the father..."

The officer swallowed. "Died a few months back." He fidgeted. "Look, Davis, no offense, but this woman's loony. She used to call constantly—reports of people trying to break in, hang-up calls. You name it. I mean who puts alarms on a gate?"

"People who want to protect their family."

"Yeah, but she... When you go in, check how many locks she has on the front and back doors—plus an alarm system. The woman's paranoid."

Davis gritted her teeth. "Don't go there."

"What? Not our first time at this house."

"I don't care if it's your millionth time. You don't take missing children lightly. Ever!"

The officer rolled his eyes. "Whatever. You deal with the woman."

"Not a problem." She rolled her shoulders and strolled around the yard, searching for anything out of place. A female officer stood beside the open back gate. Davis approached her. "Hey, Ross. This gate open when you arrived?"

"No ma'am. The neighbor brought me out here, insisting someone cut the lock."

A small patch of grass led from the yard to the alley. Possible indentions. Hard to tell, but the area looked disturbed. She squatted beside a chain and padlock. "Anyone touch this?"

Officer Ross shook her head. "No. Exactly like I found it."

Davis took a pen from her pocket and shifted the lock. "Look cut to you?"

"Yeah. Clean—bolt cutters I'd guess."

"Agreed. Make sure they get photographs. Bag it and get it over for dusting." She looked up and down the alley. "I doubt the perp left prints, but worth a shot. Maybe we'll catch a break. Anything else?"

Ross shrugged. "My partner doesn't think so, but that kinda looks like tire tracks over there."

The women moved into the alley. Fifty feet away, skid marks ran a few feet toward a side street. Davis studied them. "Could be related—or nothing." In the other direction, near the home, a white truck with a utility bucket attachment sat idle. "What about the truck?"

"Neighbors said it's been here a few days, not doing much."

"Run the plates. Not sure why workers would leave it sitting here."

The officer nodded, noted the plate number, and headed to the car.

The detective looked around one more time and went back through the gate. Two women sat at a table near the house, one holding her head. No doubt that was the mother. She took a deep breath, releasing it as she neared the patio.

"Mrs. Ferguson? I'm Detective Davis."

The woman holding her head looked up. "Please find my children."

"I'll do everything I can. Is there a place your children might go?"

"No. They don't leave the yard. I only stepped away for a few minutes. And Rita was right there."

Davis looked at the other woman. "You're Rita?"

The woman wrung her hands. "Yes. I live next door. Valorie's right. They just... disappeared."

"You didn't hear anything? A scream? Scuffling?"

"No. Nothing like that. They were playing when Bruce got out."

"Bruce?"

"The dog. Valorie went after him, but I stayed right beside the gate. I peeked through, and Michele was beside the playhouse. JR was kicking the ball around, not far from the gate. I turned back to the front, watching for Valorie." She paused. "It couldn't have been more than two or three minutes."

Valorie stood, her eyes widening. "Drake. It had to be him."

The detective cocked her head. "Who's Drake? Last name?"

The woman shuddered and wrapped her arms around herself. "Don't know. He kidnapped me. Held me in a dungeon for days."

Davis took a step toward Valorie. Her throat went dry. "When did this happen?"

"Months ago. Before Mitch died."

"Mitch was your husband?"

"Yes." Valorie fumbled with the chair and sat again.

"Did you report that kidnapping to the police?"

"No. They wouldn't do anything. Mitch didn't even believe me. Said it was a dream." Her breath caught. "I don't remember much—only bits of the whole thing. And I know it sounds unbelievable. But two women showed up when my husband died. I remembered seeing them in a dark, damp place. No details. Then we saw Drake at the cemetery. They recognized him. That's when I knew it wasn't just some dream."

Detective Davis pulled up a chair and sat facing Valorie. "These women. Where are they now?"

"Went back to Texas. Not long after Mitch's funeral."

"Have you seen this man after the women left?"

"No. We only saw him that one time."

"And these women? Any reason to think they were working with him?"

"No. They gave us the details about Drake. I didn't even know his name. They stayed with me. Took care of me for a few days." Valorie blinked, hard and fast. "Absolutely not."

Davis touched her hand. "I have to ask, ma'am. I'm covering all bases."

"Not Charissa or Shamira. They wouldn't hurt me or my kids."

"I believe you. All the same, I want their contact information. Maybe they know more about this Drake guy."

Rita jumped in. "Detective, I met those women, and Valorie's right. They're good people."

"I'll keep that in mind." She tapped her pen against the pad. "Anything else unusual?"

Valorie rubbed her forehead. "Lots of hang-up and heavy breathing calls. I thought it was just teens playing pranks. But now..."

"We'll pull phone records. See if we can find a common incoming number. You report this?"

"I tried. Same tired answer. 'We can't do anything.'" Valorie's gaze fixed on the back fence. "The police don't like me. They think I'm paranoid. Always have. But now my kids are gone. Disappeared. Maybe I'm not as psycho as everyone thinks."

"We'll see what we can find out about this Drake—and the two women." Davis started to stand, but paused. "Why would he want your children?"

"I don't know." Valorie shook her head. "Maybe because I somehow escaped from him? This is one of my worst fears. If he hurts them... I can't..." She melted into sobs, her fear and sorrow sucking air from the patio.

Rita moved to Valorie and wrapped her arms around her. "It's gonna be okay. They'll find JR and Michele."

"We'll do all we can. Have you given anyone photos of the kids?"

"Yes. The female officer asked—I think she already broadcast them."

The detective looked at the house as she stood. Not likely anyone took them for ransom. It felt personal. Still, Valorie's story didn't jive. How could she endure being kidnapped and not remember any details? She walked toward the front gate, taking one more look around for anything else she might have missed.

A tall, buff man entered the backyard. Davis drew back. "Tyler? Is that you?"

"Hey, Davis. What's going on here?"

"Looks like a kidnap."

Chad took two steps and reached her, clenching his fist and looking around the yard and then at the patio. "The kids?"

She nodded. "Dog got loose. Mom chased him down. Came back into the yard, and the kids were gone."

"Any leads?"

"Not much to go on. Looks like someone cut the padlock on the back gate. Signs of disturbance. Maybe tire tracks. Could all be unrelated. I thought you'd be long gone by now."

Chad looked over her head at Valorie. "Couldn't leave Captain Ferguson's family."

"She as paranoid as the cops think?"

"Apparently not." He ran his hand over his face. "Look, you checked out that car for me. Nothing there. Haven't seen it lately. But she keeps getting calls. Makes me wonder. They never caught the guy who murdered Mitch."

"Murdered?"

"Ran him down on purpose. I'd still swear to it."

"Was he into something bad, Tyler?"

"Not him. Straight as they come."

"Could the wife be mixed up in something?"

He peeked over her shoulder. "You're joking, right?"

Davis stared him down. "Two children missing. Not a time to joke about anything."

"Look, Davis, Valorie's scared of a bug's shadow. Can't see her involved in anything dangerous."

"What do you know about this Drake? She mentioned he took and held her for days."

Chad rubbed the stubble on his chin and glanced around the yard again. "Not much. Evil-looking man with attitude. Made his presence known at Mitch's graveside. Valorie's friends said he held them all in a dungeon."

"You believe them?"

"No reason not to."

"Did any of them report it?"

"He didn't forcibly take the others as far as I can tell. Lured and captured. Valorie seems to be the only one he grabbed." He shook his head. "Charissa talked to a cop, but they closed the case almost as soon as they opened it. No leads."

"Sounds suspicious."

"More like impossible to believe. But..."

"What?"

He rubbed the back of his neck. "Sensed they weren't lying. If it didn't happen, someone brainwashed them all to believe it did."

"I'll have a conversation with these other women. Can you give me a description of Drake?"

"About 6-2, 175. Dark hair, beard. Same as a million others. But his eyes. Even from a distance—evil. If he grabbed the kids..."

"You think he'd hurt them?"

"I don't know. Why would he want a couple of kids? Then again, why would he take Valorie?"

Davis shrugged. "Valid questions. So far, no contact. Doesn't look like someone capable of paying a ransom. Unless her family has money."

"Not much. Comfortable, but not wealthy. Gotta be something else."

She placed a hand on Chad's arm. "I'll level with you. We got almost nothing, but someone cut that padlock. So, I don't agree with my cop friends who think they wandered off. I'll give it my best."

"I know you will."

Davis walked to the gate, armed with a few notes, her head swimming with questions and the next steps.

"Hey, Davis."

She turned to look at Chad. "Yeah?"

"I'm glad you caught the case. Find them. For Mitch."

"I won't give up."

"You never did."

Davis saluted and headed for her car. Inside, she looked over notes.

Strange case. If not for the clean cut on the padlock, she might doubt the kidnapping angle. Drake or not, why would someone take two children from a backyard? Especially from one with a paranoid mom. If random, they'd pick the beach or a park.

But a backyard?

No. Whoever took them had a motive. What? No clue. If she figured that out, she'd have a better chance of finding the perp—and the kids.

Officer Ross stepped up to the window.

Davis rolled it down. "Anything else?"

"The truck. License plates switched. But I found a report of a missing utility truck and bucket from about a month ago. We're checking for fingerprints. No hits so far."

"Keep looking."

"I'm no detective, but it sure looks like someone planned this. Waited for weeks."

"Yeah. I think you're right. Keep canvasing the neighbors, will ya?"

"What are you looking for?"

"Hoping someone noticed a man or two in that bucket. Maybe get lucky with a description." Davis handed the officer her card. "Give me a call if you get anything."

"Yes, ma'am." She turned and looked back over her shoulder. "I know others think she's crazy, but I got a gut feeling. And it ain't good."

The detective lifted her chin. "I hope we're both wrong, and the kids are off at a neighbor's house playing."

But as she started the car, weight filled her stomach. Her gut agreed with Ross, and time wasn't on their side.

Chapter 30

Unreal

Couldn't think. Couldn't feel. Valorie stared across the yard, wanting the activity to stop. To wake up and find it all another nightmare.

How did this happen? What was she thinking, leaving the kids alone to chase a stupid dog?

Rita stood with a cop, nodding and gesturing with her hands. Maybe they'd believe the neighbor. Too many of them knew her. Believed her crazy. But not Rita.

A soft touch on her shoulder jolted her from the thoughts. She looked up. "Chad."

"Hey, Valorie. Just talked to Detective Davis. What happened?"

Her voice hitched as she drew rapid breaths. "I don't know. They're just gone."

"It's gonna be alright. We'll find them."

She stared at him. So confident. Yet in his eyes, glints of anxiety flashed. "I think it's Drake."

Chad blinked. "Why would he take them?"

"To get back at me. Apparently, I escaped from his dungeon and messed up his stupid game."

"You think he's been making those calls? Trying to scare you?"

"Someone has."

"Val, let's be realistic. Maybe the kids went exploring. Have you seen Drake again—since the funeral?"

She rubbed her mouth and shook her head.

"What about anyone else?"

"That man in the bucket. I told you he was watching them."

Chad sat in the chair Davis left empty. "I know. And I didn't take you seriously."

Heat rushed through Valorie as she clenched her fists. "No. You didn't. No one takes me seriously, and now my children have to pay. God only knows what those evil men will do to my babies." She wrapped her arms around herself again, sobs shaking her.

"I'm sorry. I should've paid more attention." He shifted his eyes away from her. "Did you tell Davis?"

"I think so. Don't remember. Does it matter?"

"Yeah. The truck's still there. They'll check it for fingerprints."

"You weren't here. The way they talked to me... like I made it all up." She sighed. "Maybe not the detective. She might believe me."

"I served with Davis. She's a pit bull. If I had to choose a cop, she'd be the one."

Valorie's lip quivered. "I hope you're right."

"I am." Chad rose and reached for her hand. "Let's get you inside. These cops will be here for hours. You don't have to sit and watch."

"What if they have more questions or find something?"

"They'll come inside."

Rita nodded at an officer and came back to the patio. "How you doing?"

"Are you kidding?"

"Sorry. I know. This is a nightmare. I can't... I can't believe it happened. We were only outside the gate for a few minutes." Rita buried her face in her hands. "I'm so sorry, Valorie. It's my fault. I should've come back into the yard."

Valorie embraced her friend. "No. If I had let Bruce go, it wouldn't have happened. But I couldn't let him get run over or disappear. Mitch brought him home as a puppy. I had to go after him."

Chad approached the women, placing his hands on both their backs. "Ladies, no one's to blame. If someone took the kids, that's not on either of you."

Valorie looked at him. Easy to say. He wasn't there.

He wasn't there.

What if he had been?

Would it have happened?

He'd been around less lately, choosing to text instead. Not wanting to upset Michele. She studied his face. He looked around the yard, glancing at her, but not locking gazes. His chin quivered as he paced across the concrete.

Was he thinking the same thing?

She reached up and touched his hand as he came back beside her. "Not your fault either."

His jaw clenched. "They'll find them."

She nodded. "They have to. I can't live without my kids."

The three broke from each other, standing and watching as cops moved around. Some took evidence bags and walked toward the front gate, not returning.

Chad surveyed the patio. "Where's Bruce?"

Rita grinned. "I saved him from Valorie. She looked like she wanted to beat him, so I put him in the garage."

As if on cue, a muffled bark filled the air.

Why did the dog run away? Why that day? He'd never done it before.

Still... He didn't protect them—but Bruce didn't take them. She couldn't blame him.

She moved toward the house, then opened the back door and the one leading to the garage. Bruce bounded to her, sniffing, licking. All the things she hated about dogs. Then he sat and searched her face. His stare fixed on hers, and he whimpered.

She rubbed his head. "It's okay, Bruce. You didn't know, did you?"

The dog rose and nuzzled her hand.

"C'mon. Let's go inside. I can't watch anymore."

Lead filled her legs as she moved into the kitchen, collapsing to the floor. Bruce curled up beside her with his head in her lap.

Chapter 31

Good Cop

Chad lifted Valorie to her feet. A few steps, and her legs wilted. Chad picked her up, carrying her to the sofa in the living room. He pulled a blanket over her, turning at the sound of the doorbell. Bruce stepped between him and the sofa, burying his head against Valorie's limp arm.

"You expecting anyone?"

Valorie squeezed her eyes. "No."

Rita came around the breakfast bar, a glass of water and a bottle of pills in her hands. "I called her dad. It's probably them."

Chad nodded and headed to the door. He glanced at the alarm.

"I forgot to reset it after opening it to look out front for the kids." Valorie inhaled, breaths shuddering.

"Got it." Chad opened the door and stepped aside as Mom and Dad rushed through.

"Valorie! We're here." Her dad crossed the room, pushed Bruce aside, and kneeled beside her. "It's okay. It's gonna be alright."

Mom joined them, sitting on the sofa next to Valorie. "We've been praying and calling everyone we know. People are gathering to help with the search. We'll find the kids."

She wanted to respond, but words stuck in her throat as fresh tears streamed down her cheeks.

Search for her kids? She never wanted to hear those words, though the many times she thought them beat against her brain, inciting a dull ache. With the words spoken, reality hit with the force of a bulldozer. This couldn't be happening.

An officer entered the living room. "Ma'am, I'm Officer Ross. Detective Davis requested that I stay with you—in case you get a call or anything happens."

Valorie squinted her eyes. "What?"

"There's always the possibility the kids went down the street and will come home soon. Or if someone took them, we could get a call for ransom. I'll be here if either happens."

"A ransom?"

"Yes ma'am. Is that a possibility?"

"Are you serious? I'm not wealthy." Valorie rubbed her forehead, drawing her hand down her face. "Why would someone think I can pay a ransom?"

"If you got any life insurance from your husband's death, it could happen. Someone you know might think you have money now. In that case, it's someone harmless who's out to make a buck. We have to look at every angle. Why else would someone take your children?"

"Because that man—Drake—he's pure evil. He doesn't need a reason."

Ross nodded and moved closer to the sofa. "Anyone who grabs a child is evil."

Valorie moved to the side of the sofa. "You don't understand. No one believes me, because I can't remember details. But I'm telling you—that man is the devil himself."

"I'm not here to judge, Mrs. Ferguson. I don't know your story. But we'll do what we can to find this man and question him. Can you tell me anything else about him?"

"Not really. I tried to block him from my thoughts."

Dad moved to the sofa's arm, gently placing a hand on Valorie's back. He looked at Ross. "Do we have to continue these questions? Shouldn't we be out searching for the kids?"

Officer Ross sighed. "Trust me. They're organizing volunteers and searching door-to-door. Officers have the children's photos and descriptions. Everyone on patrol has eyes peeled—looking everywhere possible. We just need a solid lead."

He sighed. "I'm sorry. These are my grandchildren, and my daughter's been through so much already."

"No need to apologize, sir. I can't imagine how you all feel."

Valorie drew her knees up to her chest. "I don't think I can stand this. I can't think. Can't feel. I'm no threat to anyone. I struggle to walk out my door. Why would anyone do this?"

"If we can figure that out, it will help find them." Officer Ross stepped back. "I'll try to stay out of your way, but if you think of anything—even the tiniest thing—let me know. That goes for any of you."

Rita offered Valorie the water. "Thank you, officer. Chad made coffee, so please help yourself." She turned to her friend. "Valorie, I found this Valium in the cabinet. If you want one to sleep..."

"I never want to sleep again. Not until I have my babies back."

Mom rubbed her back. "Thank you, Rita. Maybe later. She needs to be awake when the kids come back."

Rita turned, mumbling. "If they come back."

Chad grabbed Dad's arm. "I can't just sit here. Wanna come with me?"

"Yeah." Dad looked at Valorie. "Stay here, hon. I'm going with Chad. Maybe the kids sneaked out the back gate and lost their way home. We'll search anywhere they might go."

Fat chance. They didn't know anywhere close to go. Except...

"They always want to stop at that arcade. It's a half mile from here, but..."

Chad's eyes widened. "Worth a shot. We'll start there."

The men rushed through the door while Valorie buried her face in her arms. If only she believed they'd find her babies. Heaviness invaded her chest, squeezing hope from her heart.

What if they didn't come back?

Chapter 32

Aftermath

The clock chimed ten. The continued barrage of questions exhausted her. No, she didn't know of anywhere the kids might go. No, they never ran away. Never. They didn't leave the yard or house without her. Ever. Yes, they knew better than to get in a car with a stranger. No one she knew would take them.

Ross even dared ask if Chad might take them.

What an insane accusation. He'd never do that.

Would he?

Valorie shook her head, remembering the stinging words. No. He'd been nothing but helpful. Why would he take her kids? He cared about them all, but he also knew her deepest fear of losing her children. He wouldn't put her through this. If not for her, because of Mitch. Plus, he knew how Michele felt. Why would he kidnap them and make that worse? Preposterous.

Rita interrupted her thoughts. "Valorie, I need to go home now."

"Of course. Please. I'm fine. Mom will stay with me." She half rose.

"Don't get up. I'll be back in the morning. Do you need anything?"

"My babies back."

"I'll pray for them—and you."

As Rita headed out the door, Valorie muttered. "Fat lot of good that does."

Mom stood. "Valorie! How can you say that? All we have right now is prayer."

Valorie's jaw clenched. "God let this happen. Why should we pray to someone who allows so much pain for one person?"

Her mother took a deep breath, held it for a few seconds, and released it. "I know you're scared and hurting. If we don't have faith in God's goodness, we have no hope of seeing the children again, and I will not accept that."

"Fine. Then you pray. I can't. He doesn't hear me, anyway." With that, Valorie rose. "I'm going upstairs—maybe sleep." As she hauled her dead weight up the stairs, she knew better. Sleep would elude her tonight and every night until they found her children. But if they didn't find them, she might sleep forever.

At the top of the stairs, she peeked into JR's bedroom. No different from usual—a complete mess. Bed unmade, toys scattered. He loved his Legos—all thousands of them, and the half-built sets mocked her. Why hadn't she helped him finish the ones he started with Mitch? She peeked under the bed, walked to the closet, and opened the door. She gulped the knot in her throat.

In Michele's room, she caressed the smooth bedspread, dolls and stuffed animals lining the pillows. Several sat at the small table, laughing at her from the pretend tea party. When was the last time she partook of a make-believe scone? A vice squeezed her heart. She searched the room again, pleading in silence for the kids to come out and yell, "Surprise!"

Silence echoed against the walls.

Hugging herself, Valorie slumped to the floor beside the bed and buried her face in her arms. The tears released then, sobs wracking her body.

Why? What did she do to make someone take her kids? Was it Drake? Was this her fault?

Her body ached as she sat in the same position, time meaning nothing, until her eyes closed, and she let herself drift into restless slumber.

Valorie's eyes popped open, her head jerking upward.

What was that?

She looked around the room, searching. Her gaze returned to the bed. Empty.

Reality crashed against her, pounding her chest and tightening her throat all over again.

Voices drifted up the stairs. Dad. She unfolded her feet from beneath her body, a tingling sensation daring her to stand. She rubbed, demanding the blood to flow through her limbs. After a moment, she stood, a sense of dread telling her no one found the kids yet.

The clock downstairs chimed two times. How could it be 2:00 a.m.? She couldn't have slept that long.

She stumbled across the room, banging into the door frame, listening for her father's voice. In the stillness, she heard him. What was he saying? If they found the kids, surely, he'd bound up the stairs to tell her. The hushed tones said volumes.

The kids weren't home, and as the hours ticked by, she knew the chances of ever seeing them again narrowed. Shivers ran through her body as she dragged herself down the stairs.

In the living room, both her father and Chad slumped in chairs, holding their heads.

"Dad?"

He looked up and rose. Chad jumped to his feet.

Dad crossed the room. "Hi baby. Your mom said you fell asleep. I hoped you didn't wake up until morning."

She shrugged. "I think the car door woke me." She swallowed hard. "You didn't find them?"

"No. I'm afraid not."

Chad moved toward them. "Any calls?"

The knot in her throat tightened, her hands shaking. She shook her head.

Without warning, her knees buckled, and she grabbed the back of a chair. Her dad threw his arm around her, steadying and comforting—at least trying to. He led her to the front of the chair and lowered her into it.

Chad raced into the kitchen and returned a moment later with a glass of water. "Here. Drink this."

Valorie glared up at him and looked around the room. "What is it?"

"Just water." Chad held out the glass. "I promise."

She accepted it and took a sip. Suddenly, she bolted from the chair and raced to the breakfast bar, retrieving the phone. "Crap. I always silence it in the evenings."

Her fingers flew across the screen. What if the kidnapper called and she didn't hear it? After a few moments, she fell back into the chair and sighed. No missed calls. They didn't reach out.

The officer, whatever her name, came in from the kitchen. "Anything wrong?"

Tears fell, and she didn't stop them.

Chad said, "She silenced the phone earlier and thought she might've missed a call."

The officer nodded. "Anything?"

Valorie shook her head, the boulder in her stomach shutting off her breaths.

As if on cue, the phone rang. Officer Ross rushed back to the kitchen, motioning for Valorie to wait a second, and then nodded.

"Hello?" Valorie waited.

Nothing.

"Hello! Who is this?"

Silence.

"Please. If you have my kids, tell me what you want!"

Everyone in the room gathered around her, stealing the little oxygen feeding her. Still no response.

"Please! Where are my kids? Talk to me?"

The response came then—a low cackle, building to a crescendo before an abrupt halt. "Scared?"

"Who is this?"

"You know. Maybe you shouldn't have run. Coward. Now your children pay."

The call ended.

Valorie collapsed beside the phone as it thudded against the floor.

"Oh Lord," she whispered. "Drake has them. Drake took my babies."

Her throat closed, shutting off her air. She gasped for breaths, convulsing and unable to focus on the blurry forms surrounding her.

One face appeared before her, a voice shouting, "Breathe, Val. Breathe."

But she couldn't, and after gasping once or twice more, her world went blank.

Chapter 33

Following Leads

Det. Davis pounded the alarm. No one should face 6:00 a.m. after crashing at 2:00. Not that she slept without dreams tugging at her subconscious. She checked her phone, hoping the two women from Texas got her messages. Nothing yet. No surprise, since she left the messages late the night before, and normal people slept more than four hours. After a quick stretch and turning on the coffeemaker, she retreated to the bathroom for a quick shower.

Ten minutes later, clean and dressed, she filled a thermal mug, grabbed a protein bar, and left her apartment, convinced she'd find those kids.

Her phone rang, the old-fashioned sound meaning an unknown number. "Det. Davis."

A timid voice responded. "I hope I'm not calling too early. This is Shamira Tarquin. You left a message for me late last night, but I just heard it."

Davis' heart picked up speed. "Thank you for returning my call, Shamira. Give me one second." She unlocked her car and slipped into the seat, parking her coffee in the cup holder. Pad and pen in hand, she returned her attention to the phone. "Sorry. I need to jot down notes."

"No problem. Can I help you?"

"I hope so. Do you know a man named Drake?"

A gasp came across the phone. "Y-yes. Sort of."

Davis waited. The silence stretched. "What can you tell me about him?"

"Not much. I... Look, my story sounds insane, but I'm not the only one who can attest to what happened with that devil."

"I'm not here to judge. I just need as much as you can tell me about him."

"I met him in a Tennessee diner where I worked at one time. I had bruises from a beating at the hands of my ex. Drake offered me a way out, and I took it. But his way meant terror in a dungeon with five other women. One of them disappeared—maybe died for all I know—but four others and I escaped."

"Did you go to the police?"

"Not right away."

"Why?"

"I fell asleep in the back of a sheriff's SUV and woke the next morning beside my passed-out boyfriend. After taking money I hid from that abuser, I went to pick up my last paycheck and hightailed it to Texas."

"Why Texas? Is that where the dungeon is?"

"I have no idea. But one woman—Charissa—lived in Texas, and I knew if I could find her, it might all make sense."

"You found her."

"Yes ma'am. We're roommates now. She helped me find a job and gave me a place to stay so I could get on my feet. She confirmed what I remembered from our captivity, so we went together to the police."

"And?"

"They didn't believe us. They agreed to investigate, but with so little to go on, the case went cold within hours."

Davis glanced around the parking lot and took a sip of coffee. "Do you know Drake's last name?"

"I'm not sure he ever gave me a last name. Charissa said Hannibal. But the cops didn't find anything."

"Hannibal? Like *Silence of the Lambs*?"

"Yeah. Crazy, huh? I don't think he ate any humans, but he was no less evil."

At least the dungeon piece of the story matched. “In this dungeon, you knew a woman named Valorie Ferguson?”

“Valorie? Yes. Oh no. Is she alright?”

“I’m not at liberty to discuss Ms. Ferguson.”

“What do you mean not at liberty?” Shamira’s voice shook, the tone and volume rising. “You can’t ask me about Valorie and not say anything else.”

Davis swallowed. “She’s not harmed. I can tell you that. This Drake is a person of interest in an ongoing investigation. What else can you tell me?”

“I don’t know much about him. Out of all the women in the dungeon, Charissa probably knew him best.”

“Is she there with you?”

“No. She pulled a double shift, so she’ll be here in about an hour. I’ll make sure she calls you.”

“Thank you. I appreciate that.” The detective jotted down a few notes and shuddered as a cool breeze blew through her open car door. “Do you remember any other names of women held captive?”

“First only. Drake kept us in the same large room. Our interactions weren’t... friendly. We didn’t exactly trade phone numbers or addresses.”

“Anything could help us.”

“The three others were Arianna, Diedre, and Edna. That’s about all I know. Edna betrayed us when we escaped. When we left, she stayed behind. But...”

“What?”

“For some reason, I think she was from New York or that area.”

“Good.” Davis took another sip of coffee. “How did you reconnect with Valorie?”

“I can only attribute it to God. I took the long way from Tennessee and stopped at a grocery store in Gulf Shores. When I saw Valorie choosing fruit, I recognized her. Neither of us wanted to believe the other was real—but how could we deny what we both remembered?”

"Valorie doesn't remember much."

"Most of the time, she stayed curled in a tiny ball, terrified of everything. Almost in a trance. I think it all sent her into shock. She was there longest, and Drake relished terrorizing her. He raped her in front of us all."

"That couldn't be easy to watch."

"No." Shamira's voice barely came through the phone. "He had us all chained. We couldn't do anything."

"I want to talk to this man. Please be sure to have your roommate call me as soon as she can."

"K."

Davis disconnected the call. As far-fetched as the dungeon story sounded, pieces coming from both women matched. Was it possible this Shamira and her friend made up the story and fed it to Valorie? Could they be the ones who took the kids and concocted Drake as a cover? Or maybe they were working with him.

She shook her head. Not plausible. The emotions in Shamira's voice seemed authentic. And Major Tyler vouched for them. He didn't know them well, but she always trusted his instincts. He'd know if they meant evil for the widow.

As she closed her door, a chill encompassed Davis. If Shamira leveled with her, the kids could be long gone and in trouble. Hopefully, Charissa would call soon and give her more on Drake. She needed a break in the case.

Chapter 34

SHAMIRA

VALORIE PACED. A DIFFERENT police officer lounged at her kitchen table, sipping coffee. Why did they still have someone there? Not like he did anything. Besides, Drake didn't want a ransom. She knew that when he called the previous night and didn't demand money. They all knew. But no one did anything.

What could he possibly want from her?

The phone rang. Her heartbeat quickened. The officer held up a finger and prepared his equipment then nodded.

Valorie's hand shook as she held the receiver. "Hello."

"Valorie?" The voice sounded familiar, but she couldn't place it.

"Yes?"

"It's me. Shamira. Are you okay?"

"No." She held back a scream and nodded at the officer.

"What happened? I just spoke with a detective—Davis."

Valorie swallowed hard. "My kids. They're missing."

"NO!" Shamira gasped. "Was it Drake?"

"I'm not sure." Valorie slumped onto a barstool. "No one saw anything. But I think he called last night, taunting me."

"That's why Davis questioned me about him. She thinks he did it, yeah?"

"Maybe. But we have no leads on where he'd take them." She straightened. "Did you give her any information?"

"I tried, Valorie. Charissa should be home soon. She knew Drake better than the rest of us. Maybe she can help more than I did."

She looked around the room, blinking back fresh tears. "He'll kill them. Won't he?"

"I... I...I don't know, hon. Maybe they'll find them before he can hurt your babies. I'm praying for it."

Valorie huffed. "Fat lot of good prayer does anyone."

"I know you're upset, but you have to trust the Lord. You know that."

"No, Shamira. I don't know that. Mitch prayed every day. Did it save him from death? Now my kids are gone. If God exists, He hates me."

For a moment, nothing came over the phone. Finally, a whisper. "I don't believe that, Valorie."

Whatever. Shamira could believe all she wanted. Valorie didn't care about God. He hadn't been there for her, no matter what anyone said.

"Listen, Shamira, I appreciate the call. But I need to free up this line in case the kidnappers—Drake or whoever has my kids—calls."

"Alright. I'm so sorry this is happening. Keep us updated."

"Yeah." Valorie ended the call, looking at the officer.

"Legitimate call?" He searched her face.

"Yes. A fri...acquaintance."

He nodded. "If the kidnappers call, we need to keep them on the line as long as possible—try to get a trace. Anyone else, keep it short, like you did just now."

She tilted her head back, her stomach clenching as she tried to breathe deep. But her throat remained tight, stealing oxygen from the air and blocking it.

A gentle hand caressed her shoulder. "Morning, honey." Her mom's soothing voice melted into her.

"Where's Dad?"

"He and Chad went out early this morning. Still looking. They thought maybe the kids hid somewhere, and they might find them in the light. It's possible. JR always protects Michele. If someone tried to grab them, they'd run. And you know he's great at hide-and-seek."

Valorie's thoughts drifted back to a few days earlier when she distracted them by suggesting the game. JR hid so well she almost panicked, fearful he sneaked outside. Except for the armed alarms, she would've called the police then. As her voice reached a high pitch, he jumped behind her and almost made her wet her shorts. She smiled at the memory.

Almost as fast, she looked at the officer watching her. Reality crashed against her brain. She squeezed her eyes, half expecting to see the children sitting at the table instead of the uniformed man. But when she opened her eyes, only the cop remained in her kitchen.

She bolted from the room then, her stomach roiling and threatening to heave the emptiness. She made it to the bathroom as the first wave pushed up her throat. The little she'd eaten spewed.

Chapter 35

Dead End

Det. Davis strode through the precinct to the back area dotted with desks. With a half-full mug of coffee, she bypassed the break area and headed straight for her spot, praying for some break in the kidnap case. Should she be out on the streets, canvasing neighbors again?

She shook her head. Already done. Follow-up planned for the day. She reached for the desk phone receiver, punching in the speed dial extension for the lab. They came in early—eager to gaze into their microscopes. Maybe they had something for her.

Misty answered on the first ring. "Lab rat at your service."

"How'd you know it was me?"

"New phone system—shows who's calling. I have your number, Davis." The young technician giggled.

"I like you, Rat. Not sure why you call yourself that. But whatever."

"You guys started it. I overheard and figured might as well beat you to it. Besides, we are kinda lab rats. I mean, we don't get out of here much, except going home. Never-ending cheese trails to follow that too often leave us with empty traps."

"You're sick. You know that?"

Misty chuckled. "Look who's talking. Detectives see the same junk we do—only up close and personal. I just get the forensic clues to analyze."

"True enough." Davis glanced up as another detective entered. She nodded, trying to remember the new guy's name and coming up blank. “Speaking of clues... The fingerprints from the kidnap. Did you get a hit on them?”

“Nah. And I so hoped... Wait a second.” A quick gasp trickled through the phone.

“What?”

“Wow. Just got a match.”

Davis clutched the phone. “And?”

“Found your unsub.”

“Where? Who?”

“In the morgue. Tagged John Doe.”

The detective froze. “How’d he die?”

“No clue. I just got the match.” Misty sighed. “I’m sorry, Davis. If he was involved, it’s a dead end.”

“Not funny, Rat.”

“Sorry. Too much time with fingerprints and tissue samples?”

“You should get a life. Maybe get a cat—a big one.”

“Yeah, I always wanted to run for my life.” Misty laughed. “We both have frightening humors. Maybe we both need a break.”

“After I find those kids. For now, guess I’ll skip over to the morgue and see what I can find out.”

“I’m sure that’s your perfect idea of starting the morning right.”

“Of course. Glad I skipped breakfast.” Davis blew out a breath of air. “Thanks, Rat. At least you found him for me.”

“I hope you find those kids soon.”

“Me too. And not in the morgue.”

Davis didn’t work homicides. She stuck with missing persons. If they ended up in the morgue, she relinquished the case without a fight. But she didn’t have any other leads. She needed answers, and the land of people on ice might hold one or two.

As she stepped through the door, she took a breath and regretted it. Death permeated the air, mingling with antiseptic and formaldehyde. Worse than a hospital and nursing home combined. Davis shuddered and looked across the room. A man in a white lab coat spoke with one of the homicide detectives. Peters? Maybe. Not sure.

They looked up, and the detective smiled. "Detective Davis. Right?"

"Yes. Peters?"

He nodded.

"That your John Doe?"

Peters said, "Yeah. Pretty sure he's part of several petty thefts, one which left a man dead. Something Jones."

"That's original."

"Isn't it? Never ID'd him but caught his mug on a camera. Been asking around working the case. Jones is all we got so far."

"So, how'd he die?"

Peters gestured to the doctor, who responded with a flat tone. "Definite broken neck but also signs of struggle. Homicide."

"Are you sure?"

The doctor's nostrils flared. "I don't claim murder without being sure."

"Sorry. It just adds a layer of complexity to my case. He's our best lead. And if someone murdered this jerk..."

Peters nodded. "Then you have one mother... of a storm cloud."

"Exactly." She rubbed her forehead. "Do you have an ETD?"

The coroner scratched his bearded chin. "Not the exact time, but someone killed him late Thursday. Probably dumped him not too long after. Not much exposure."

Davis gasped. "The same night the kids disappeared."

Peters nodded. "Lots of foot traffic in that wooded area—dozens of hiking trails. They didn't care if someone found Jones—maybe wanted it. Hiker discovered the body early Friday."

"Why would they want someone to find this guy? They had to know we'd get fingerprints from that truck."

"Maybe. Why not get rid of a potential link to the mastermind?"

"But we didn't have the fingerprints in the system yet."

Peters looked down at the corpse and shrugged. "Wanted to make sure? Maybe the big man doesn't know the area. Thought no one would find the body."

"Maybe." Davis massaged the ache covering her neck. Too early in the day for mounting stress. "Peters, Doc—let me know if you get anything else. Please."

"Sure." Peters waggled his eyebrows. "Maybe we could compare notes over dinner."

Davis shook her head. "Are you seriously flirting with me?"

He cocked his head and grinned.

She turned and rolled her eyes. Jerk. "I'm not stopping to eat until I find those kids."

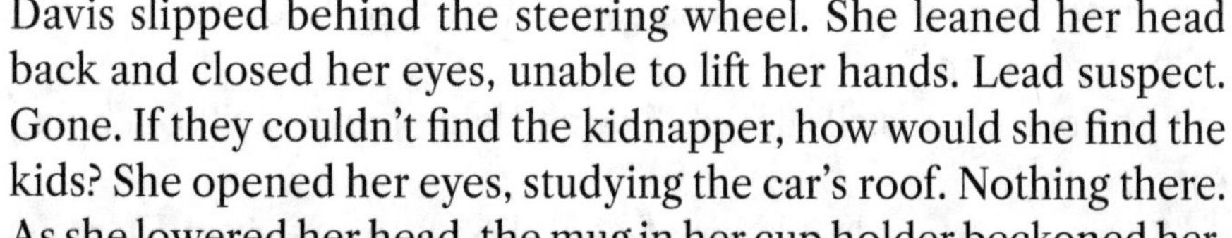

Davis slipped behind the steering wheel. She leaned her head back and closed her eyes, unable to lift her hands. Lead suspect. Gone. If they couldn't find the kidnapper, how would she find the kids? She opened her eyes, studying the car's roof. Nothing there. As she lowered her head, the mug in her cup holder beckoned her. Coffee. Her arm ached as she reached for the promise of caffeine. Not that it would energize her much.

"Lord help. I'm lost on this one, and I gotta find those babies—before something terrible happens to them."

Not much of a prayer warrior, but she grew up in church. Tyler reminded her of the many times she watched her grandmother on her knees. Did prayer work? Maybe. She had nothing else.

Her phone blipped. Ross. She liked that woman.

Got another hit. Partial on the gate and lock.

Yeah. That guy's dead.

Different one-with a match.

What?

Interpol. Dagon Ivanov. Known assassin. Stays just out of reach. He disappears fast.

If he has the kids…

Someone hired him.

Drake guy with suspicious last name?

Maybe.

I don't suppose we have a last-known address?

No record of him coming into the US.

Of course not.

Any more on Drake?

No, haven't gotten the second call back yet.

I'll try again. Good work, Ross.

We gotta stick together, girl. I'll send you the Interpol photo.

Davis smiled. "We gotcha, sucker." The smile plummeted. "If we can find you."

She put on her seatbelt and started the car, eager to talk with Valorie. Maybe she knew something about Dagon. Doubtful. But it wouldn't hurt to ask.

The old-fashioned ring tone stopped her from moving.

"Detective Davis."

"I'm glad I caught you. I'm Charissa Imani. My roommate told me about Valorie's kids and that you wanted to talk to me about Drake."

Yes. Maybe this woman had something. She took a deep breath. "Thank you for calling me back. I'm hoping you can give me more about Drake—maybe a location of where he held you and the others."

"I wish. My friend, Haniel, and I have searched several times. But we've never found the trails or any roads."

Figures. "Do you remember anything else about the dungeon?"

"It was beneath a castle—or what looked like a castle. He had lots of men guarding it. Burly men."

"I don't suppose you got a photo of Drake."

"No. I'm afraid not. I wish I could be of more help. I can't believe this is happening to Valorie."

"I know. It's a tough one. If you think of anything else, please call me. Any little thing might help."

"Absolutely. If you need anything else, please call."

Davis disconnected. Not much help. Of course, Drake kept bodyguards. Why wouldn't he?

Her eyes widened. The man Tyler kept seeing in the neighborhood. She scrunched her forehead, eyes shifting. Dark-haired, burly. Wasn't that how Chad described him?

Her phone blipped again. She opened the text and stared at the photo. Possibility. Big one.

She peeled out of the parking lot. Arms tingled as she raced toward the Ferguson house. It had to be this guy. She needed a break in the case.

Maybe prayer worked after all. A solid lead didn't mean she had the kids back—yet.

Chapter 36

THE FRESH LEAD

VALORIE STUMBLED TO THE kitchen, ignoring her mom. She stood at the window and looked across the yard, shivering. Her stomach churned, clenching nothingness. She went to the counter, filled the electric teakettle, switched it on, and reached for a peppermint green tea bag.

Mom joined her. "Can I make you something to eat? Toast maybe?"

How could she think of food?

Valorie shook her head. "Not hungry."

"You should eat something, honey."

"Mom... You can't feed this one away."

Her mother looked down. "I don't know how else to help." She sighed. "Go sit in the living room. I'll bring your tea when it's finished."

Without an answer, Valorie went to the living room, using anything to steady herself. Her legs wobbled, determined to keep her upright, but she couldn't shake the chill snaking through her body.

Before she reached a chair, the doorbell rang. She crossed the room and checked through the peephole. The detective—what was her name?

Davy?

No. Davis. Yeah.

She disarmed the alarm and threw back all the deadbolts.

Why bother? What else could Drake or any evil person do to her? If her kids didn't make it, she wanted to die with them.

She shoved aside the thoughts and opened the door.

"Hi, Valorie. I'm sure you had a rough night, so I won't insult you by asking how you are."

"Thanks." She stepped back and motioned the woman inside.

"We identified fingerprints in and on the truck—but he... I'm not gonna pull punches. Someone killed him."

Valorie's stomach lurched.

The detective steadied her, directing her to the nearest chair. "Please."

The room swam as Valorie tried to focus her eyes, determined to stay conscious. But she couldn't control the violent shaking. She slumped.

Davis touched her arm. "That doesn't mean they killed the kids. This guy—a loose end. One of our cops recognized him as a petty thief."

Valorie glanced at the woman.

The detective continued. "I have a new lead—a partial fingerprint match." She pushed buttons on her phone and held it out for Valorie. "Do you recognize this man?"

She studied the photo. Familiar. Maybe? "I'm not sure."

"Take your time."

Mom came into the room, tea in hand. "Detective Davis! Do you have news?"

"A new lead, ma'am."

"That's good. Right?"

"Any lead is good."

"Would you like coffee or tea?"

"No, thanks. You might look at this photo, too. See if he looks like someone you've seen around here."

Her mom looked over Valorie's shoulder. "I don't think so. There was a man in a car, but I didn't see him close up. Not like Chad did. He's the one who told me to keep an eye out."

Davis stiffened. "Have you seen Chad today?"

"Yes. He and Ted—my husband—went out early. Still searching."

Valorie handed Davis the phone. "He looks familiar. Could be the man in the utility bucket, but... I'm not sure." If she could identify the man... She swallowed a sob. *If only* never meant squat. She buried her head in her hands.

As the front door opened, Valorie gasped and scrunched back in the chair. She left it unlocked?

Her dad, pocketing keys, entered, and Chad followed him.

Chad's gaze settled on Valorie. "Ladies? What's going on?" He moved toward them.

Dad kneeled beside Valorie. "Honey, what happened? Did they find the kids?"

A quick head shake. She couldn't muster more than that as tears again prickled her eyes.

Davis held up her phone. "Chad. Do you recognize this man?"

Valorie watched as Chad took the phone and studied the photo.

His eyes widened, blinking fast. "Yeah. The car I called you about. That's the guy."

"Are you sure?"

"One-hundred percent." He handed Davis the phone and glanced over at Valorie. "Who is he? And how's he involved?"

"We got a hit on partials from the gate latch and lock. Lucked out. Name's Dagon Ivanov."

"Russian?"

"Yes."

"I knew it. Should've decked him when I had the chance."

"And end up in jail?"

"Better than him ending up with the kids."

Valorie rose and paced. "Is he connected with Drake?"

"Not that we can find, ma'am. We're still searching."

Chad rubbed a hand over his face. "What about the Honda?"

Davis shook her head, her jaw tightening. "Nothing. I'm sure he ditched it somewhere—probably driving a different vehicle by now. We searched through traffic camera videos in the area. Came up empty."

Valorie stepped between the two. "So, find him. You know who took my kids. And you can't do anything? Don't you have a last-known address or something?"

Creases lined Davis's forehead as she pinched the bridge of her nose. "It's not always that simple. He moves around—no permanent address anywhere that we can find." She smiled—one that stopped below her nose. "We won't give up, though. Sooner or later, we'll spot him."

Chad swallowed.

Valorie held back a scream and retreated to the sofa, where she drew herself into a ball.

They might not have a later.

Chapter 37

TRAPPED

JR TWISTED THE DOORKNOB. Locked, of course. They wouldn't toss them in a room and leave it unlocked. Not after stealing them from the backyard. Even a kid like him knew that.

Michele sat in the corner, whimpering. "JR. Why did they grab us?"

"I don't know, Chele. But don't worry. I'll take care of you."

He slumped beside his sister. "Are you okay?"

"My face hurts."

"Yeah. It hurts me all the time."

She huffed. "Not funny. You yanked tape off my mouth."

"Well, maybe I should've left it on there."

"No." She crossed her arms, puffing out her lips. "But it ripped off the skin. At least say sorry."

"I am sorry. It's a little red, but no blood. You'll be fine."

"K." She peeked around him toward the door. "Are they coming back?"

"Dunno. Who are they?" As if his little sister would know.

"It's the man."

"What man?"

"The 'lectric man. From the bucket."

"Well duh. I KNOW that much."

"I seen him. Lots." She shrugged. "He waved at me a few times. Seemed okay. But Mama didn't like him."

"Mama doesn't like any stranger."

"Well. Maybe she shouldn't. A stranger stole us." Red rimmed her eyes. "What are we gonna do, JR?"

"Don't cry. I'll get us out."

JR walked around the room, opening a door. Closet. He backed out and looked around. No windows. No escape. Other than the door, they couldn't get out. He sat beside Michele again, trying to think. How could they get free?

With just one guy, they could kick him and run. But the second guy might catch them. Maybe Chele could run fast and get away. Go for help.

He looked at his sister.

Not a chance. Too little. And she was about as fast as a turtle.

He might get away, but he'd never leave her. He had to be the man. Protect her.

At the sound of the lock turning, JR jumped to his feet, staying between the door and the little girl. The big man who threatened them came in. "I go talk to my boss. Don't try anything. You can't break out of this room. No one can hear you scream. You understand?"

JR nodded.

Michele whimpered. "I want my mama. I want to go home."

"Shush. Be good. I take you home later."

JR caught his bottom lip between his teeth. "Mister, I gotta pee."

"Me too. And I'm hungry." Michele stood and grabbed JR's hand.

The man looked around the room for a second and rubbed his beard. "Is this game?"

"No, man. I gotta go bad." JR's brain whirled, wondering if they might escape through the bathroom window. If it had a window. Had to. Didn't it? He squeezed his legs together, hoping the man bought it.

"Girl go first. Hurry up."

Michele's voice quivered. "I need help. I can't go alone."

Good. Maybe she understood his thinking.

JR chimed in. "I'll help her."

"No. Only one. Not both."

"But..."

"Only one, or you pee your pants. I no care either way."

JR glanced over his shoulder. "Go ahead, Chele. You'll be okay."

Her bottom lip stuck out. "I'm scared, JR."

"I know. But it's okay. Go potty."

She trudged through the door, hugging the sides, avoiding the big man's body.

JR waited his turn, and when Michele came back, he rushed across the hall, taking in the bathroom while he took care of business. If they could both get in there and lock the door, they might make it through the small window. He couldn't see through it, but maybe...

His shoulders slumped. Who was he kidding? Even if he could get Michele up and out, he might not know the way home.

Crossing the hall again, he glimpsed the kitchen. No one. No sounds. "Where's the other guy?"

The big man laughed. "I lose him. Cops find him, maybe before animals eat, and match fingerprints in truck. I go free."

JR's throat clinched. "You killed him?" He pulled in quick breaths, trying not to shake.

"Yeah. No big deal." The man shrugged. "You behave, I not leave you for animals."

"Yes, sir."

Michele moved beside JR, grabbing his arm. "I'm still hungry. And I want Mama."

"I bring food—maybe. Forget about Mama. She not coming. At least, not yet. Maybe I bring her later. Now, get back in room. And no yelling for help."

Both children shuffled through the opening, clutching each other's hands. The door closed behind them, the sound of a key turning.

"Is he gonna kill us, JR?"

"No. I won't let him."

"How? He's ginormic."

"That's not even a word."

"Yes, it is."

"It isn't!"

Tears trickled down Michele's cheeks. "You're so mean."

JR put his arm around her. "I'm sorry, Chele. I'm..." He stopped. No use telling her the truth. The man scared him. But she didn't need to know that. "I'll think of something."

Chapter 38

Baby Monitor

Darci peered into the crib and blew out a soft breath. Sound asleep.

Finally.

She checked the baby monitor. On. She rolled her neck, tiptoed into the living room, and picked up the parental unit for monitoring. Not the best brand, and so old she didn't trust it half the time. But with her husband in school and training people at the gym most nights, she thanked God for the garage-sale find. Don agreed. At least she felt better having the baby in a separate room.

She switched up the volume, smiling at the recorded lullabies. Time for a movie, popcorn, and soda. Even the best mama needed a little me time. With her snack in hand, she settled on the sofa and checked the monitor again.

Still music. No rustling or crying.

Halfway through the movie, Darci paused the video and headed to the bathroom, stopping for a throw blanket on her way back. Curled up on the sofa, she picked up the remote. Before hitting play, a man's voice drew her attention.

What the...?

She grabbed the baby monitor and turned up the volume, her heart revving from zero to 60 in seconds.

Her baby.

Who was in her house?

She bolted down the hallway and swung open the baby's door, ready to pounce on the intruder.

The infant stirred.

Lullabies continued playing.

A man's voice—on both monitors.

Darci crumpled into the rocking chair, taking deep breaths, commanding her heart to slow down.

She listened.

What you doing here?

The boss sent me.

Why? He thinks I not handle two kids? I find monitor, so I hear what they say. They not know, though.

He said you might need a break. Doesn't want them left here alone. Where's Guy?

Lost. Permanently.

Geez. Drake that paranoid?

Of course. The man snickered. *He trust no one.*

So what's next? A ransom?

No. He say wait.

Wait for what?

Who knows? He crazy. Obsessed... mama... want...

The monitor stopped for a moment, followed by the soothing sounds of lullabies.

Darci covered her mouth. Did she just hear what she thought they said?

The baby stirred again and whimpered.

She crossed to the crib and pulled a light blanket over her sleeping child, a knot filling her belly. The men had kids. And the word ransom echoed in her brain. Could it be kidnappers? No way. They lived in a safe neighborhood. No one would hold kids against their will here. Would they?

She paced. They might want more babies.

Blood pulsed against her temples.

Did she leave that baseball bat in the hall closet or bedroom?

They wouldn't take Sunny without a fight.

Checking her daughter one more time, Darci tiptoed from the nursery, her mind swirling. In the hall closet, she wrapped a fist around the solid wooden bat and took a deep breath in. She stepped out and headed back to her sleeping child.

Two steps. And...

The soft click of a door.

She spun, hoisted the bat, and rounded the corner. Don dropped his keys on the counter. "Hey, honey." He froze. "What's wrong?"

She lowered the bat, her breaths quickening. "You scared the bejeebbers out of me!"

He chuckled. "Ahh. Been watching thrillers again?"

"NO! Well, okay. I might've been." She glanced around the kitchen. "But that's not it."

"What? You're as pale as a corpse."

Darci grabbed his arm with a trembling hand. "Come sit down."

Don shook his head but let her drag him to the sofa, eying the empty bowl and can. "I knew it."

"Forget that. I paused the movie for a potty break."

"Potty break? Hon, you gotta spend more time with adults."

"Whatever. I had the baby monitor on, and a man's voice came over it. Scared me worse than you did. I thought someone was trying to take our baby. So I ran in there."

Don stood. "Did he hurt Sunny?" Darci pulled him back down.

"No one there. She's still fast asleep."

He sighed. "That's a relief. You had me going for a second."

"But that's not all." Darci bounced on the sofa. "I heard two male voices, Don. Two."

"They talked to you?"

"No. To each other. Something about kids and a boss." She swallowed hard. "I heard the word ransom. Then it changed to static and stopped for a minute before going back to the monitor in Sunny's room."

"Do you know how insane this sounds, Darci? Are you sure you didn't fall asleep and dream all this? You watch way too many cop movies and shows."

"It may sound crazy, but I didn't imagine it."

Don reached across Darci and picked up the receiver. Soft music drifted through it. He turned it over, moved it around. Nothing changed.

Without warning, static cut through the music. Bits of male voices crackled.

Darci placed a hand on her chest. "See?"

Through the static, they caught sounds, but nothing intelligible. Then the music returned with a soft rustle of their daughter's movements.

Don ran his hand through his hair. "I don't know, Darci. It could just be someone's TV bleeding over. These old monitors... they pick up stuff like that."

"But what if it's real, Don? What if someone really kidnapped kids, and they're nearby?" Darci stood and paced in front of the sofa. "If it were Sunny being held, wouldn't you want someone who heard this to call the cops?"

"Sure. But this isn't enough to make me think we have kidnappers down the street."

She crossed her arms. "You didn't hear the conversation I did. Their voices... They didn't sound like nice men. One sounded foreign, even."

Moving off the couch, Don put his arms around Darci. "C'mon, honey. You're overreacting. Probably some movie or something. I mean, they'd need an old monitor, too. Right?"

She pulled away and snapped her fingers. "He said that. He found a monitor."

"One as old as we have? That's unlikely."

"Not if he found it in an old house. Some people keep things like that, you know."

Don chuckled. "I still think you're letting your imagination run wild. But if you hear them again, then, yeah. Call the cops. Tell them what you heard." He stretched and cracked his neck. "I'm bushed. Let's double-check the doors and get some sleep. I'm sure you'll feel better about it all tomorrow."

While Don went to check doors, Darci looked at the monitor again. Nothing but soft lullaby sounds.

Maybe he was right.

Nah. She knew what she heard. And it didn't sound like a TV or anything innocent.

Her gut twisted and clenched. The sinister tones of those men replayed across her brain. Don might be right, but she didn't think so.

Chapter 39

Useless Voices

All night, Darci dreamed of voices coming over the monitor and evil men coming after her precious daughter. More than once, she woke with perspiration beading across her forehead while she shivered from an unseen coldness.

She threw off covers and picked up the monitor, hearing only soft movement and lullabies. Still, she crept from bed and tiptoed across the hall, then peeked into Sunny's room. Nothing stirred—not even the baby.

She returned and curled up in her bed next to Don, snoring beside her. After listening to the monitor, waiting for strange voices, she finally dozed off, only to repeat the cycle again. And again.

When the alarm finally sounded, she dragged herself from the bed. Despite the exhaustion, she didn't want to sleep any more. Dreams of hands clutching her baby—grabbing, pulling Sunny from her. Men breaking in, using the bat on her head, and stealing the sweet infant. Various scenarios—all with the same outcome. Losing her baby.

Enough of those visions.

She shivered and pattered to the kitchen.

Showered and dressed for work, Don whistled as he entered. "Hon, you look exhausted. Did Sunny keep you up? I never heard her."

He never heard anything once he went to sleep.

"Sunny slept like her usual angel self. I, on the other hand, had nightmares all night. Not that you had a clue. You didn't miss a beat in your snoring."

He wrapped his arms around her as she perched on a barstool beside the breakfast bar. "I'm sorry. You could've woken me."

Darci sipped her coffee. "It wouldn't have helped. It was those voices, Don. I can't get them out of my mind."

"It shook you that bad?"

"I didn't think so, but yeah. Apparently, it did."

Don retrieved a travel mug and filled it with coffee. "You still want to report it?"

She shrugged. "Maybe. Should I?"

"Not sure they can do much with it. But if you need to, call the cops. At least you'll feel better."

Men. The situation didn't concern him a bit. Did it?

A soft murmur came across the monitor. Darci hopped off the stool. "Sunny's up. I'll get her fed and then call."

"Do I need to stay home today?"

"No. We're fine. Like you said, probably just my overactive mother imagination."

He smiled and gave her a kiss. "Let me get our precious girl. I need her hugs today, too."

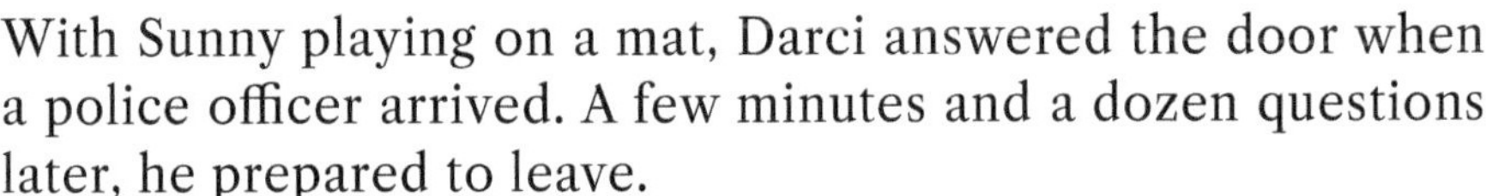

With Sunny playing on a mat, Darci answered the door when a police officer arrived. A few minutes and a dozen questions later, he prepared to leave.

"Nothing much we can do. Not sure what you heard, ma'am. Could've been a movie, like your husband said."

"It sounded real, though. What if those men really have children they took? Do you have a recent kidnapping?"

The police officer shrugged. "I can't comment on any ongoing investigations. It's possible. But where did it come from? Who were the men? Or the kids, for that matter?"

"I don't know." Darci rubbed her forehead and looked at her baby, who cooed at a stuffed animal. "I keep thinking how I'd want someone to say something if my daughter was missing."

"And you did the right thing." The officer stood. "For now, keep your ears open. If it happens again, try to record it somehow."

Darci rose from the sofa. "Does that mean someone might tap into our house?"

"Not sure. Maybe. If I were you, I'd ditch the old monitor and invest in a more secure model."

"Yeah. Kinda freaky, isn't it?"

"At least it isn't the video one. Heard of a ton of problems with that type." He moved to the door. "If you hear anything else, call immediately. If what you heard was real, it's likely they've moved on. I don't think you have anything to worry about. You're safe."

Darci nodded. "Okay. Thank you, officer."

She closed the door behind him, scooped up Sunny, and retreated to the nursery where she rocked her child.

What if it was real? Was it too late? She should've called when she heard them.

"Lord, protect those children, if they exist. I don't want to hear those men again, but if I do, give me courage to do the right thing. Immediately."

Sunny smiled up at her. But the heaviness in Darci's heart made it difficult to smile back.

Chapter 40

HOPE

CHAD STRODE BETWEEN THE living room, kitchen, and back. He should go search again. But where hadn't they looked?

The photo Davis showed him beat against his brain. Why didn't he take that jerk down? Put the fear of God and the USMC in the SOB?

Dagon. What a name.

How did Mitch's family get so messed up? Was Valorie hiding something?

Chad glanced across the room at the woman curled in a fetal position on the sofa. Her mother sat beside Valorie, rubbing her back like a traumatized little girl. Her dad leaned forward in a nearby chair, his hands cupped over his mouth, eyes closed. Praying, no doubt.

Chad threw back his head in a silent prayer.

"Lord, I should be on my knees seeking your help. You know me too well. That's not how I operate. I'm a man of action. I need to move—do something. Show me what. I'm helpless here, and I can't stand it."

A soft thud interrupted Chad's prayer. His head jerked up. Mrs. Daniels tiptoed toward him on her way to the kitchen.

He tried to smile at her. "You need something?"

"I'm just gonna make tea for Valorie. She won't eat anything, but I can at least put milk in tea."

Chad followed her to the kitchen. What else could he do?

She opened the refrigerator and removed the milk jug. "Oh no. It's almost empty."

"Is there enough for a cup?"

"Yeah. Barely. I'm not sure how I missed it before."

"Other things on your mind, ma'am. I'll run to the store."

"Thanks, Chad. You've been such a good friend to Valorie and the kids." She swallowed. "I know some neighbors had unkind words, and Valorie said Michele's given you a rough time."

"She's a little girl dealing with her daddy's death. I wanted to give her space, so I quit coming over as much. Maybe I should have shrugged it off. If I'd been here..."

"Don't. This isn't on you."

"Yeah. It is. I was supposed to protect them. And that man took them. On my watch."

Mrs. Daniels put a hand on his shoulder. "You did what you thought was best for my granddaughter. And based on those circles under your eyes, I'd wager you haven't slept since they disappeared."

"A little." He shrugged and looked around the kitchen then through the back window. "I have to find them."

"I know. But please don't blame yourself. You didn't take them." She dropped her hand. "For now, go get milk. You're wearing a hole in the carpet, and your constant pacing makes me nervous." Her tiny smile didn't fool him. "We're gonna get through this. Keep praying."

"Yes ma'am. Be back in a few. Need anything else?"

She surveyed the fridge. "No. I think that's all. No one seems interested in food." She gave him a quick hug. "Thanks again."

Chad hurried into the grocery store across from the gym. What he wouldn't give for an hour to work off some tension.

Not today. Milk and back to the house. He needed to be there. If anything developed.

Rounding the corner to the refrigerated cases, he bumped into Don. "Hey dude."

Don nodded. "What's up, brother? Haven't seen you at the gym for a couple days."

"I know. My friend's kids went missing."

Don froze. "What?"

"Kidnapped. Got a worthless lead. No one can find the dude."

"No way." Don shifted his weight.

Chad nodded, not trusting his voice to carry around the knot in his throat.

"When did this happen, Chad?"

"About 24 hours ago. You didn't hear?"

"Nah. Working double shifts. New baby and all. We barely watch news. Thing is..." He rubbed his lips.

"What?"

"I don't know, bro. Sounds crazy."

"Crazier than a man taking two kids from a locked yard?"

"Valid point." He paused. "My wife... heard something."

"Heard what?" Chad's heart pounded. "Spill it!"

"We have this garage-sale, ancient baby monitor. I was at work. Came home to find her frantic. She almost decked me with a bat."

Chad gritted his teeth, motioning for Don to wrap up his story.

"Darci thought she heard two guys talking. They mentioned kids, ransom. Stuff like that."

Unbelievable. Chad clenched his fists. "And you didn't call the cops?"

"Not that night. Darci called them the next morning, though. They took a report. Basically, said what I did."

"Which was?"

"Not much they can do. No probable cause. No definite direction. I believed it was random TV coming through. But now..."

"Thinking otherwise?"

"Maybe. They'd have to be close. But if they had an old monitor, too? Possible. Isn't it?"

Chad pulled out his phone and added a contact. "Type in your name and address. It's a lead. I'll case the neighborhood—get the info to the cops."

"Dude. Did we mess up?"

"Lost some time."

"I'll keep my eyes open. So will Darci. If we see anything..."

"Call 9-1-1. And convince them the kids are nearby."

"Gotcha. I'm done here and heading home."

"Me too."

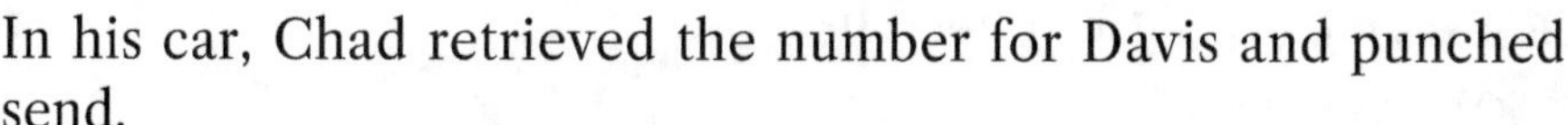

In his car, Chad retrieved the number for Davis and punched send.

"Hey, Tyler. You got something?"

"I just talked to a guy from the gym. His wife heard men over a baby monitor. Sounded suspicious."

"A baby monitor?"

"Yeah. Old one. Maybe bleedover. But it could be Dagon with the kids."

"You know that's a long shot, right?"

"It's something. They could be in that neighborhood."

"Without probable cause or a warrant, we can't do more than a door-to-door canvas."

"I know. Me? I got nothing but time. I figure a few blocks' radius. Drive by. Check potential places."

"Tyler—don't you dare get in trouble. If you find anything, call me or 9-1-1."

"No problem. Don and his wife will keep their eyes open, too."

"I pray it goes somewhere. But I gotta be honest, Chad. Not hopeful. Shoot over the address. I'll get patrols going."

"Got it."

Chad disconnected, his heart still thundering. Davis never called him Chad—unless something awful happened. He swallowed hard, willing the bile not to rise.

Back at the house, he slipped through the door and found Mr. Daniels in the kitchen. After sharing what Don told him, he said. "I'm going over to that neighborhood. Maybe nothing, but it's better than sitting around here."

"I'll go with you. Should we tell the girls?"

"No. I don't want to get their hopes up."

"Get our hopes up about what?" Mrs. Daniels came into the room.

Chad sighed. "A lead. Long shot. I let Davis know. But getting through red tape takes time. I got no red tape, but plenty of time."

"Then go. Both of you. I'll stay here with Valorie. She took tranquillizers, so she's sleeping. Call if you find anything."

"We will."

Mr. Daniels kissed his wife. "Pray, honey. That's all I know to do right now. Maybe God's answering our prayers and leading us to our babies."

"I hope." She pushed away from his chest. "Go on, now. I'll see you both soon."

Chad led the way. If they saw anything—the kids, the big man, anything—God, and the cops, would just have to forgive him for taking action.

Whatever that looked like.

Chapter 41

Awakening

Valorie's eyes fluttered. For a moment, she fought the drowsiness sucking her back into oblivion.

Why did she want to sleep?

Fog crept through her brain, its tendrils beckoning her to surrender—refuse to move—let sleep retake her conscious thoughts. Keep the eyes closed. Ignore life.

So sleepy. But why couldn't she focus on anything?

A thud broke through the fogginess of her mind. Her eyelids flew open as she bolted upright. Across the room, Chad and her dad glanced at her, talking in whispers.

Chad attempted a smile. "Hey, Valorie. Sorry. We didn't mean to wake you."

She took a deep breath. Chad. Her dad. Reality crashed against her as memories created a tsunami of emotion. Her jaws clamped tight. Her stomach roiled. She forced a whisper. "Where've you been? Did you find the kids?"

Dad crossed the room and sat beside her on the sofa. He shook his head. "Afraid not, hon. We'll go back and scout the same area tomorrow."

She scrunched her forehead. "What area?" She swung her feet to the floor. "Did you get a lead? Something..." Valorie couldn't finish the thought that banged around her head. She didn't want to know about a possible dump site. If that's what they knew but didn't dare tell her.

Chad moved closer. “I ran into a friend from the gym. His wife heard something suspicious over a baby monitor.”

“That doesn’t make sense, Chad.” Valorie leaned forward. “Are you saying she heard the kids?”

“No, not the kids. Men. Talking about kids. Ransom. Stuff like that.”

“Over a baby monitor?”

“Yes.”

“I guess. But it only happened with OLD monitors.”

“They’re young. Broke with a new baby. Garage sale deal.”

Valorie stood, moved away from the furniture, and paced. She stopped, turned, and stared at Chad. “You think it’s possible?”

He shrugged. “It’s all we got.”

Dad nodded. “We drove around the area where this couple lives. Figured it’s worth a shot.”

Valorie crossed her arms and rubbed her shoulders. “But you didn’t see anything?” She dared not let herself hope.

Both men shook their heads.

Valorie narrowed her eyes. “How long did you look?”

Chad leaned back in the chair. “Not too long. We mapped out a viable area. Met Detective Davis there.”

Hope drifted upward, but Valorie squashed it. “So, she has the area staked out then?”

Chad crossed his arms, looked toward the window. “Lot of houses in that neighborhood. No positive lead on any.”

Valorie said, “But they could be there. My kids could be in one of those houses.”

“I know. Davis has extra patrols on it. My friend and his wife are on high alert. Your dad and I will go back after we get water and snacks. We’ll stay on it all night.”

A savory smell drifted from the kitchen, making Valorie’s stomach grumble for the first time since... She didn’t remember the last time she ate or wanted food.

Her mom entered the living room, drying her hands on a towel. “I have stew and cornbread ready. Why don’t y’all come get a bite.

While you're eating, I'll pack up some snacks and bottled water. Maybe fill some thermal mugs with coffee." She sighed. "You can't stay out all night without sustenance. Although, at some point, all lights in the neighborhood will go out. That might be your signal to come back and rest."

Valorie nodded. "You're right, Mom." She turned to Chad and swallowed hard. "I... want to..."

What? She wanted to go. But what if they called with a ransom demand and she missed it? Did she want to see it if they found the kids too late? Fear gripped her mind, squeezing all reasoning from her.

Chad stood. "What, Val?"

She turned to the kitchen. "Thank you. That's all. Let's get you guys ready for tonight."

Valorie walked to the kitchen. Wait! What day was it? What time? How long had she stayed on the sofa in a stupor? As much as she wanted to crawl back into that denial space, she couldn't.

"Chad, Dad. When you go again, take me with you."

Three heads turned her way, gazes boring into her. Six eyes widened. Lips parted.

Finally, her dad responded. "Okay, hon. But not until you eat something. I can't pick you up if you faint from hunger."

Chapter 42

Civilian Stakeout

Valorie followed Chad and her dad out the front door. She looked both ways down the street, her heart pounding against her ribcage. Everything looked normal. But her mind wandered back two days earlier. Nothing seemed wrong when she sat on the patio, the kids playing in the backyard. The one protected place she liked for her kids to play. Secure at home. So she thought. Nowhere felt safe anymore.

She glanced at the two men in front of her. Chad's head shifted. Did he feel it too? That uneasiness that gripped her heart, forcing it to pump harder?

He opened the rear door of the car.

Valorie sped up. "I'll take the back seat."

"You sure?"

"Yeah. You need the leg room up front. The back's more comfortable for me."

He shrugged. "As long as you can see."

She slipped into the car and hunched down, a bigger knot tangling her guts. "I'm good." She pulled her door shut. Discussion done.

Chad slid into the front passenger side. Her dad already had his seatbelt on and the car running.

Valorie pushed down the urge to fling open the door and race back inside. What kind of mother didn't want to go search for her children? She looked out the window and blinked rapidly, hoping her dad pulled out before she bolted. He didn't hesitate, and her stomach clenched as sweat covered her body.

Minutes later, they entered an unfamiliar neighborhood. Rows of older but well-kept homes lined both sides of the street, sentinels for the trio as they edged along. Each yard, mowed and welcoming, decried the possibility of anything sinister.

Valorie squinted, looking closely at every house. "Is this where the couple lives? The ones who heard something?"

Chad nodded. "They're a block from here."

"Doesn't look like a place where kidnappers would hide."

Dad shrugged. "Looks can be deceiving."

One house caught Valorie's attention. Weeds and tall grass covered the yard, blinds closed against prying eyes. Odd. It looked out of place in the otherwise pristine neighborhood. Movement drew her attention to the opposite side of the street. A woman with a stroller half-jogged on the sidewalk.

Chad held up a hand. "I think that's Darci."

Her dad pulled across the street and stopped at the curb, rolling down his window.

Chad leaned toward him. "Hey. Are you Darci?"

The woman peeked into the car. "Yes." Her eyes widened. "Are you Chad?"

"Yes, ma'am."

"Don told me about seeing you in the store. I've not heard anything else." She glanced into the back seat. "Are you the mom?"

Valorie nodded, the chunk in her throat keeping her silent.

Tears pooled in the younger mother's eyes. "I'm so sorry to hear about your kids. I can't imagine how you feel, but I'd be devastated if something happened to my little Sunny. I keep looking outside, going for walks, and watching. Nothing out of the ordinary, though."

Swallowing hard, Valorie pointed at the forsaken house. "What about that place?"

"Oh. Poor Mrs. Jackson. She died about a month ago. Her kids came, of course, but they don't care about her lovely home. I guess they'll come back eventually and clean it out—then probably sell it."

A soft light filtered through one blind as dusk covered the street. "But there's a light on."

"I think they didn't want it to look abandoned, so they left on one light." Darci peered over the car. "I don't remember seeing anyone coming in or out. You'd think they'd at least mow."

With a backward glance, Chad said, "Looks abandoned."

"Maybe." Valorie stared at the windows, wishing for a shift in the blinds. Nothing happened. She watched for another minute, ignoring the continued conversation between her dad, Darci, and Chad. Something about the house made her keep looking.

She shook herself.

Needed to get a grip. Kidnappers wouldn't hole up in an obvious place. Especially not where someone might see them.

"Valorie?" Chad reached back and touched her hand.

"Sorry. I was lost in my thoughts."

Darci smiled at her. "I'll keep watching and praying. But I have to get this little one in before dark."

"Thank you. Keep a close eye on her." As much as Valorie hurt, she wouldn't wish that pain on another mother. Ever.

Darci retreated down the block, almost out of sight.

The trio drove through the neighborhood, making turns but staying near their ally's home. Same pattern for hours. Valorie stayed alert, but as darkness fell, nothing questionable popped up. One-by-one, lights went out in houses. Part of her wanted to go home, pop a pill or two, and slip back into oblivion. But if they had a chance of finding JR and Michele, she wouldn't give up.

Chad broke the silence that pressed down on the three of them. "Looks like most have called it a night. Maybe we should, too."

A look passed between him and her dad. She suspected they'd take her home and at least one of them return. Hoped they planned that, although as another day ended, she wondered about her babies. Were they still alive? Was Drake involved, and if so, where did he have them?

So many people praying. What was the use? If God existed, why didn't He let them find the kids? What did she do to deserve all of this?

If God was real, why didn't He prove it? End this nightmare?

She silently asked, "Could you stop this, please?"

As so many times before in her life, He didn't respond, and her hope waned. Maybe she should take some tranquilizers—the rest of the bottle.

She quivered and drew her arms around herself. With her luck, a suicide attempt would leave her a vegetable instead of killing her. Until they found the children, she'd not let herself entertain that thought. For the moment, she only longed for home and sleep.

Chapter 43

Escape

"JR, I GOTTA PEE."

"So go." Why was Chele in his room, waking him up? JR rolled over, blinking sleep from his eyes.

Wait. Not his room. What the...

Oh yeah.

Kidnapped.

"JR! I'm hungry, and I want to go home."

Ugh. Would she ever quit with the whining? "What do you want me to do about it, Chele? It's not like I have a key to the door!"

His sister's chin shook.

Not good.

Major meltdown warning.

"I'm sorry, Chele. Please don't cry. It won't help." He jumped from the bed. "Let me see if I can get the guy's attention. Okay?" He searched Michele's face. The chin continued quivering.

He hurried across the room to the door and tried the knob. Still locked. Of course. Worth trying. He sighed and lifted a hand, ready to bang and face the mean man.

Muffled words filtered through, bringing JR to a halt. "Hey, Dagon. I'm hungry, man. When are we doing something besides sitting here?"

"Shut up. You wake the kids! And no use my name."

"Whatever. Get us some food."

"You go get food. We need it for kids, anyway. Go."

JR sucked in a breath. Dagon? Why did he know that name?

"JR? I gotta GO!"

He shrugged. "Yeah, yeah."

He made a fist and pounded on the door. "Hey, mister. We're awake."

"Pipe down pipsqueak. I coming."

"Well, you better hurry. My sister needs the bathroom, and if you wait, you have to clean up the mess. I'm not gonna do it."

He hopped backward as the lock clicked. A door between them gave him a sense of bravery, but with it open...?

The big man appeared in the doorway. Dagon, huh? The name rolled around his brain. He shook it off and motioned for Michele.

"Let's go, Chele."

She scampered across the room and brushed past the big man. Sometimes, her potty needs took out all fear. JR grinned at her sudden bravery. He looked up. Dagon seemed far less amused.

"No try anything brave. Little girl—she get away with it. I squash her with one hand."

"She won't try anything. I promise." JR willed his bladder to hold tight.

Michele opened the bathroom door and peeked around the corner. "JR?"

"I'm here." He moved toward her and grabbed her hand. "Wait in the room. I gotta pee, too."

His sister looked up at the man then ducked back into the room, raced to the bed, and jumped onto it. "Can we have some breakfast, please?"

That tremble in her voice—subtle. He hurried to the bathroom. No time to wash hands, but Mama would be mad if he didn't. He skipped the towel drying though, wiping them on his jeans as he flung open the door and tore across the hall back to his sister.

He looked up at the man he knew as Dagon. "Can we have breakfast, now?"

Dagon laughed. "I not starve you. Though it might be easier than constant bathroom breaks."

"You could just leave the door unlocked."

"I not stupid. Then you escape."

JR shook his head. "No. You'd catch us before we got free. But if it's unlocked, we could take ourselves to the bathroom."

Dagon snorted. "No." He moved to the door. "Breakfast come soon." He closed it with a bang, the turn of the key louder than normal. Footsteps clunked down the hall.

JR shrugged at Michele. "I tried."

"I know." She drew her feet to her chest. "JR, do you think he's gonna kill us?"

He slid onto the bed beside her. "Of course not. He needs us alive, or he would've already done it."

"Are you sure?"

JR swallowed a lump, his stomach clenching. "Yeah, sure." He chewed on his thumbnail. "I heard another guy call him Dagon. That name sounds familiar."

Michele brightened, bouncing up and down. "Ooohhh. It's like that story Gramps told us. 'Member?"

"Story? What story?"

"From the Bible." Chele's eyes sparkled. "The bad guys—Philis something—took God's ark to a temple, but not His. They bowed to a Dagon there. But he wasn't God."

"Oh yeah. Now I remember. The next morning, they found the statue on its side. Gramps said it must've freaked them out."

"Yes." Michele clapped her tiny hands. "And they put the statue back in its place."

JR nodded. "But the next day, they came again. Not only was the statue knocked down, but its head and hands were cut off—lying beside the door." He bounced off the bed. "God did that, Chele. Not any man."

"Do you think God might do that to this Dagon?"

JR shivered. "That'd be cool... But kinda gross, too." He looked around the small bedroom. "But He could make me strong like David. If I just had a sword..."

He lifted his right arm, fist clenched around a blade of his mind's making. "Take that, you mean man."

He swished around the room, slicing, cutting, stabbing the air. But in his mind, the Dagon holding them stood before him, receiving every blow. He bled and clutched his belly. JR didn't give up.

"No mercy for you. Die! You should not have taken me and my sister."

JR finished with a swift flourish of his imaginary sword, and a final downward plunge.

Footsteps echoed against the door. The lock clicked, and the knob turned.

All bravery slipped from JR as he turned and vaulted back to the safety of the bed.

"What all that racket?"

Chele grabbed JR's hand. He swallowed, wiping beads of sweat from his face. "Just making my sister laugh. She's scared of you."

"And you not?"

JR clenched his teeth, refusing to lie, but not wanting to admit the truth.

The man threw a bag at the bed. "Eat. I be back to let you take potty break—again."

The door closed, the lock turning again.

Michele snatched the bag and opened it. "JR, donuts."

He peeked inside. "Mama would insist we have something healthy with them."

His sister pulled out two small bottles of milk. "At least he got us some milk. That's healthy."

JR nodded. His brain argued against the unhealthiness of the breakfast, but his stomach gurgled. His mouth watered. Besides the two donuts, he spotted holes and two sausage-filled rolls. "Chele, eat these first."

"No. I want a donut."

"You can have a donut, but eat at least the meat first. You don't have to eat the bread."

"You sound like Mama." Her eyes glistened. "I miss her, JR."

"Me, too."

She set the bag down and slumped into a tiny ball. “I’m not hungry now.”

“Chele, you gotta eat. One of these times, when Dagon opens the door, we’re gonna make a break for it. I’m gonna get you outta here.” He pulled food from the bag and put it in her hand, then opened her milk. “We gotta be strong enough to run.”

She nodded and took a tentative bite. After chewing for a second, she gobbled the rest of the sausage roll and snagged a donut. JR smiled and helped himself to the contents, wolfing down the healthier of the two options first, then digging into the treat his mom seldom allowed.

With a full stomach, JR leaned back. Neither of them touched the donut holes, but he folded up the top of the bag, unsure of when their captor might bring more food. When Chele whined again—which he knew she would—he’d let her have the rest of the morning treat.

He drifted around the room, looking for any possible escape. What kind of room had no windows? How could they get out? He glanced over at his sister. She twirled beside the bed until she got dizzy and fell. Too much sugar. He paced around the room.

Not near the door. Those big hands that grabbed him in the backyard. Too strong for him to fight.

Dagon.

An evil name. In that moment, though, the door drew him closer. He tiptoed to it, a sliver of light creeping through. He touched the knob, turning it. Locked. But then, it moved—not like a turn. More like...

Could it be?

He nudged the wood. It moved. Only a little.

He nudged again. The door moved.

“Chele.” He motioned for her.

She kept twirling.

C'mon. Listen to me for once. "Ugh!" No time for a bear hug to stop the ridiculous circles.

Six-year-olds and sugar. Not a good idea.

"Chele." He tried to keep his voice low.

She fell to the bed and started to fling herself backward. She stopped and her eyes widened as JR beckoned her toward himself. "What?"

He put a finger to his lips like Mama did in church—when they went.

She nodded and tiptoed across the room.

He pushed on the door. It opened.

His sister gasped.

He whirled, bringing his finger to his lips again.

Chele's eyes grew wider, a visible breath entering her body.

JR grasped her hand, and with the other pushed the door a little more.

He hesitated, listening. Noises in one room—sounded like a TV. No voices. No footsteps. He edged forward, looking down the hall.

Nothing.

He let air escape from his lungs, then took in a deep breath and ventured farther. At the end of the hallway, he peered around the corner. To his left, the two men slouched in chairs facing a television, eating. He glanced back at his sister, again shushing her.

She nodded.

JR turned his head to the right. A closed-off kitchen. If they stayed quiet, they might make it. Maybe a back door or at least a window. He glanced over at the men again. Then, with a deep breath, he pulled Chele across the opening and through the open kitchen door. He considered closing it, but dared not. It might squeak like the one in the den at home. Mama always knew when he tried sneaking in there to watch TV when he wasn't supposed to. If he just got home, he wouldn't ever do that again.

The two children scooted across the kitchen floor. Chele's hand trembled in his. Or was it his hand trembling? Across the room, a window beckoned him, despite the closed curtains. He suppressed the desire to bound across the floor, fling open the curtains and window, and scream for help.

That wouldn't work. They had to stay quiet. He slipped to the window, pulling his sister behind him.

The TV continued playing in the other room. Shaking, JR pulled back the curtain and twisted a rod to open the blinds. Chele peeked out beside him. A van eased down the street.

His sister gasped. "Mama!"

"Shhhh." JR covered her mouth.

She squirmed away from him and pounded on the glass, screaming. "MAMA!"

"Chele. Be quiet."

Too late. A booming voice slid around the door frame. "What going on in here? How you get from room?"

The two men lurched across the kitchen, each throwing an arm around a child.

Michele kicked and screamed. "No. That was my mama. Let me go. I gotta catch her."

Not to be outdone, JR kicked as hard as he could, but Dagon squeezed him.

"Stop kicking me, brat!" He twisted the rod back and stepped away from the window.

JR didn't stop. He kicked harder. If he could just get away. He bent over, trying to bite the man, but Dagon threw his free arm around him.

"I break your neck if you keep fighting."

JR slumped. It didn't matter. If that was Mama, she didn't see them. The van didn't stop. She didn't come running. But then again, would she? Afraid of everything, she couldn't rescue them. He fought back tears, refusing to let these mean men see him cry.

Michele wailed, though. The other man shushed her, even covering her mouth. She bit down hard. "You little b..."

"You stupid to put hand on mouth." Dagon laughed. "Get them back into room. And for that little trick, you no get lunch."

JR's breath hitched as Chele continued sobbing.

The men took them back to the room and threw them on the bed.

"Make sure you lock door good this time." Dagon glared at the other man.

"Me? I haven't even been in here today. This is on you."

Dagon threw a punch, but the other man ducked, turned, and drew back his fist.

"Enough." Dagon glanced back at JR. "No more try to escape. Next time, I kill you both." He exited and slammed the door.

JR wrapped his arms around Chele, both shaking. "It's okay, Chele. It's okay."

"But I know that was Mama, JR. Wasn't it?"

"Maybe. Looked like our van. But it could've been anyone."

She shuddered. "Do you think they'll really kill us?"

"Not on my watch. I'll keep you safe."

"How? They're too big."

"I don't know. But we'll figure something out. If that was Mama, maybe she'll come back."

Michele slipped off the bed and planted herself on her knees. "I'm gonna pray, JR." She bowed her head and clasped her hands. "God, please send Mama back to save us. Let her have saw us in the window, cos she just had to."

JR wiped tears with his sleeve. He hoped God listened. But he had to figure out something. He didn't count on Mama to do anything. Not with all her fears.

Chapter 44

Mother's Intuition

VALORIE'S EYELIDS FLUTTERED OPEN, her heart pummeling her chest. All night, in dreams, the house reappeared with its weeds and tall grass swaying in harsh winds. Michele and JR staring out a window, terror filling their eyes. The man in the picture popping up behind them. Repeatedly, the scene beckoned her, daring her to save her children.

Her.

The one almost too afraid to open the front door. Too afraid even to go search for her babies. And somewhere in those dreams, Drake's face appeared, taunting. Always with that sick sneer and his tongue darting across his lips. He tormented her even in restless sleep.

The deep gray of first light peeped through the open blinds. When did she leave the blinds open at night?

It didn't matter. What if someone saw into her bedroom? What more could anyone do to her?

She curled into a tight ball and closed her eyes, wanting nothing but more sleep. In her stomach, a hard knot weighed down her body, but just as she almost drifted back to sleep, the voices of her children screamed for Mama. She bolted upright, threw back the covers and stomped to the bathroom, stopping to grab jeans and a T-shirt.

Enough.

The kids needed her, and despite any fear, she could no longer sit idly watching the days pass. That neighborhood—maybe the abandoned house. Could her dreams hold the answers? It seemed far-fetched, but she remembered the dungeon—at least pieces of it. Drake might not have taken them, but she couldn't shake the feeling it all somehow involved him.

Within minutes, she dressed, washed her face, and brushed her teeth before slipping down the stairs. Without a sound, she grabbed two bottles of water from the fridge and keys from the hook beside the garage door. Just a quick drive. That's all.

The sun peered over houses, many of them with pinpricks of light in various windows. Most of them remained still in the early morning. At one time in her life, Valorie loved getting up early and jogging along the ocean at sunrise. Maybe she would again—someday.

She willed her hands not to shake. Instead, she tightened the grip on the steeling wheel and turned down the street with the abandoned house. She eased her car past it. One light burned, just like the previous night. Nothing else. She studied the windows, watching for any sign of life.

Nothing.

A breath expelled from her lungs. How long had she held it? Who knew—or cared? Gentle breezes rifled through the grass and weeds. No harsh winds. No evil faces in the window, nor the faces of her beautiful children.

Tears welled in her eyes, but she raked her hands over them. Not now. She didn't have time to cry. Her pulse quickened as her mind pictured her children nearby. Michele crying for her while JR played the part of hero, always the brave protector—even when he instigated the tears. A smile played at her mouth as she remembered the many times he sped between antagonizing and comforting his little sister.

Oh, how she missed even the bickering.

She tried to steady her breathing, but her pulse raced on, throbbing against her temple. Was she losing it? No time for a panic attack. After checking the rearview and side mirrors, Valorie eased down the street, taking in everything around her.

At the end of the cul-de-sac, she circled and headed back the way she came. More lights switched on in homes, the sun rising higher. It didn't brighten Valorie's mood, though. She glanced over at the abandoned house again.

Still nothing.

Valorie looked back just as a car pulled out in front of her from a side road. She stomped the brake, wanting to curse, screaming. "You idiot."

Her knuckles white, hands aching, she swallowed whimpers.

Wait.

That road.

Did they drive down it the night before?

Of course they did. Chad and her dad wouldn't have missed it. But she couldn't remember.

She shook out her hands and returned them to the steering wheel, trying not to squeeze it again. She maneuvered the car to the right, looking at each house. In every home, blinds raised, curtains opened, revealing people at breakfast. All but one. Odd. Despite the manicured yard and inviting exterior, it looked empty—abandoned even. Maybe the family already left, but something drew her.

Sweat beaded on her upper lip. She slowed, waiting, watching.

How silly of her. Obviously, no one lived there. She looked at the other side of the street. A family hustled out the door loaded with backpacks and lunch boxes. She retrained her eyes to the road in front of her.

From her right peripheral, a flash. She jerked her head to the right and back. Two small faces—a girl hitting the window. Michele? No way. Making a U-turn, she pulled up to the curb across from the blinds-drawn house.

It sat in silence. Nothing moving. No open blinds. No children's faces. And no car in the driveway.

Did she imagine it? Did she want to find Michele and JR so much she imagined seeing her baby girl?

She stared at the house for what seemed like an eternity. A few minutes passed, but still no movement. She looked around the corner, where the weedy abandoned house taunted her. The obvious place, but not where she saw that face. She closed her eyes, breathed deeply, and sighed. Did she see her daughter, or did she imagine it?

Her phone chirped.

Chad. Looking for her.

She didn't respond to the text, but bringing up her camera she snapped a picture, capturing the number. Then she turned the phone to catch the weedy house and corner street sign. She snapped again.

Maybe she imagined it all. But what if she didn't?

She wouldn't take that chance.

After a few more seconds, she responded to Chad.

Out for a drive. On my way home. Meet me there.

Valorie checked the empty window one more time and headed home.

Chapter 45

Chad in the Neighborhood

CHAD STARED AT THE photo on Valorie's phone. "You're sure you saw Michele?"

Valorie shrugged. "I thought I did. But..."

"But what?"

"It was out of the corner of my eye. And a quick glimpse of something." Valorie covered her eyes. "Could it be I wanted to see my baby so badly, I imagined it?"

Her mother moved beside her and slipped an arm around her shoulders without saying a word.

Valorie shook her head. "It's just... I... I didn't sleep much last night. Every time I dozed off, this same dream haunted me. That house. With the weedy yard... It kept popping up with both JR and Michele's faces in the window." She moved to the chair and sat. "But it wasn't that house where I thought I saw my daughter."

Chad studied the picture again. "You parked across the street to take these, right?"

"Yes."

"You can see that abandoned house from where you parked."

"But it was the house across from where I parked that the blinds opened." Valorie brushed strands of hair away from her face.

The doorbell rang, and Mr. Daniels opened the door. Detective Davis stepped inside.

"Morning, y'all. I went by the address you gave me. Nothing. No response, no movement. A neighbor said the owner left unexpectedly several weeks ago." She turned to Valorie. "You sure you saw your daughter?"

"Maybe. I thought... Oh, I don't know." Valorie whimpered.

"I know this is frustrating. If I could go inside the house for a thorough search I would, but I can't get a warrant on 'think I saw Michele.' It's just not enough probable cause." Davis placed a hand on Valorie's arm. "Sometimes we want to see something so much our mind sees it. Doesn't make it true, even if we believe with all our hearts."

"So now what?" Chad gritted his teeth. He didn't like Davis's implications. What if Valorie saw something? What if the kids were in that house?

"We'll keep patrols going—continue watching the neighborhood. I'll add this house to places of interest. Beyond that, I can't do much. Not unless we have something definitive. Get a picture of one of the kids at the window, and we'll go in."

"Great." Too much sarcasm. It wasn't the detective's fault. The system—messed up. Marines didn't wait for probable cause. They went on intel—not always correct intel, but that didn't matter. It ended up as the right decision more often than not. The law protected too many guilty people. By the time they got probable cause, Dagon could move the kids—or worse. Not going there.

"I'm sorry, Chad." Davis shook her head. "I get it. Laws sometimes stink, but we can't just barge into someone's home. You know that."

"Yeah, I know."

Davis headed for the door. "Call me if you get anything else. I'm sure you're about to head back over there and do some recon."

She knew him well. And yes. No law would keep him from staying on that house like a bee on a soda can.

Chad chose a spot where he could see both houses, but not in front or across from either. Unconvinced Valorie saw anything, his gut said the kidnappers had the kids in the area.

Despite Mr. Daniels and Valorie wanting to come with him, he convinced them both they needed to take shifts. He'd watch 24/7 for a day or two. He could. Weary eyes missed things, though, causing the 'I think' instead of certainty.

He offered to cover this first shift of the day. Valorie and her dad could take the afternoon and early evening. Mrs. Daniels kept food and water ready to go. She hit her knees more than any of them, praying for the kids and for everyone else looking and watching.

But overnight belonged to him.

Overnight. Darkness. His specialty. Evil lurked in the darkness. And he smelled evil surrounding this situation. No information on Dagon. Little on the Drake guy. Was he involved? His mind veered back to the few interactions with Dagon as he parked near Valorie's house, never trying to conceal himself. Moron. Or maybe he did that on purpose for a time—trying to put more fear in her.

Why didn't he pay more attention? Insist Davis do more to check the guy out? Why hadn't he snapped a picture himself? He pounded the console with his fist.

"I could've stopped this whole stupid thing."

A gentle voice soothed his mind.

Grief doesn't always think straight.

Mitch told him that after they lost half their platoon, and then he missed a hostile that almost took out more of them.

He couldn't save the world. Didn't want to anymore. And Michele didn't want him around. He honored that, didn't he? Why? Could it be the little girl sensed something he wouldn't admit? He cared for Valorie—as a friend, of course. He protected them because of Mitch. Right?

He never had much of a family. Valorie and the kids... Comfortable. The few times he embraced her...

What was he thinking? She was Mitch's wife. And it hadn't been that long. He shook his head, chasing away any thoughts beyond duty to his friend.

A dark sedan passed him and turned on the side street. He shifted to full alert. The driver pulled into the house's garage where Valorie saw Michele.

Chad rushed from his car, trying to get a glimpse of the man.

Too late.

The garage door hit the pavement. He skidded to a stop, not wanting anyone in the house to see him. Backpedaling, he retreated to his car, pulled out binoculars, and zoomed in on the house.

No movement. It still looked deserted, but he knew better.

"Gotcha, sucker." Maybe. If he spotted that Dagon character, he didn't need probable cause.

He waited, praying someone gave him a reason to go into that house. His gut clenched. Not so different from recon in the military. Wait, and before long, the enemy appeared—every time. He focused on the target, searching every window for movement.

Just wait. He had nowhere to go.

A motor hummed outside his window. Chad glanced from behind the binoculars and retrained his eyes on a familiar face.

"Hey, Tyler." Davis smiled from her cruiser's rolled-down window. "Got something?"

He looked back at the house and pointed. "Not empty. Saw a sedan pull into the driveway about 12 minutes ago."

"Was it our guy?"

"Not sure. The door closed before I could see anything." He licked his lips. "Dark sedan, though, so it could be."

Davis rolled her shoulders. "I wish you got a glimpse of him."

"But you know someone's there. Can't you pay them a visit?"

She nodded. "I could knock on the door again. Doubt anyone will answer."

"Let's go, then."

"You can't insert yourself into my investigation, Tyler. Not happening."

"Why not?"

She ducked her head and raised her eyebrows.

Yeah, not the best idea. Still... A piece of Dagon. Just one.

"Brother, I know you're looking to crack his skull open. I don't want to throw you in jail while a scumbag gets away with kidnapping. Please stay here."

"Alright. But if I see trouble..."

"Stay put and call for backup. That's what you do."

"Davis, you are no fun since you put on that badge."

"Different place, new rules. This one goes by the book."

"Yeah, yeah. I hear you."

Davis shook her head, backed up the cruiser, and headed down the side street, parking at the curb.

Chad pulled up the binoculars again, zooming in tight on the doorway. He waited, breath held, shoulders taut. Davis rang the doorbell and knocked. She waited a minute. Knocked again. Chad jerked back and then adjusted the zoom. He looked again. Someone opened the door? His pulse pounded against his temple as he stared. Not the right man.

"Grrr." Where was Dagon?

He watched as Davis returned to her car and drove away from him and the house. Why did he believe Valorie? She even said it could've been her imagination. But something wasn't right.

"Get a grip, man."

No signs of the kids or Dagon. No reason to watch. And no reason to believe they held the kids in there.

Then why did his skin crawl every time he looked at the house?

Chapter 46

Trouble

Dagon peeked between the blinds. Was that military guy? Not possible. How he find him?

A key turned and the front door banged against the wall. He shook his head and pulled away from the window. He turned.

Drake. Crap.

His muscles tightened.

"Where are the brats?"

Dagon shrugged. "Locked in room where they should be."

"Hmmm. Then why did I get a report of cops coming here?"

"They checking all houses. Not just this one."

"Are you sure about that?"

"Of course." Dagon licked his lips and gazed around the room. No way he would tell Drake they escaped for few minutes.

Drake sank into a recliner. "Have you seen the mother?"

"No. She still locked away at home."

"I'm not so sure. You know I have people watching her—and you."

Dagon clenched his jaw for a moment and then crossed his arms. "You no need watch me. I do what you tell."

"I'm bored with this game. Maybe I misjudged the mother. Have you done anything to frighten her more?"

"You not tell me do anything else."

"Must I tell you everything?" Drake steepled his fingers and leaned back. "We need a plan for the rest of this game."

"Da." Dagon sat on the sofa. "You want I grab mother?"

"Maybe. But not here. Too many nosy neighbors." Drake ran a hand over his lips and beard.

Dagon waited, heat rushing through his body. Boss enjoyed these sick games—most of all torturing those who worked for him. He knew better than to push.

Drake snapped his fingers. "Tonight, put the kids in the car's trunk. Make sure you pack up all your mess. Leave nothing behind. You will bring the kids to my castle."

"Boss, that long drive."

Drake's eyes narrowed. "Then I guess you might want to take a nap before you leave."

Oh, how he detested this man. Dagon shoved down thoughts and leaned forward. "Then what we do?"

"After I lock them in my dungeon, we'll work on Valorie. Raise her fear—make her believe we will kill the brats. She'll beg me to take her back and let her become my servant." He cackled. "Only when she gives in to me, I won't kill them. I'll sell them right in front of her and let her live with that horror. That will teach her to run from me."

The other man scratched his jaw. "Is that what this is about?"

Drake squinted his eyes. "It's always about the game. I don't like losing. And you won't like it if I lose, either."

The guy nodded. "Got it."

What a wimp. His friend's eyes spread and shifted around the room. Better watch him. He'd run if they had trouble.

Drake stood. "Wait until midnight. No sense in alerting any neighbors." He walked toward the door, then turned. "And Dagon, you better not mess this up. I won't show you the mercy of a quick death."

Visions of Smitty with a hole in middle of the forehead flashed through Dagon's mind. He shuddered. "Da, boss." His blood burned. Maybe he should leave evidence implicating Drake, off kids, and escape back to Russia. Or leave kids here, sneak into castle and off boss. Not bad idea.

Drake exited, leaving Dagon with orders. Might or might not follow them. He, too, tired of this game.

Chapter 47

Probable Cause

Valorie's dad pulled up behind Chad's car. She glanced around the neighborhood. Not much movement. Wait. A black Explorer—in the driveway of that house.

She bolted from the vehicle. Chad motioned for her to stay low.

At the window, she locked eyes. "What's going on, Chad?"

"Not sure." He looked through the binoculars. "A man pulled up a few minutes ago. He looked like the same guy from the cemetery—the Drake guy."

Valorie gasped. Ice crept up her neck and arms. "Drake's here?"

"Not positive, but it could be him."

"I knew it."

Dad appeared at the window and squatted beside her.

"What's up?"

Chad looked over at him. "Maybe nothing."

How dare he say it's nothing? If Drake was in the house...

She drew in a deep breath. "Chad thinks that SUV in the driveway belongs to Drake."

Her dad peered through both windows and looked at the vehicle. "That doesn't sound good."

As they watched for a few more minutes, the front door opened, and a man dressed in all black stepped out. Valorie froze, her pulse roaring in her ears. A whimper eased from her throat. "It's him."

Chad looked over at her. "You sure?"

She nodded. Everything in her screamed, "Run!" But her feet stuck to the grass beneath them.

He held up his phone and snapped several pictures. "Mr. Daniels, if he leaves, follow him, but do not engage. Just find out where he goes."

"Got it." Dad retreated to his car.

Drake got into his SUV and backed out of the driveway, heading their direction. Valorie slipped lower, and Chad pulled up his phone, pretending to have a conversation. She peeked. Drake ignored them. An engine engaged behind them. Valorie stood and watched as her dad did a three-point turn and followed the Explorer around the corner.

"Chad, if Drake's here, my kids gotta be in that house."

"I know. We'll keep watching—for a while."

"Then what?"

He shrugged. "Playing it by ear. Might have to get closer." He motioned to the door. "Get in."

Valorie fumbled with the handle. After a few times, she opened the car door and slipped inside. Her hands refused to quit shaking, no matter how hard she tried to control them. How would they get to the kids and rescue them? She tucked her hands beneath her quivering legs.

We? Chad, maybe the cops, but her? No "her" in the "we."

They watched in silence while the sun drifted toward the horizon. The scent of meat cooking on a nearby grill turned her stomach. She couldn't think of food. The house remained still, abandoned to anyone not watching.

Chad turned toward Valorie. "Val, my gut says the kids are in that house. But I haven't seen any sign of them."

"But I feel them, Chad. They're there. They have to be." She shoved down the ache in her throat. Not a time to blubber all over the place.

"When it gets dark, maybe before, I'm moving in, try to see inside."

She nodded. "What am I supposed to do?"

He looked at her and shook his head. "I'd say let's double team them."

"But?"

He scrubbed his hands over his beard and hesitated. Then he continued. "Look, Val. I get that you're scared. Not totally. But let's face it. I don't know if you have the courage to go near that house."

Shudders took over her body. "I don't want to be afraid—of everything."

He touched her arm. "But you are. And I can't fix that for you."

A teardrop slipped down her cheek. "How do you do it? You're not afraid of anything."

Chad tilted his head back. "Huh." He looked into her eyes. "We have nothing for the cops, which means I get something, or I simply barge in there. But what if Michele and JR aren't there? What if I'm too late?" He swallowed. "I'm terrified of failing—of not saving the kids or failing to keep you and them safe. I owe that to Mitch."

Her tear became a stream. "You don't look terrified."

He looked away from her, his view turned back to the house. "I learned long ago to take back the power fear tries to steal."

"What?"

"Fear takes away your power only if you let it. Circumstances come with anything from anxiety all the way to horror—sometimes even with the best situations. When it shows up, we can't stop it. But we can refuse to let it immobilize us."

"Sounds nice. But it isn't that easy."

"Didn't say it was easy." He looked at her again. "Back in the day, I dreaded every mission. Sometimes, I could barely move. Would've stayed put except for my platoon urging me forward." He drew a deep breath. "Then I met Mitch. He led by example. Prayed us through the toughest times. After he told me about Jesus, I tried it. Scared sugar-honey-iced-tealess many times. Prayed." He shook his head. "I still can't explain it. But the fear... Poof! Gone."

Good for him. Never worked for Valorie. How many times did she beg God to take away the fear? Maybe He listened to Chad...

and Mitch. If God existed, He turned a deaf ear her way. Oh, how she wished He'd hear her—just this one time.

She stared back at the house. Waiting. Always waiting. For what?

The sun disappeared behind trees and houses.

Chad opened his door. "Wait here. I'm gonna sneak around to the back of the house. Has to be a window—something. Gotta see what we're up against."

Valorie trembled. "Are you sure you should do that?"

"No choice. We need to know what's going on in there. Don't worry. I'll be right back."

Chad darted down the street and disappeared between houses. She chewed on her thumbnail, her stomach cartwheeling. She checked the time. 5:48. Shifting, she tried to see in the growing darkness. Minutes ticked by.

"C'mon, Chad. Where are you?"

She glanced at her watch again.

5:56.

She should call for help. Shouldn't she?

No sign of Chad. One more minute...

Chad sprinted from between the houses and back to the driver's side.

"Well?"

"Got 'em." He held up his phone, revealing a picture of two men behind a sliding glass door.

One she recognized as Dagon from Det. Davis's phone. The other—just a scrawny younger guy. "That's Dagon isn't it?"

"Yeah. Hang on. Gotta get this to Davis. Probable cause. If nothing else, he's wanted by Interpol."

He sent the text, then turned toward Valorie. "Something's going down. They're packing up like crazy."

PLOP!

Chad looked at his phone. "Davis agreed. But she needs a warrant."

Movement at the house squeezed Valorie's heart. The garage door lifted. Her chest tightened. "They're leaving!"

The dark sedan eased from the garage, down the driveway, and headed away from them. Chad put the binoculars to his eyes. "Just one. Dagon I think."

"What if he has the kids, too? Maybe in the trunk."

Chad tossed the binoculars aside. "That's **my** probable cause. I'm going in. Wait here for the cops."

He didn't wait for a response, but bounded from the car and raced to the house.

Valorie's fingernails dug into her hands. "Lord, I often doubt you. But hear me this time. If my babies are in there, keep Chad safe and let him get them out. Please."

She waited, wondering what the heck was going on. One minute... two... five. "Come on!" Just as she reached to open the door, a dark sedan wheeled around the corner.

"Noooo!"

The vehicle pulled back into the driveway, and Dagon got out with bags from a fast-food place.

Valorie screamed.

Chapter 48

Rescue

CHAD RUSHED TO THE patio door, determined to get inside, and grab the kids in under five minutes. He peeked through the glass. The smaller guy darted around the room, grabbing various items and stuffing them into a duffel bag.

Good. With the man distracted, he could flip the lock and catch him off guard. No hesitation. The door wouldn't be quiet. Suddenly, the man left the room, heading to the front of the house.

Yes.

Chad pushed on the door handle, hoping they forgot to lock it. Not. He pushed up and jiggled the door. It slid open, and he entered. He glanced over the room. A rope and roll of duct tape sat on an end table. Convenient. He snatched them and slipped across the room in silence. Around the corner, a door opened. The man appeared, zipping his trousers.

"What the...?"

Chad landed a blow on the guy's jaw, driving him backward.

He recovered, ducked his head, and charged at Chad. He sidestepped and let the guy crash into the wall. The man stood and shook his head. Chad hit him with a jab and cross, followed by an uppercut. He fell, moaning.

Chad flipped him to his stomach, dug a knee into his back, and tied his hands. He yanked the guy's feet up behind him and secured them to his wrists. Ripping off duct tape, he covered the man's mouth. "Don't move."

The man grunted.

"Where are the kids?"

"Ummumum."

Chad pulled back a fisted arm. The man winced and nodded down the hall.

"Thank you for your cooperation." He coldcocked the guy and sprinted down the hallway.

Several closed doors greeted him. He turned the knob on one and opened the door to an unmade bed. Same thing at the second door. When he tried the third one, it didn't budge. He put an ear to the wood. Muffled voices drifted through. Not sure, but it could be JR. He took a chance.

"JR? You in there little brother?"

"Chad?"

"Yeah, buddy. It's me."

Michele's quivering voice broke the barrier. "Chad, please take us home. I want my mommy!"

"I got you, sweetheart. Just need the key to get in."

He felt above the door—obvious place. No luck. He turned a full 360. Nothing. He darted back into the nearest bedroom and scanned the sparse furniture.

Crap. No place to put a key.

His heart beat faster. "Gotta be here somewhere."

Across the hall in the first room, he looked on the nightstand and a dresser. Still nothing.

"God, please. Help me."

He took a deep breath, easing his frantic heart. He pivoted, searching the room again. No key. His gaze fell to the floor. Paper clip. That'd do. He retrieved it and raced back to the locked door. Kneeling, he inserted the paper clip, easing his way around the keyhole.

Precious moments ticked away. He took a deep breath.

"Chad? You still there?" JR's voice trembled.

"I'm here, buddy. Give me another minute."

"Hurry!"

Sweat poured down Chad's temple. He steadied his hand and tried again.

CLICK.

"Thank you, Lord." He turned the knob, and the door opened.

Michele jumped into his arms. Tears streamed down the little girl's face, wetting his shirt. He patted her back. "It's okay. I'm here now."

She pulled back. "I'm sorry I treated you so mean."

"No problem. All's forgiven." He looked her over, then glanced at JR. "Are you both alright? Did they hurt you?"

Both kids shook their heads.

JR took a shuddering breath. "A little hungry, maybe, but not hurt."

"Good. Let's get out of here."

"Wait!" Michele ran toward the bed. "I gotta put on my shoes."

Chad slapped his forehead. Of course she did. He glanced over his shoulder and then looked back at JR. He already had his shoes on. "Michele, I'll just carry you."

"No. They're my favorites."

JR grabbed his head with both hands. "Chele. We gotta go. Now! Forget the stupid shoes."

Chad's eyebrows raised as he took in the girl's pout and shaking bottom lip. He'd seen that before—just prior to a meltdown. No time for one of those. "It's okay. Let's just get them on. Quick. Can I help?"

She nodded and skipped across the room, reached down to get her socks and shoes, and plopped on the bed.

Chad rushed forward and knelt in front of the child. He bit his bottom lip, trying to be gentle, yet hurry. While Michele struggled with one sock, he put on the other and a shoe. He waited, his finger tapping the second shoe until she finished. Then he shoved the shoe into place, tied the lace, and scooped her off the bed.

"Let's bug out."

With JR close behind, Chad hurried down the hall. The tied-up man moaned but stayed put. JR pushed past Chad and grabbed his hand.

"The kitchen's that way."

Chad looked at JR. "Is there a door?"

"Yeah—I think it goes to the garage."

Not the best choice. Dagon left from the garage. He glanced around. Back through the sliding glass? Maybe. No. Front door. Fastest, most direct. "This way."

He pulled JR, his arm aching from holding Michele. Who knew such a little thing could be so heavy?

At the front entrance, he threw the deadbolt and opened the door wide.

"Well, well." Dagon filled the doorway, hands full of paper sacks. "What have we here?" He dropped the food and pulled a gun. "Leaving without me, Mr. Military Man? I not think so. Should've killed you when I ran over husband." He raised the gun, aiming it directly at Michele's temple. She buried her face in Chad's neck, sobbing.

"Easy, man. Let's not do anything rash." He backed into the house.

"Give me girl." He wrenched her from Chad and raised the gun, aiming the butt at Chad's head.

He shifted his weight. Not fast enough. Pain seared through his temple. The room whirled and went dark.

Chapter 49

FEAR

DAGON GLANCED OVER HIS shoulder. Valorie slumped farther down in the seat, praying he didn't see her. She could barely see him.

He shrugged and headed to the front door.

No, no, no. He couldn't be back so fast.

She grabbed the binoculars. Call Chad. Warn him! His phone sat on the console beside her. Not good. Maybe he came out the back. Just hadn't come around the side yet. He'd had long enough to find the kids and sneak out. Right?

She focused on the front door.

Moments before Dagon reached it, the door opened. Chad stood there with Michele in his arms and JR clutching his hand.

"Oh, Lord. My babies!"

Sobs pushed up to her throat, but she squeezed them down.

Dagon dropped the bags and whipped out a gun.

"NO!"

He pointed the weapon and moved forward.

Did he raise the gun? She stared harder through the lens, but with them halfway inside, she couldn't tell for sure. Then the door closed.

Her knees bounced. Sweat poured down her back despite the chill of the evening. Now Dagon had Chad and the kids. Should she do something?

"Oh, Lord. Help them. Please." Her shoulders drooped as she bowed her head and clamped her hands over her mouth. Scenarios ran through her mind, flashing scenes of horror with

Chad and her kids all bleeding. Would that evil man shoot them? Even the kids?

She wanted to run. Save them. Paralyzed, she couldn't think. Couldn't make her body move. The sobs overtook her.

A still small voice resounded through the car.

Peace. Be still.

Valorie looked up. Her hand wrapped around her phone. Of course! Call Det. Davis.

She punched in the detective's cell number.

It went to voicemail. After what seemed a long message, she got to the beep.

"Detective Davis, this is Valorie Ferguson." She choked down a lump. "You gotta get to that house. Now! Chad went inside, but Dagon came back and caught him trying to leave. I saw the kids. But he has a gun and... and... just get here. Please hurry! It may already be too late. Hurry!"

She ended the call.

Her belly filled with bile. She wanted to puke. The house stood quiet again, only the car as evidence of anyone inside. Would a neighbor help? Did she dare to endanger one of their lives?

She couldn't.

Minutes ticked by.

Dad. He'd help. But where was he?

Following Drake still.

She peered at her watch. No sign of Chad or the kids. No sign of movement.

Tiny squeaks forced themselves from her throat between gasps of air trying to move in and out.

The front door opened and a man—the younger one from Chad's picture—ran out, dragging a bag. He disappeared into the shadows of darkness.

Valorie's vision narrowed. Her mind grew numb. She couldn't stop her entire body from shaking.

Chad's words drifted into her mind. "I prayed."

But didn't she just pray and ask God to keep them safe? What good did that do?

She chewed on her thumbnail. Her heart pounded as she drew ragged breaths. If she only knew what was going on inside. But she didn't. She checked her watch again.

Five minutes gone.

A breeze drifted through the window, ruffling her hair.

Peace. Be still.

"Lord, is that you? Are you even real?" In the silence, she shook her head. "I can't do this." She stared back at the house, waiting, hoping. "Chad, where are you?"

He could take down Dagon. But the gun...

Why wasn't Davis there yet? She had plenty of time to get a warrant. Didn't she?

The house loomed in the darkness. She had to know—had to see inside.

Valorie took a deep breath. And another.

If Dagon shot Chad, he needed help. And he wasn't coming out with her children.

She glanced around the neighborhood. Empty streets teased her. No one to help.

Alone.

Terrified.

The memory of Chad holding Michele and JR grasping his hand washed over her. No one there to help. Only herself.

"I can't let them die. Dagon will kill them if I do nothing." She bowed her head. "God, I need you. I'm scared to go—terrified to stay. If Chad's right, you're my hope. You're my strength. My courage." She sobbed. "Please help me."

The wind trickled across her face, kissing her tears away and ruffling her hair again. Words swished through her mind.

Do not fear. Only be strong and courageous. I am with you always.

Words from various scriptures. If Chad, and Mitch, could face unknown enemies in foreign lands, she could at least sneak up to the house and peer into the back door like Chad did earlier.

“I have to try, Lord.”

She took a deep breath and blew it out, then opened the car door.

Chapter 50

PLAN B

"YOU KIDS. BACK IN room."

The boy glared at Dagon. "You hurt Chad."

Dagon bent toward the kid. "And I hurt you unless you do what I say. Now move."

The kid leveled his eyes at Dagon, glints of anger flashing in his eyes. The little girl slipped her hand into her big brother's. "JR. We should go in there." She scrunched next to the boy.

"You listen to sister."

"I won't leave Chad behind. I won't let you kill him." The boy shoved away his sister's hand and crossed his arms.

Dagon laughed. "What you do, pipsqueak? Huh?" He shrugged. "Gotta admire spunk. If you can drag him, go for it."

JR grabbed the unconscious man by the hands and tugged. "Chele, help me."

The girl grabbed Military Man, too. They strained against the weight, pulling. Trying. He moved a centimeter—maybe.

Dagon huffed. "We be here all night. Move."

He pushed kids aside, grabbed one arm, and dragged the man to the back bedroom. He shoved him inside. Never liked quick deaths. He pummeled Military Man in ribs, putting as much power as he could behind fists and heavy boots. Bones snapped. Good. Kill him now? Maybe let suffer. Maybe not. He pulled the gun and aimed at the man's forehead.

Both kids raced past him and stood in front of the gun.

"Oh. I so scared." He laughed.

The boy squinted at him and crossed his arms. "We may be little, but you need us alive. You will not shoot Chad."

Dagon kicked the man's foot away from the door and landed one more whack to his head. Blood trickled from both temples.

Incapacitated. For while.

He looked at the kids. "Because of little escape stunt, you get no supper. It on porch now, anyway."

The girl's lip quivered. He didn't care—as long as she didn't start wailing.

He closed, then locked the door. A twinge of pain crossed his forehead. Drake wouldn't like this.

Back down the hall, he ripped the duct tape off his friend's mouth. "What happened?"

"I don't know, man. After filling the duffel bags, I went to piss. When I came back, that dude landed punches. He asked about the kids, then coldcocked me. My head still hurts."

"He should've killed you. Save me trouble."

"No way, man. You didn't tell me some military dude would show up." He squirmed. "Untie me. I didn't sign up for this sh..."

"I not have time to untie you." He rubbed his forehead. "But I still need help to get kids out of here."

He stooped and surveyed the rope. Could he cut and still use it to confine kids? Probably. Or just use tape. Easier.

He pulled a knife from his boot and sliced through rope. "You do rest. I call Drake."

Dagon walked to the kitchen and punched buttons on the burner phone, dreading the conversation. One ring, then two.

A deep voice boomed. "How can you already have an emergency? I haven't been gone an hour."

"We need move up time."

"No. I said midnight. Why would I move my timeline to please you?"

"Military Man showed up."

"What? How did he find you?"

"I not know."

"Where is he now?"

"Locked in room with kids."

"He got into the house?" Even through the phone, boss's voice sent shivers down Dagon's back.

"I went for food. Not sure how he got in, but he knocked out man. Tied him like pig."

"So you just put that Marine in the room with the kids? Did you bother to secure him?"

"I knock him out with gun butt and many kicks. He not moving."

"You idiot. He's a trained career Marine. Do you really think a few kicks and a couple of punches will stop him? Do you for one second believe he won't be waiting when you open that door again?"

"Many bone-breaking kicks to ribs. If he can move, I put gun against kid's head. He back off."

"Not when he takes you down before you get to a kid. You are a worthless imbecile."

The room blurred. Nostrils flared. "He not move." Dagon shook. "Besides, I almost shoot him, but kids stand in front of gun. You want me kill them? I can. All. Maybe I kill you, too."

"Kill me?" Smooth as rich vodka. No good. "Just try."

Dagon ran a hand over his head. Quick breaths. "I not mean, boss. I mad at worthless friend. Should shoot him."

"Moron. People hear gunshots."

"What I do then?"

"Slit the man's throat, get the kids, and go now. I'll tend to your friend in the morning."

"I leave in minutes."

Dagon disconnected the call and stomped to the living room. He gazed into the backyard. Oh, if Drake stood on the other side of that glass door. He'd risk cops to shoot the boss and flee, leaving captives in the bedroom. The vision of the boss slumping to ground flooded his brain, a welcome image of defeating one he detested. Too long with him. Time to leave. Russian government would welcome him back. Give him reward maybe. Why he ever leave?

Eerie silence pulled him back to reality. He scanned the room, his gaze lingering on each area as he turned. One duffel bag remained on the sofa. The other nowhere in sight. He strode to each room, searching for the younger man.

After retracing his steps, he headed to the entryway. Door closed, but the lock disengaged. Dagon shook his head. Stupid. Drake could find anyone. If he didn't find idiot first. But Drake didn't need to know this. Not now. Maybe never.

He slipped back into the living room and shouldered the bag. Put in car first, then deal with Military Man and kids.

Unless he changed his mind and headed for the airport instead.

This game? Not boring. Bothersome. Dumb. No money was worth this mess.

Chapter 51

The Mind of Babes

JR knelt beside Chad.

Michele whimpered behind him. “Is he okay, JR? He’s bleeding. Bad.”

“I know Chele. Grab one of those napkins.”

She scurried over to the dresser and ran back to her brother. “Here.”

Chad groaned and tried to sit up. “Mmm.” His head dropped back.

“Chad? You okay brother?” JR dabbed at the blood streaming down the sides of his face.

Stupid question. He wasn’t okay. No one bleeding, moaning, and unable to sit up could be okay. Chad’s forehead wrinkled like his mom’s when she had a headache. That stinking Dagon hurt his friend, and JR wanted to punch him somewhere. How and when, not sure, but he had a secret and maybe a plan.

“Chele, come hold this napkin at Chad’s temple, where it’s bleeding the worst.”

“Ooh. No way. It’s icky.”

“C’mon. It’s just a little blood. I need to listen at the door.”

“What good will that do?”

“I dunno. But I gotta try.”

Michele ventured toward them and squatted beside Chad. “I don’t wanna get blood on me.”

“You won’t. Just hold the napkin here and press—but not too hard.”

"Oh, alright. But if I get blood on me..."

"Quit being a baby. Chad came to save us. The least you can do is take care of him for a minute."

She stuck out her tongue and then made her fish lips face. What a bratty kid.

JR tiptoed close to the door and placed his ear against it. A muffled voice drifted through. No idea what Dagon said. He pulled open the door a crack.

Chele gasped. "Hey! How'd you do that?"

"Shhh. You want him to know?"

Michele dropped her voice to a whisper. "No. But how'd you open the door? Does that mean we can get out?"

JR shook his head. "Not yet. We gotta give Chad a minute. Wait for a chance to catch Dagon by surprise—have a plan." He peeked through the crack and then back at her. "And you gotta keep your pie hole shut."

She glared at him and snuffed. But she kept quiet. Wonder of all wonders.

He kept trying to see Dagon, listening for his voice again. He still couldn't catch all the words, but something about the guy. Kill. Nothing sounded promising. The other rooms grew silent. Where did Dagon go? Did he dare open the door any wider? He couldn't see their captor, but the sound of a door closing drifted through the house. Maybe he left.

A moan behind him drew his attention. He needed to see if Chad could get up. If Dagon left, this might be their chance, but he and Chele couldn't carry him.

He gently pushed the door to a closed position and turned. Kneeling beside his sister, he touched Chad's cheek. "Chad?"

His eyes fluttered. "Hey, little brother. You alright?"

"I'm good. You?"

"Yeah. Other than a splitting headache and this vice squeezing my ribs."

"I think Dagon plans to kill you—maybe all of us."

"I'm surprised... he... didn't already."

"He has a gun. But I don't think he wants to shoot it."

"Neighbors might... hear."

Chele lifted the napkin. "Still bleeding. You don't sound right, Mr. Chad."

He held up a hand and brushed the hair from her eyes. "Just... hard to... breathe."

JR looked around the room, wishing for a weapon. Useless. He already searched everywhere. What if he sneaked out, got to the bathroom, and climbed through the window? That might work.

He shook his head. Chad would never agree to that, but if he didn't tell him...

While he pondered the idea, Chad's eyes closed again. He needed to get help. If his plan worked, what then? Go to a neighbor's house? Someone he didn't know? Would they help them? And what would he do with Michele when he left? No way she would let him go without her, even with Chad there.

They had to escape. But how?

"Oh, Mama." He whispered. "I wish you were here."

She might not have any courage, but she knew how to comfort him, and more than anything, JR wanted her reassurance.

Chad moved and groaned. JR looked over at him. "Hey, buddy. Help me get up. We need... a plan. When he... comes back, we... we need to take him... down. Somehow."

JR pulled on Chad's hand.

"Mmmm."

JR stopped. "Sorry, Chad."

"It's okay. Just hold... steady. I'll pull." He sat upright, breathing hard and fast. He pushed himself backward toward the wall. Sweat dripped off his forehead, the blood trickling faster.

Michele gently moved with the big man, still holding the napkin to his head. "Mr. Chad, what are we gonna do?"

With his back finally touching the wall, Chad looked at her. "I don't... know yet, honey. But I'm not... gonna let him hurt you."

JR shook his head. How would Chad stop Dagon? He could barely move.

Chad's eyes closed again, lines forming across his forehead. JR clenched his teeth, making a decision. Time to get help. He whispered, "Chele, you stay here with Chad. I'm gonna get help."

"No, JR. He'll kill you."

"Maybe. But maybe I can get out the bathroom window. You take care of Chad, and stay quiet.

Chad's eyes fluttered, but didn't open. "No..." He tried to move and moaned.

"It's ok, Chad. I'll be fine."

JR moved to the door and took a deep breath. He could do this. He had to.

Chapter 52

Mama Bear

Valorie approached the house, careful to stay in the shadows. Where were the cops? Chad and the kids still hadn't come out. Not good.

Her stomach clenched as visions of possibilities ran through her mind. Chad—lying on the floor in a pool of blood. Her children bound and stuffed into the car's trunk. Maybe she should go back and wait for Detective Davis. But she couldn't. She reached the side of the house just as the garage door went up.

She pressed against the brick, gasping for breath. No one came out, and she didn't hear the car starting.

Blood rushed through her ears, the world slipping into fuzziness.

A thick, accented voice came from the garage. "Yeah. Loading now. We leave five minutes."

Five minutes?

Valorie froze. She fought for breath. In the shadows, her breaths came faster. Thoughts swirled.

Breathe. Just breathe.

But she couldn't.

Suddenly, a voice whispered. "Peace. Be still."

Valorie jerked her head. Who said that? Her glance darted around the yard.

No one there.

She took one step forward and peered into the garage.

Empty.

Warmth enveloped her, memories of self-defense classes flashing like lightning across her brain. She knew the moves. Could do all of them.

The last class invaded her thoughts. Standing behind a massive man, she kicked the bend of his knees one at a time. He fell to the ground. Then what? She closed her eyes, trying to envision what she did next. "Lord, help! I need courage, and it's not there. Help Chad. Help my babies. And help me."

She raced to the back of the house and spied the sliding door. She peeped inside where a big man shouldered several bags and left with them.

Now.

She pulled the door open, slipped inside, shut it behind her. A thud sent her behind the drapes. Footsteps. Movement. More bags? Maybe. As they retreated, she rushed from behind the drape, searching for a place to hide and attack from behind.

Her hands trembled, her heart pounding against her ribs. This time, the world didn't tilt.

Footsteps—around the corner. Hide. She sprinted across the room and pressed against the wall. One chance. If she didn't take him down...

Don't think. Just react.

A long hallway loomed before her. Soft sounds drifted. What was that? A door? Quiet footsteps.

Heavy footfalls neared the corner.

"What... how?"

The big man rushed past her just as her gaze landed on JR.

The man took two steps toward her son.

Oh, no you don't. Valorie moved, her feet connecting with the back of the kidnapper. He fell forward, hitting his knees against the floor. Before she could reach him, he somehow spun and drew a gun. She kicked again, knocking it from his hand. She landed a blow to the side of his head with her other foot.

The man's eyes blinked, his balance wavering for a moment. Then he shook his head.

A slow smile spread across his face. "Well, well. Mama found some courage." His eyes smoldered, piercing holes in her bravery.

As he moved to stand, JR bent and picked up the gun. What was he thinking? Her throat tightened. Keep the man's focus on her. She glanced down the hall. Chad leaned against a wall, blood streaming down the side of his face.

Her lungs froze.

His eyes opened.

Good. He wasn't unconscious. If JR took the gun to him... But how could she convey that to her son without tipping off the man? He lowered his brows and turned his head in her son's direction. Valorie took three steps back. As the giant began turning his body, she ran a few steps and launched a drop-kick. The man stumbled against the wall.

"JR. Run to Chad. Run!"

Her son bolted down the hallway, but the man grabbed him. "No. You not get away."

Something came over Valorie at that moment. Visions of a dungeon and unspeakable things flooded her brain. Memories of Mitch's motionless body tore at the fabric of her heart. And this man's hand touching her son merged as the worst of what life could bring.

"Take your hands off my son."

Dark eyes refocused back to her. "Who will make me?"

She took a step toward him. "Me."

He laughed. A booming, menacing laugh she might never forget. The boiling rage inside Valorie grew. Every muscle tightened as she envisioned the terror this man caused for her babies. No matter what happened to her, he would not touch her kids again.

A few steps and a knee came up and connected with his groin.

He winced, but stayed upright.

That wasn't supposed to happen. He ought to be on the ground. Instead, he growled. She backed up and went in for a kick. The man grabbed her ankle with one hand and foot with the other.

SNAP.

Excruciating pain raced up her leg. Valorie screamed. Her back hit the floor as the man shoved her away. He pounded toward her. One fist punched her in the stomach.

"No woman ever kick me there and live." He sneered down at her. "Now, you die. I no care what Drake wants."

She raised her hands and clawed across his face.

The back of his hand connected with her jaw.

Massive hands closed around her throat.

She kicked. Hit him with her fist. Squirmed, trying to break his hold.

No good. The pressure increased.

Air. Not. Coming.

Get his hands off her throat. Couldn't.

She grabbed his hands, digging fingernails in as deep as she could.

Still, he squeezed.

No air. Gotta breathe. Got to...

Don't give up. The kids...

Tears welled in her eyes. How could she fight this beast? Her surroundings faded.

"Mama!"

No. She couldn't die like this. Not with JR watching.

Was that a soft click?

For a moment, the hands loosened. She caught a hint of air before they tightened again.

"Let my mama go."

A loud boom.

Black.

Chapter 53

ALIVE?

AIR. VALORIE GULPED BREATHS despite the ache in her throat. Weight pressed against her body. Was this death?

"Mama?"

Her son. She must be alive.

"Is she okay, JR?"

Michele? Her babies.

Another breath. Rank. What was that smell?

She couldn't move. Something weighed her down. She tried opening her eyes, but a rough texture pushed against her.

"Get him off her, JR."

"Help me, Chele."

Grunting. Her children struggling. Near, but so far away.

"He's too heavy." JR's voice broke through the fog. "Mama? Mama. Say something. Please be alive. Please don't leave us!"

Valorie forced her eyes open. Dark. Cloth?

Her mind cleared. To a point. Hands no longer choked her. The clothes. The kidnapper? But...

She shoved. Too much weight.

"JR? Michele?"

"Mama!" Both of her children. Beside her. Safe.

"Where's Chad?"

JR answered. "He's in the bedroom. Hurt bad."

Valorie summoned all her strength and pushed against the weight again. Not much, but something. "Lord, please help." She moved her head, getting it out from under what lay on top of her.

Her children knelt on the floor. A flood of emotions flashed in their eyes. She knew the answer—in part. But she asked anyway. "What's on top of me?"

JR's eyes narrowed. "Dagon."

"The man who took you?"

"Yes."

"What happened?"

"I shot him."

"You? JR..."

"He was killing you, Mama. Choking you. I couldn't let him do that. I didn't mean to kill him, but I had to protect you."

"It's okay, baby."

JR huffed. "I'm not a baby."

She chuckled. "Alright, big man. Maybe if you help me, I can get out from under this beast. On three, we both shove him toward the wall. Okay?"

"Okay."

"One, two, three."

Valorie pushed with all she had and scooted away from the bulk. Just enough she could take a full breath. "One more time, JR."

"I'll help, too, Mama."

"Good, Michele."

She counted again, and repeated her movements, this time breaking free. Her ankle throbbed, but she sat tall enough to see the man beside her. Blood matted the hair on the back of his head. He didn't move.

She glanced down the hallway, spotting Chad again. Was he dead? She looked over at JR. "What happened to Chad?"

"Dagon hit him with the gun. Then he kept kicking him in the head and his side. He kicked him so many times."

Michele chimed into the conversation. "He couldn't talk right, Mama. And his head hurt."

Valorie stood, pushing against the walls with both hands and not putting weight on her right foot. "JR, help me get to him."

Using her son as a crutch, she hobbled down the hallway to the room. She reached Chad and lowered herself to the floor beside him. “Chad?”

His eyes opened to slits. “Valorie?”

“Yeah. I’m here. You’re gonna be alright. Hold on.”

She needed help. How? She wouldn’t send her son, and she wouldn’t leave him or Michele.

Chad breathed. Shallow, but a breath. “Where’s the bad guy?”

Valorie swallowed hard. “Dead.”

“Dead?”

JR joined his mom on the floor. “I took him out, Chad. I protected my mom and sister. And you.”

“Good man.” He reached up and grasped JR’s hand in the same grip Mitch used often with military friends. JR’s face beamed. “We’ll talk. Later.”

The labored breathing. Not good.

The sound of a door crashing filled the house. Stomps. Shouts. A woman’s voice.

Detective Davis. Finally.

Valorie leaned her head against the wall beside Chad and breathed.

Chapter 54

Waiting

Detective Davis waited impatiently. Chad's text gave her all she needed. With or without the kids, Dagon was inside that house. She knew the Marine. If he said going in, he went. Was he armed beyond his bare hands? If the kids were there, he'd stop at nothing.

She gathered her team in a conference room. "The warrant's not through yet, but we need to be onsite when it does. We have no verification of children in the house, but we suspect it is where they're being held, so go in with caution." Davis pointed at two men. "Jackson, Peters. When we get there, I need eyes inside. Need to know what we're up against."

"Copy that."

She turned to the other officers gathered. "Take no chances, but when we breech, don't hesitate. Lives are at stake."

They rushed through town, lights flashing but sirens silent. All vehicles cut the lights two blocks from the target and before entering the neighborhood. A lone vehicle sat at the curb with a view of the house. Chad's car. Empty.

Her heart beat faster. Deep breaths. Slow the rate.

They pulled over and exited vehicles without a word.

Hated scenarios like this one. Loved her team.

Jackson and Peters slipped between houses toward the backyard.

Other officers went in low, peeking into windows. Several of them shook heads.

Not good.

Jackson sprinted back to her. "Sliding door. Unlocked. We couldn't see much but sounded like a scuffle."

Peters joined them. "No one in sight. We should go in."

Davis nodded. "Agreed but take it slow. We don't know where Dagon is or the kids."

Her team continued unloading gear. She motioned for them to take their places. Before they reached their spots, a loud boom echoed in the stillness of the night.

Unmistakable. "Gunshot. Go, go, go!"

The team scurried to their places. Too slow.

She joined men at the front door.

A battering ram demolished it. The team poured through the opening, guns raised. Hands, fingers motioning to each other.

Precision. Chaos yet order. Perfect entry. Still, too much time wasted.

No chances, though. They had to slow down—keep kids out of crossfire.

She scanned the entryway and room in front of her. Emptiness and silence screamed back.

Her team moved through each room, maintaining silence.

Were the kids there?

Where was Chad? And where was Dagon?

Someone shouted, "Hallway."

Shouts of "Clear" reverberated through the house.

Another voice boomed. "Back room. Need a bus. Stat!"

A lump formed in Davis's throat. An inner groan begged for release. Please, God. Not those innocent children and not my friend.

At the entry of the hallway, she froze.

In a back bedroom, Chad leaned against the wall. Pale. Bleeding.

Two small children huddled around him, Valorie beside him, not moving.

Metallic notes assaulted her nose. She looked down at the massive hulk in the hallway. Blood pooled around a dark form, lying still. She lifted her gaze to the officer bent over him. He shook his head.

Her legs wobbled. She had to know. Swallowing a lump, she moved along the hallway until she reached them and squatted beside the children.

Chapter 55

At the Hospital

Valorie's eyes flew open. How long had she slept?

The children! Where were her children?

She looked around the room until her gaze fell on her dad's face, his eyes closed, and a soft snore slipping from his mouth. She moved.

Bad mistake. Every muscle in her body ached.

Her ankle screamed, "Stop!"

So, it wasn't all a bad dream.

Her father stirred and woke. "Morning, hon. How do you feel?" He rose and came to the bedside. "That's kinda dumb. I'm sure your ankle hurts."

"All of me hurts, Dad. Where are the kids?"

"With Mom. The doctors checked them out. No physical damage. A bit dehydrated, still shaken, but for all they endured, they're remarkably well."

"No... you know."

"Neither was sexually assaulted."

"Thank God!"

He smiled. "Yes. And thank God you are safe."

"Chad?"

"Beat up. But he's young and strong. In better shape than most people. It may take a while, but he'll recover." He reached out and took her hand. "JR told us what happened. Honey, what you did was insane. You could've died."

She nodded, tears pooling but staying put. "I know."

"Still, you kicked that Dagon's butt. From what JR said, you're his new hero." Dad laughed. "He demonstrated your moves. Fortunately, Michele took five steps back when he started."

Valorie laughed, then groaned. "My throat feels like... nothing I've ever known."

Her dad nodded. "Yeah. I imagine. Between that guy choking you almost to death and the tube for surgery, it may take a few days for that to feel better."

"Surgery?" She didn't remember surgery.

"Um hmmm. The jerk broke your ankle. They set it."

She glanced down at her foot, hanging in a sling.

"They'll put a cast on it today or tomorrow. It's still swollen."

Valorie nodded. Moments from the previous evening tugged at her brain. She looked into her father's eyes. "Dad, did JR...? Did he shoot that gun? Hit that man?"

Her father nodded, tearing up. "He said the man wouldn't let go of your neck. He didn't have a choice. The cops said it was a lucky shot. I don't think JR aimed for his head. But that's what the bullet hit."

"But he's still a baby."

Dad perched on the bed beside her. "Hon, he grew up the day Mitch died. The little man of the house."

"I don't want that. I want him to be an innocent little boy."

"I know. Death of a parent matures kids at exponential rates, and someone taking you and your little sister from your safe backyard? Well, that just took away a chunk of his childhood. I'm sorry, but it did."

"Can I get it back for him? And for Michele?"

"A social worker spoke with us last night. I'm sure she'll come back and talk to you. The kids will be okay, but they need professional help to deal with all this." He patted her hand. "Give them both some credit. They're pretty tough kids. You, on the other hand, may need someone to keep you from tying them to your hips."

They both laughed, and joy spread through her. Joy. Something she hadn't felt in years. "I faced a fear, Dad. It may have taken a little more of JR's innocence away, but I didn't let it paralyze me this time."

"I know. For that, I'm thankful and so proud of you. Don't be surprised if reporters start calling. It's all over the news—how you took down an international hit man."

"What?"

"Yep. Go figure. That Dagon guy—wanted in multiple countries for assassinations and attempted ones. Big bounty on his head."

"No way."

"Yes, way. The detective said it might go to you and JR. Wouldn't that be something?"

"I'd put it away for his college."

"I figured as much. You can worry about that later."

He let go of her hand and stood. "You hungry? You slept through breakfast, but I can ask the nurses to get you something."

"Not really."

The door burst open, JR and Michele traipsing into the room, each with a giant bouquet accented with balloons. "Mama!" Their chorus soothed her aches and brought a smile to her face.

"Hi babies." She held out her arms.

Both children ran across the room and bounced on the bed.

Valorie gritted her teeth and threw her arms around JR and Michele, drawing them as close as she could.

"Mama. You're squeezing too tight." Michele squirmed.

"Sorry. I'm just so happy to see you." She looked over both children, inspecting them for bruises, cuts, any sign of abuse. Pale maybe, but good.

JR hopped off the bed. "Not as happy as I am to see you."

"Did you have breakfast?"

"Of course. Gramps wasn't there to make pancakes, but Grams did alright with them. No chocolate chips, but she did let us have chocolate milk."

"Really?"

Michele bounced. "Yeah. Two glasses, plus the one last night."

Valorie looked at her mom and shook her head.

Mom grinned. "They needed liquid. Dehydration from not enough to drink the past few days."

"I'll let it slide this time. But you two know we drink water, not sugary stuff."

"Yeah, yeah."

She leveled a look at them.

"Sorry. Yes, ma'am." Both the children smiled at her. Their sweet faces beamed with love.

How would these events shape their future? Neither seemed bothered. Was it only the calm before a hurricane? Memories had a strange way of working themselves to the surface when least expected. Counseling—definitely in order.

A soft knock and the door opened again. Detective Davis peered into the room. "May I come in?"

Valorie nodded. "Of course."

"How are you, Valorie?"

"Sore. My ankle hurts like the mother of all pain."

"I'm sure." Davis stood at the end of the bed and cleared her throat. "What you did at that house—you should've waited for us."

"He was about to leave with my babies. I didn't know what happened to Chad, but I knew he wasn't alright. The last time I saw Dagon he had a gun. My kids were in there. I had no choice."

"I get it." Davis looked into her eyes. "You are a brave woman."

"Me?" She laughed. "I'm anything but brave. Ask anyone who knows me."

Davis shook her head. "I'm not sure I'd face Dagon alone. He was a giant of a man—and super strong. I think he underestimated you, and he made a big mistake in thinking JR a coward." She turned toward him. "Just one question, young man. How exactly did you get out of that room?"

JR shrugged. "Easy. When Chad took us out, we almost got away. But Dagon caught us at the door and knocked out Chad. I picked up a piece of tape from the floor while he dragged Chad into the room. He never saw me." He shifted his weight between his feet. "In the room, while he kept kicking Chad, I couldn't stop him. But I put the tape over the thingy that keeps doors closed. He locked it, and I pushed against the door so it didn't come open when he left. He thought it was locked. But I fooled him."

"You sure did."

"I figured we could sneak out. But with Chad not moving much, I came up with another plan."

"Really?"

"Yes, ma'am. I was gonna sneak out, go in the bathroom, and lock the door. Then I could climb out the window in there and get help. Maybe from a neighbor."

"But that didn't happen."

"No. Mama was there kicking butt. When the gun landed near me, at first, I just stood there. But then he started choking her." Tears filled his eyes, and his voice quivered. "We already lost our daddy. I couldn't let him kill Mama. Her face was red—purplish. I told him to stop. He just laughed at me." JR looked up and took a breath. "That's when I picked up the gun, pointed it at him, and pulled the trigger. He slumped while I kinda crashed against the wall."

"The gun's recoil."

He nodded. "I didn't know it would do that. I have a BB gun. It doesn't knock me back. I just wanted to scare him. Get him away from Mama."

Davis crossed to him and put a hand on his shoulder before bending to eye level. "You did good, JR. You saved her. Probably Chad, your sister, and yourself, too."

She turned to Valorie. "I'm gonna go check on Chad. They say he's doing well, but I want to see for myself. We've been friends a long time. We need an official statement from you when you get out of here. Just come by the station so we can take care of that."

"And the kids?"

"We have all we need from them. With what JR told me just now, I can close the case. He acted in self-defense, so we're all good."

She turned to leave and then turned back. “If you need anything, call me. I can give you a list of counselors if you need them.”

“Thank you, detective. I appreciate all you did.” Valorie swallowed. “You believed me from the beginning, even when some cops didn’t.”

“I saw the anguish of a mother whose children were missing. How could I not believe you?”

She left. Not for the last time. She could become a close friend. And for a change, the idea didn’t scare Valorie.

Chapter 56

Statement

Valorie read over the statement Davis had prepared. Everything sounded right, so she signed it and laid the pen on the desk. "Is that it?"

"Yes. We'll close the case."

"What about Drake? He was at the house, too."

"Chad's pictures weren't clear, so we have no proof of his involvement. I'm sorry."

Valorie shook her head. "My gut says he instigated it all."

"I can't disagree. The part of my job I don't like—my hands are tied. If I knew where to find him..." She shrugged. "I've seen his name pop up before. But we don't even have a photo of him. No clue what he looks like beyond a general description."

Valorie glanced around the small office. Stacks of paper. Empty coffee cups. Davis didn't let up. "I'm glad you caught my case, Davis. My memories of Drake are fuzzy. I think my mind doesn't want to remember him."

"That's not unusual. Self-protective mechanism." She raised her eyebrows. "Guess that's good. But don't worry. He'll mess up one day, and we'll be there to pick him up." She leaned back in her chair. "Did you see Chad before you left the hospital?"

"Yes. I suspect they'll beg him to go home within a day or two." Valorie chuckled. "He had those nurses almost hopping to attention."

"Sounds like Tyler. He's one of the best, Valorie. He may be big and gruff, but he's got the heart of a lamb. Big ol' teddy bear. But

I'll deny ever saying that." She wrinkled her nose. "I didn't know your husband, but Chad often spoke of Mitch. He admired him more than anyone. I think he feels responsible for you and your children."

"He's been amazing. Taking good care of us. In some ways, he blames himself for the kidnap."

"Why?"

"Michele had a hard time. She still expects Mitch to come home, but I think reality might be catching up with her. She told Chad she knows he's not trying to take her daddy's place."

"He never thought he measured up to your husband's standards, but he tried. Drove us crazy talking about Jesus, which he learned from Mitch. But he had it right."

"Well, he sure helped me overcome fear because of his relationship with Jesus. I had that a long time ago, and I miss it. I know he's right, and I'm better. But fear is a powerful enemy."

"The most powerful. But we can stand against it and not let it keep us from living. We can face it, knowing man cannot take our salvation even if he takes our lives."

Profound words. She needed to grasp them and hold on tight. "So true. Thanks for reminding me of that, Davis. I hope we become friends. I need women like you in my life."

"I concur with that." Her eyes twinkled as they both nodded.

"I should go. Dad's waiting across the street at the coffee shop."

Both women stood, started to shake hands, but went for a hug instead.

"Keep in touch, Valorie, and I'll check on you soon. I'm here if you need me."

Valorie didn't trust her voice, so she nodded and left.

She waited for the elevator doors to open. With the cast, she couldn't take the stairs. Just as well. Another fear she needed to conquer, anyway—the what if of elevators kept her off them. Several people shifted to make room. One floor down, all but one exited. The door closed, and Valorie's skin crawled. She didn't like being alone with a man in any enclosed, tight space.

"Hello, Valorie."

Her eyes widened, her throat constricting. She knew that voice. It dripped with evil. She gripped her phone. Would it even work in there?

"Fancy meeting you here. How are those children of yours?"

Valorie spun, ready to gouge him with a crutch.

"Come, come, my dear. We're at a police station. You think I'm stupid? I just wanted to see you again. I so love playing with your mind—keeping you all wrapped up in unrealistic fears."

The fury Valorie experienced in the house returned. "You did all of this, didn't you?"

"Nothing you can prove. Not with a kidnap, or with your husband."

Her hands clenched the bars of the crutches. "Why? I didn't do anything to you."

"You got away with the others. They'll have their turn. In time."

"You won't get away with it."

"I already did. And you may have won this battle, but the war isn't over. You'll always wonder if I'm coming back. You'll never stop looking over your shoulder or running in fear."

She locked eyes with the evilest man she ever knew. "I'm. Not. Afraid. Anymore. Not of you. Not of any man."

"Good for you. We'll see."

"No. We won't see. I'm not alone now. And in Jesus' power, I don't have to fear you. I don't have to cower before you. And I won't. Get away from me, you vile, evil man. And leave my family alone!"

Was that a twinge of fear in his eyes?

Yes. She recognized it from years of looking in the mirror.

She smiled then. "You can't hurt me anymore, Drake. You've already done everything I feared most. And I survived."

The doors opened and Valorie backed out. She raised her phone to her waist, hit a button, and snapped a picture before turning and hobbling away as fast as possible. Footsteps fell behind her while an officer held open the station door. She glanced over her shoulder. No one there. Where did Drake go?

Coward. No doubt he disappeared out a side door.

Her heart raced as she crossed to the coffee shop. At its door, she held out her trembling hand. Dad approached and held it open for her.

"You okay? You look like a demon's chasing you."

She swallowed, panting.

Breathe.

Better.

"Maybe. But I think it was just a man."

Dad pulled out a chair for her. "Have a seat." She slumped into it.

Pulling up the picture on her phone, she held it for her father to see. "His name is Drake. I think Detective Davis can use this."

She punched a button to share the photo, found Davis's number, and typed a quick message.

Maybe he just messed up.

She hit send. In seconds, the reply came.

Drake? Where?

He was in the elevator. Long gone by now.

You okay?

Yes. With Dad.

Good.

Funny thing. He still terrified me. But I didn't show it. Jesus was there too.

I'm so proud of you.

Discovered something.

What's that?

Evil men don't like the name of Jesus… or a display of His power.

No, they don't. You go girl.

And thanks for the picture. Priceless.

Go get him.

Oh, the look on Drake's face if he ever met Davis.

He'd go underground for a long time. But he'd come back out one day. He didn't know the detective like she did.

Valorie breathed in the aroma of coffee. Machines gurgled and spewed. Tension melted from her body as she leaned back. "Dad, do we have time for a latte?"

"Of course. Are you alright?"

"Never better. All along, you and Mom told me to trust Jesus with my fear. I finally learned you were right. I should have listened years ago."

He bit his bottom lip, a sure sign he wanted to cry but wouldn't. Strong men. Why were they so afraid to let emotions go? She reached across the table and touched his hand. "Thank you, Dad, for never giving up on me. I love you."

That did it. Tears trickled from his eyes. He flicked them off his cheeks. "I'll get that latte for you." A slight quiver sneaked into his voice, but as he crossed to the barista, he stood tall and straight.

Although the moment passed, neither would forget it.

Never.

Chapter 57

Drake's Report

Drake sat at his desk, a bottle and glass within easy reach. He failed with Valorie. Lucipheus didn't waste a minute before chastising him.

No big deal. Despite losing this skinny wench, the games continued with millions of other fearful people—not only women, but men too. He especially loved the cowardly ones who let fear of their women control them.

His master, on the other hand, didn't like losing one soul. He fumed over Charissa. Now he added Valorie to the list, and Lucipheus waited for the report. He always wanted it in writing.

Drake opened the bottle, filled the glass, and took a long sip of smooth scotch. He picked up the pen, drew in a deep breath, and looked at the blank paper for several minutes before writing a single word.

My lord,

With you, I regret losing the woman known as Valorie. The Marine got to her, although we tried our best to keep him from influencing her for the enemy. I failed you and acknowledge your rage. I disappointed myself. I admit poor choices of men to do the work I should have taken care of myself. Nevertheless, you have Dagon in the abyss now and can torment him at will. As for the one who ran... I have loyal servants looking for him as I write this report. No one will ever see him again, nor will authorities find his body. His soul is yours.

I continue playing the game of fear with millions on this earth, toying with their minds and guarding against those who try to convince them turning to our enemy will ease their anxieties. Both legal and illegal drugs and alcohol help many of them cope with their fear—or so they believe. But in the dead of night, they run through nightmares. I, as always, continue finding ways to keep their fear alive and well. You must admit, I win this game more often than I lose. We lost a soul, but a weak one at that. I won't make the same mistakes.

The fear provides only one outlet to win for your glory and honor and keep them from our enemy's camp. Of the women who I held for a time, I have chosen the next one to pursue. Although she doesn't have fear working against her, she maintains unforgiveness and anger, producing a nice root of bitterness. Taking her should be no problem. Already, I have a plan in place to destroy and pull her from the enemy's grasp. She will not set an example for others to follow him.

The kidnap of Valorie's children gnaws at this woman's brain, and when she returns home to find her child, we can watch those bitter emotions until they dig so deep, she'll never rid herself of them. In that state, as a follower of our enemy, she makes a perfect tool to turn others from him. Who wants to follow a "believer" who hates her father? Even now, it skews the way she sees the enemy. And I intend to drive these doubts and bitterness to a cavernous level.

Rest assured, oh great one, I will defeat this one. Shamira will fall.

Chapter 58

One Year Later

VALORIE CHECKED HER LIST one more time and zipped the suitcases. "If we forgot something we can always buy it. Not like we're broke. Right?"

JR and Michele bounced on the bed.

JR said, "Mom, you've double checked everything 20 times. I seriously doubt you forgot anything."

"Just making sure smartypants." She grinned at her son and ruffled his hair. "Are you excited about this trip?"

"Yeah."

"Hey! What about me?" Michele tumbled off the bed.

"I already know you're excited, baby."

"I'm not a baby, Mama. And how do you know I'm excited?"

"You will always be my baby. I know because you haven't quit hopping around since you woke up this morning."

"Oh." Michele shrugged. "I'm gonna get my toy bag."

"Good idea. JR, why don't you go get your bag, too? Both of you take them to the front door. I'll lug these suitcases down."

JR joined Michele.

Had she lost her mind? Traveling to the Grand Canyon alone with two children. Maybe she should have insisted Mom and Dad went with them. Chad offered to accompany them, too. But how would that look? Besides, who'd keep Bruce? Mom and Dad tolerated him when they visited, but they didn't want a dog digging up their yard. She didn't blame them. Bruce loved to dig holes she always managed to find. Usually with the lawnmower.

Coming up on a year since Mitch's death, Valorie enjoyed having Chad around. He took care of all the man stuff she needed done. And he never minded helping with the kids, hanging out with JR, going to school activities. Even Michele warmed up to him after the kidnapping. With the counselor's help, she finally admitted Mitch lived in Heaven.

For a moment, Valorie's heart clenched. A cloud of sadness descended over her. Only for a moment. She missed Mitch every day. But she learned to cope with the sorrow and pain. Hence the trip. They always talked about visiting the Grand Canyon when the kids got a little older. Well, they were older, weren't they?

She picked up the photo from her nightstand. "Oh, Mitch. I wish you could see them. JR reminds me so much of you. I'm sorry I put you through so much with my unreasonable fears. I still struggle some days, but I'm better." She wiped away a tear. "I'm glad you sent Chad to us. He and Detective Sheree Davis made me see how much I let it control me. But I faced it—still do."

Her thoughts drifted to Chad. Despite major differences, he had many of Mitch's best traits. She couldn't deny their deepening friendship. Maybe someday they'd be more. Not yet.

After taking a deep breath, Valorie picked up suitcases and carried them down the stairs.

JR and Michele sat in the den, mesmerized by the TV. Valorie shook her head.

"Kids, go use the potty and grab your water bottles. I'm loading this all up, and then we're on the road."

She opened the front door and stepped outside. What a feeling. Breathing in the morning air, she smiled. To think going into the front yard used to terrify her. No more.

All suitcases in the car, bags placed strategically where the kids could reach them, she loaded one more bag between them and an ice chest filled with water in the middle of the backseat floorboard. Done. As she closed the door, she glanced around the neighborhood, waved at the old couple down the street taking their walk.

Rita rushed across the grass. "Hey, girl. All packed and ready to head out?"

"Yep. Just waiting for the kids to join me." JR and Michele ran through the door just then.

"I baked some cookies for you to take for a snack. You sure you want to do this, Valorie?"

"Not really, Rita, but in a way, I do. Hard to explain."

"I know." Her neighbor and friend folded her arms around her. "I'm proud of you. For so many things. Be safe, and check in with me every night."

"Yes ma'am. You and a dozen other people."

"I bet. Like the hunky Marine?"

"Stop it! But yes, he made me promise. Besides, I have to make sure Bruce isn't giving him any problems."

"He's keeping him for you?"

"Yes. I think they have similar mindsets."

Rita laughed. "I can see that." She gave each of the kids a hug. "You mind your mama, behave yourselves, and have a fun trip. I can't wait to hear about it when you get back."

They both waved and JR jumped into his seat, pulling the seatbelt tight.

Valorie turned as Chad jogged up the sidewalk.

"Hey. Bruce ready to go?"

"Yes. I left his food, leash, and everything out for you. The fridge is loaded, so help yourself."

"You didn't have to do that."

"You're watching my dog and house sitting. It's the least I can do."

"Okay." He gazed into her eyes. "Are you sure about this, Val? I can have a bag packed in five minutes. Seriously. I'm sure Rita would take care of Bruce."

Rita nodded in agreement.

Valorie sighed. "Tempting. I never traveled alone, Chad. I was always too scared something awful might happen. So, I stayed home, and terrible things happened anyway." She glanced around the neighborhood again. A gentle breeze blew across her face, warmth flitting through her body. Was that what peace and joy felt like? She looked back at the honey-brown eyes studying her. "I need to do this—prove to myself I can take care of the three of us."

"And when you get back?"

"I hope you stick around, Chad Tyler. I mean, you might need me to rescue you again."

They both laughed.

"Maaammma." Michele tugged at her sleeve. "Can we go already? I want pancakes like you promised. At the pancake place. And I'm starving."

"Nope. You're not buckled in your booster yet."

Michele hopped into the backseat. "I got it. All by myself."

Chad leaned into the back seat. "Bye JR. Take care of Mama. Michele—you just be your sweet little self. K?"

"K. I will. You take care of Bruce. He'll miss my hugs."

"I'm sure he will. I'll do my best to fill in, Michele."

He straightened and smiled at Valorie. "Take care. Call to check in. I'm here if you need me."

"I know. And I appreciate it. We'll be fine."

One last hug, and Valorie climbed beneath the steering wheel and blew him a kiss. "See you soon."

She glanced in the rearview mirror. Both JR and Michele had on seat belts. Content, she waved at Chad again, looked both ways, and pulled out of the driveway.

What adventures might wait for them? No idea, but she looked forward to finding out—for once without stressing and filled with fear for the entire trip.

Afterword from the Author

A LINE OF THUNDERSTORMS approached from the north, moving rapidly—never a good sign on an unseasonably hot winter day. Ominous clouds loomed over the horizon as the wind shifted, bringing the strength of a giant. I stood to look out, watching the temperatures fall five degrees in under five minutes.

"Storm's a comin'," I whispered to the emptiness of my 33-foot RV. I crossed the eight feet, prepared to close the door, and keep out the imminent rain. The wind, harsh gentleman as it was, beat me to it, shoving the door closed before I reached it.

My youngest daughter called. "Just checking on you."

"Rocking, but I'm good." I peeked out the window while the skies grew dark, shutting off the remaining light of dusk. "No roiling clouds. I'm not seeing green in the sky." The combination of those two, and I might have made a run for it.

"OK. If you need anything, we're here."

Interrupted by an incoming call from my sister, I switched over. "Hello."

No greeting. "You might want to go to the RV park's community room. They're saying strong winds up to 60 mph. Those in RVs and mobile homes should take shelter in a sturdy building."

"I might do that."

By that time, rain pummeled my roof louder than any thunder. "I haven't heard of any tornadoes in the area." In north Texas, we get warnings—usually minutes before a tornado rips through.

"No, but the wind is blowing hard."

"OK. If anything happens, and they find my body, you know where I am." For me, death on Earth meant a new home in Heaven. Not suicidal by any means, I didn't fear death.

"It isn't the death; it's how much pain you endure before it comes." My sister, always the nurse at heart, AND the big sister.

"Valid point."

We disconnected.

I looked out again, not relishing the thought of a cold, rain-drenching shower. The RV rocked, but in the 18 months of living in it, I experienced worse.

Perhaps I should've run out in the storm and taken cover. Instead, I retreated to my sofa, finishing the journal entry so rudely interrupted by a springlike winter storm. Then I picked up my laptop and commenced playing games to exercise my brain and distract me from the gusts swaying the tiny place I called home. Over the next 30 minutes, the temp fell from 74 degrees to 54. Another frightening thought with a line of clouds hovering. Still, no rotation, despite an atmosphere ripe for creating a funnel cloud.

No fear.

I can't explain why, but the storm didn't frighten me. Sometimes, I wondered if I might be too foolish to feel fear in the face of danger. A sense of peace overwhelmed me, chasing away any temptation to panic.

Through the rocking, thunder, and heavy rain, I remained calm. I can only attribute that type of peace to faith in Jesus Christ, who more than once calmed literal and figurative storms in my life.

Perfect love casts out all fear. As I rest in His arms, I need not fear. And in my gut, I know. If I need to take shelter, Holy Spirit says, "Go. Get out now."

'Tis so sweet to trust in Jesus—especially during a Texas storm.

In *Fear's Game*, Valorie battled overwhelming fear, much of which came from her imagination. The things she feared most happened while this character cowered in her home. No number of locks protected her from the evil of this world. In the end, she had to overcome her fear and trust in God's power to rescue her children.

Once she learned to control fear, Valorie could move in bravery, as her name suggested. She learned about peace that passed all understanding.

If you never experienced this type of peace, Jesus offers it.

He said, "I am the way. I am the truth, and I am the life. No one comes next to the Father except through union with me. To know me is to know my Father too." (John 14: 6 TPT)

"And everything I've taught you is so that the peace which is in me will be in you and will give you great confidence as you rest in me. For in this unbelieving world, you will experience trouble and sorrows, but you must be courageous, for I have conquered the world!" (John 16:33 TPT)

Jesus gives peace the world cannot comprehend. Should I sit still while a storm approaches? Well, God provides common sense, and if needed, yes, I will do my best to outrun a deadly tornado. But I will not live in fear, cowering before a "possible" wind-filled thunderstorm. That's the beauty of trusting in Jesus—not only for salvation and eternal life, but also for guidance in this one.

If you don't have an intimate relationship with God through Jesus Christ, you can. Prayer—communicating with God—means talking and listening. Admit you are lost without Jesus, filled with sin, because we all sin and can't measure up to God's holy standard. Believe Jesus, fully man and fully God, died to cover the penalty of your sin and rose again on the third day. Ask for His forgiveness and guidance for your life. And the peace that passes all understanding will fill you. Jesus promised it, and He never forgets His promises.

Fear not. He will abide with you.

ACKNOWLEDGMENTS

My brother-in-law recently asked, "How does your mind go to such dark places?"

I have no answer. Perhaps it's a gift (or a curse). Truthfully, we live in an evil world, and although my mind sometimes dwells on these 'what if" scenarios, I'm grateful I have a savior who gives me the way out. Without Jesus, I could never write dark tales that end well because my characters find Him along their journeys. Any gift for writing I have comes from the Lord.

A lone pursuit, writing well requires the support of those who understand the process and who share honest feedback. Thank you to the members of Living Waters Writers, Heart & Soul Writers, and The Heights Small Group for Writers and Aspiring Writers. I may lead the groups, but you all provide feedback that keeps me on my toes and makes me a better writer. Thank you for catching many of my errors.

To my BETA readers, Amber Whiteaker, Wanda Strange, Kerry Strange, Cindy Tippett, Dee Dee Ward, MT Webb, Sarah Olson, and Vicki Woodson, thank you for the final perusal of errors and comments to take me to a higher level of excellence.

I can't leave out my precious grandchildren, especially those who hover around that six and eight age range. Your input (intentional or otherwise) helped me craft the characters of a little boy growing up too fast and a precocious little girl who knows well how to act bossy and morph from adorable to mean and back again. Sometimes being six isn't easy.

Thank you to my friends and family who nudge me to finish and encourage me daily. I am blessed beyond my greatest desires because of you all.

And finally, thank you to my readers. Without you, why would I write? May God continually bless you and remove all fear from your life.

About Lisa Bell

Lisa Bell is a published author of fiction and non-fiction books. As a former community editor for NOW Magazines LLC (*BurlesonNOW* and *WeatherfordNOW*), she published hundreds of articles. Besides personal publications, she also has stories in several *Chicken Soup for the Soul* titles and other anthologies alongside developmental editing for numerous clients. After retiring in January 2023, she focuses now on personal writing, freelance work, and encouraging writers.

Lisa works with writers to encourage and help improve their skills. She offers her expertise to those who desire to pursue independent publishing. Providing coaching, editing, formatting, and cover design as well as assistance with uploading documents to chosen platforms, she supports writers who want to use cost-effective publishing options while creating quality products.

Lisa leads a small group of writers through her church (The Heights, Granbury, TX) and two writing groups that began under North Texas Christian Writers and continue under a general Radical Writers (www.texasradicalwriters.com) umbrella and as part of Roaring Lambs. She speaks and teaches whenever the opportunity arises. She holds a BS in Business Management from University of Phoenix, is a CLASS alumnus, a panelist for The Writers View, and active in other groups and her community. A single mother and grandmother, she lives southwest of Fort Worth, Texas.

For more information about the author, please visit www.bylisabell.com or email LisaBell@bylisabell.com.

About Radical Women

Owner of Radical Women, Lisa Bell, lives in Granbury, Texas. She retired early in 2023 from her position as an editor for NOW Magazines, LLC, covering two of nine markets. She still offers freelance editing of all types (including developmental editing), interior book design, custom cover creation, and she strives to guide and assist writers in publishing their stories independently or with traditional publishers. Whether fiction or non-fiction, Lisa has experience and knowledge to make a story its best possible version.

Lisa also serves as a coach for three writing groups. She strives to teach writers the skills of writing so their work becomes the best they can achieve. Through writing groups, individual coaching, editing and more, she takes pride in finished products that rival any book regardless of the publisher.

Lisa has published hundreds of articles and multiple books. To learn more about Lisa, contact her by phone, text, email, or visiting the bylisabell website.

www.bylisabell.com.
lisabell@bylisabell.com
www.texasradicalwriters.com
(817) 269-9066

Other Books by Lisa Bell

Littleness of Faith
Homeless Hearts
Out of the Dungeon
Journey to Senility
My Inner Nemesis
The SWORD and a Pen

Included in the following anthologies:
The Plight Before Christmas
Christmas Love Through the Ages
*Memeories and Revelations**

Walking in Freedom Series
Fear's Game: Book 1
Broken Wagons: Book 2*

*Forthcoming

Visit www.bylisabell.com/books for additional information and purchasing options.

BONUS CONTENT: OUT OF THE DUNGEON

IF YOU LIKED *FEAR'S Game*, consider reading the book before Valorie's story. Go back to the dungeon with Valorie and her friends. And it all started with a gunshot wound...

by Lisa Bell

ISBN-13: 978-0615731421
For purchasing options, visit
https://www.bylisabell.com/books/out-of-the-dungeon/

Out of the Dungeon-Chapter 1

"Someone help. My buddy's been shot."

Charissa's head snapped up from a patient's chart.

A man staggered through the doorway under the weight of his friend, who looked more like a dead body than someone in need of the ER. The chart in her hands clattered against the floor. Memories of long nights in Dallas flashed as comprehension of the scene before her unfolded. This couldn't be real – not in her safe little hometown.

The man's eyes drilled into her. Pain streamed over his face, teeth clenched and struggling to speak. "Help...me."

Charissa stood, her legs moving as if immersed in molasses. Then with a blink and shake of the head, her mind shifted into crisis mode.

She grabbed a gurney and propelled herself toward the two men yelling, "GSW! Code Blue!"

After nursing school, she spent five years in Parkland's ER. They treated more gunshots in a single night than most hospitals saw in a year. But the child...

Not now. I can't think about that right now.

Procedures for a gunshot wound raced through her mind as she reached the patient. She slipped an arm around him, moving the limp body onto the gurney. A camouflage jacket covered a blood soaked t-shirt. She pushed aside the jacket and cut away cloth. Warm ooze from his abdomen mingled with cold clamminess of skin.

So much blood.

The stench hit her nostrils catapulting her stomach into a double somersault. The nausea caught her off guard. It wasn't her first time to smell blood gushing from a hole in someone, but this time was unexpected. She still hated the tang of senseless death hanging over someone.

As Charissa bent down to check for breathing, hands gripped her shirt. She pulled back, filled with apprehension, but the grip tightened.

"Don't let me die." The man's chest rattled with rapid, yet labored breaths, as if he sucked through a straw covered with water. "I can't die...you have to save me."

Compassion pushed down every ounce of dread. She covered the man's hands, forcing calmness into her voice. "You're not going to die. We'll do all we can for you. Stay with me and don't worry. We'll take care of you."

His eyes pleaded for mercy. "Please." His voice shook. "I need...to see my wife. Don't let me die."

Double steel doors banged against the wall as her supervisor, Ann, ran into the reception area with another nurse at her heels. Fresh out of nursing school, Kim's eyes widened. The area around her lips turned pale.

Ann fired questions at the victim's friend. "What's his name? How long ago was he shot?"

"I only know him as Bubba. An hour ago, maybe longer. We were out hunting; took a while to get back to the truck."

"Any drug allergies?"

The man shrugged his shoulders.

God help them if they saved him from the gunshot and then killed the man because of a drug allergy.

Ann's irritation slipped through in her tone. "Great. We know nothing about this man. Don't suppose you have any idea about his blood type?"

"No. Sorry."

The supervisor turned her attention to the nurses. "Let's get him into a room and start an IV. Cross and type match. He'll need blood."

Kim froze.

Ann bellowed orders. "Kim, wake up. Move it. He's in shock. Be sure to warm both the IV and blood. Dr. Stone is on his way from the cafeteria."

Charissa grabbed Kim's sleeve and thrust her toward the doorway as she shoved the gurney through and down the hall.

Inside the trauma room, Charissa grabbed warm blankets and covered the man, noting the distension of his abdomen and bluish tint of his fingers. She suspected a liver wound – not good, especially if it happened more than an hour ago. Her only gunshot victim since coming home, and the situation looked bleak. Kim's hands shook and fumbled with an IV kit. Charissa snatched it from her and tore open the wrapper.

Calm down. You can handle this.

Taking a deep breath, she prayed for steady hands and a good vein. She found none. "Ann, I'm going for the subclavian vein. Kim, we need vitals stat."

Ann shook her head. "You better know what you're doing."

"I've done it before. Don't worry."

Ann drew a small amount of blood and thrust it into the hands of a waiting tech. "Cross and type match, priority."

Kim fumbled with wires and connections. Charissa threw a pulse oximeter on a finger and slapped a blood pressure cuff around one arm. With connections to a monitor, the steady bleep representing heartbeats filled the room with a welcome sound. Dr. Stone rushed in and demanded stats.

Charissa responded. "BP 50 over 30. Pulse—irregular, weak, about 175. Oxygen—70 and dropping, respiration—50."

"Heart rate's too high, and I don't like any of those levels. He's in hemorrhagic shock." The doctor did a quick exam. "Without a scan, I can't be sure, but it appears the shot hit the liver. Has he been typed and cross-matched?"

"The tech just left."

"Fine. Get O negative going until we get results. Ann, do you have a surgeon on the way?"

"Yes, but he's about thirty minutes out."

Sweat popped out on Dr. Stone's forehead. "Great. I haven't seen too many gunshots."

Charissa whispered. "I have – far too many. Move him to OR. We'll have him prepped by the time the surgeon gets here."

Dr. Stone shook his head. "We should stabilize him first."

She whispered. "He's not getting more stable."

"You're right. Let's move."

Bubba's eyes shot open and he touched Charissa's arm. His pale face took on a grey pallor, deepening with every breath. He whispered, "Tell my wife...I love her...and I'm sorry...for everything."

She looked into his eyes. A small sliver of green surrounded his dilated pupils. Not even a hint of a sparkle appeared, but the glassy appearance against his grey skin spoke volumes. They needed to move fast.

Emotion squeezed her throat until it ached. "Just hang on. We're taking you to surgery."

"Just...tell her." His voice dropped. "Promise."

She managed a weak, "Okay."

He drew in a deep breath filled with a pronounced rattle. She knew that sound. The monitor changed to an unbroken whine, alarms sounding loud and long.

"No. Don't you dare die on me."

She looked at Kim. "Get an ambu bag on him. Now."

Out of the Dungeon–Chapter 2

Kim didn't move. Charissa grabbed an ambu bag and slapped it on his face, then jumped onto the bed, hit his chest and started CPR compressions. She kept working—willing the man to live. Sweat and tears combined and ran down her cheeks as she alternated chest compressions and pumping the bag.

A flurry of activity filled the room, but she didn't care. She glanced at Dr. Stone and Ann who both wore panic as a facemask. Neither of them ever worked in a city hospital. She wondered if either saw a gunshot before.

Charissa yelled, "Do something."

The doctor and supervisor moved beside the gurney and sprang into action. Charissa paid little attention to what they said or did other than a vague awareness of someone packing his injury. Her primary concern was keeping this man alive. She had to trust their knowledge, even without experience.

Please, don't die.

Faces swarmed through her mind. Men and women wearing the same gray color, covered in blood. She'd seen far too much death. But the last one—a little boy—was too much. She moved home after he died. No more.

She willed away the faces and kept pushing on Bubba's chest, hoping for another breath—even a rattled one.

After a few minutes, Dr. Stone rested his hand on her shoulder. "Charissa, stop. We can't do anything now. Let it go."

"No. He can't die—not from a gunshot wound. I'm not giving up." She reached for the man's chest again. Kim stepped beside her and took over the ambu bag pumps.

Dr. Stone said, "We got him too late."

"No. We have to get his heart going again and get him to surgery."

"The surgeon's still at least ten minutes out."

"Then you do the surgery."

"I'm an ER doctor, barely out of residency from a small community hospital, not a surgeon. I can't handle this kind of wound. You know that."

"You can try."

"And lose my license? Let it go." He pulled her arm. "Kim, what's the time?"

"No. I won't give up. I won't let him die." Charissa shrugged away his hand and yelled at the patient. "Can you hear me, mister? You hold on—for your wife. Don't you dare give up."

Dr. Stone surrounded her with strong arms and pulled her from the patient. She fought and almost broke loose before he hauled her off the bed. "You've done enough. I'm calling it."

Charissa wilted. "Why? This isn't some big city. Llano is a little town with good people. How could this happen?"

Dr. Stone shook his head. "Hunting accident maybe. People get careless."

"I grew up in this town and heard of hunting accidents, but not this bad. It's just wrong."

"I know." He caressed her shoulder. "It seems so senseless, but accidents happen."

He nodded to the other nurse. "Time?"

"Eight seventeen, doctor."

"Note the time of death. I'll go tell his family."

Charissa glared at him. "And what will you tell them?"

"The truth—the same thing I'm telling you. We did everything we could, but he lost too much blood before we got him."

Turning to go, he paused and then glanced back over his shoulder. "Don't beat yourself up over this, Charissa. You gave it your best shot. More than most would have done."

Dark emptiness settled over her mind. *My best still wasn't good enough, was it?* The lifeless face blurred behind tears as she stared down.

She'd returned home to avoid this kind of trauma. Sniffles, broken limbs, maybe an elderly person with a heart attack, but nothing prepared her for this. Her hometown; secure without big city crime or gangs, where eagles nested nearby, and seasoned hunters went out prepared for anything. It was supposed to be a refuge from senseless deaths.

Too many experiences with brutality suffocated and drove her home. An innocent boy died in her arms the day she resigned from Parkland. She ran like a frightened child back to safety. As she looked at Bubba, reality bit her as terrifying as a copperhead. Violence again, and all of her efforts made no difference. The years of training meant nothing. She didn't even know his real name. The still body taunted her. Sorrow washed down, pushed her to the brink of despair. The blank stare condemned.

"I tried," she whispered and bolted from the room.

She ran through the hall into the staff restroom, a thin door providing shelter from reality. Locked inside, she slid down the door. Faces flitted from her subconscious mind to the surface. Memories of wounds, unnecessary yet fatal, sickened her. And the little boy's face came again with eyes pleading for help. Tiny eyes, so similar to Bubba's, wanting to survive, yet a life cut short by a bullet not intended for him. In both instances, nothing she did mattered. It didn't help whether she wanted desperately to save them, or kept trying after everyone else quit. In the end, both still died. Waves of grief shook her entire body, engulfed by sobs. Fear that someone might hear suppressed the idea of banging her head against the door.

Why? This is too much watching a man die from a gunshot again in the middle of my secure world. So fast and all alone.

The sobs subsided as she wrapped arms around herself and rocked back and forth. The cold, hardness of the tile floor merged with a growing numbness inside.

The little space isolated her from feeling, alone and trying to make sense of the situation. Asking why seldom brought answers, but she wanted to ask. Minutes clicked by.

Enough.

She pushed herself off the floor and washed her face. The man left a message for his wife. How could she comfort a young widow with so much grief pouring over her heart?

Blast this stupid job. It isn't what I want for my life.

She longed for a pair of tiny arms from a Honduran orphan around her neck at that moment. She never witnessed any of them die, and at least she could take care of those little ones. Food and love came easy. But no arms, tiny or otherwise, comforted the pain.

She looked up, alone in the stark bathroom. Dim light bounced off the mirror. She didn't look, knowing its inability to hide red-rimmed eyes laced with anguish peering back. She forced a slight smile, splashed cold water over her face and patted it dry. Get over it. You have a job to do. Self-pity swallowed, stale air filled her lungs.

She pulled a lab coat from the shelf, put it on and buttoned it over red stains.

Outside of the restroom, Haniel McCrae leaned against the wall. She knew this man well, although never quite understood why he spent so much time in this God-forsaken place. Still, she thanked God for his presence. His towering, muscular frame looked intimidating, but those chocolate eyes twinkled as he looked down at her. The peace that exuded from him held her attention, comforted her.

"Charissa, are you okay?"

She nodded, not trusting herself to speak.

Haniel raised his eyebrows. "Are you sure?"

"I'm a little shaken. We treated a gunshot victim tonight, but he didn't make it." Hot tears stung again. "I tried, but it wasn't enough."

"I heard. I'm sure you did all you could. Don't blame yourself for his death. People die sometimes. It's part of life."

"He was young. People around here die from old age, not gunshot wounds. It isn't as though we have gangs or drive by shootings. I came home, sick of that kind of death. I saw too much of it, and never expected it here."

Haniel touched her shoulder. "I know. I'm sorry."

Charissa inched closer and melted into Haniel's hug. "I have to work through this. I'll be okay when I get home and process everything."

"I'm here if you need to talk."

"I know. Thank you, Haniel. You're a good friend."

His smile strengthened her spirit and renewed peace. She gave her best. No one asked for more, but defeat and weariness hung over her head, a dark storm cloud ready to burst with a deluge of hopelessness. She stepped back and forced a smile for him.

"I need to go find this man's wife and deliver a message. Thank you for caring. Really, I'm fine."

He didn't look convinced. She headed to the nurse's station.

Ann sat in the swivel chair. The victim's friend leaned against the desk. His broad shoulders blocked her view of the waiting room, and his relaxed stance made her wonder if something delayed Dr. Stone. Surely, he'd already delivered the bad news.

At the desk area, Ann's giggles revolted her. The other woman's eyes drooped as she placed a hand on the man's arm. Unbelievable. This man just lost his friend. How could she flirt with him at a time like this? The huskiness in his voice left the impression he didn't mind.

Disgusted with the whole scene, Charissa pushed past the man and glanced over the waiting room. Empty seats lined the walls.

She turned to Ann. "I'm sorry to interrupt. Has Dr. Stone talked to the family?"

Ann rolled her eyes. "No family. Only Drake here and yes, he's been notified of his hunting buddy's death."

She faced the man. “I’m sorry for your loss, sir. He spoke of his wife. Have you been able to reach her?”

He held out a hand. “Hi. I’m Drake Hannibal. Bubba’s wife left him years ago. I never met her—but from what he told me, she’s no big loss. He never got over her—always seemed depressed. Maybe he’s better off dead.”

Charissa gasped and gawked into the man’s eyes. Dark brown ice peered back. She shuddered.

Drake said, “Sorry. I guess that seemed rather heartless. I barely knew the man. We hunted together sometimes. He always said maybe he’d get shot. I think he hoped for it – didn’t have the guts for suicide but wanted to die. You know what I mean?”

He moved nearer and put a hand on her shoulder. The tone of his voice mesmerized her – smooth as honey. Musk, pine and earth all comingled and drifted from his body. She grabbed onto the desk and steadied herself.

Ann interrupted the downward spiral. “I’m sure you can make it your mission to find the widow and offer her some comfort. Such an easy task for a sweet little Christian like you.”

Charissa bristled and pulled away from Drake’s touch. I’m about to show you a sweet Christian. She hesitated, used every ounce of strength to control the mounting flame, sighed and spoke through clenched teeth. “She deserves to know.”

Drake agreed. “Yes, she does. I think there might be a kid too. Maybe I can find out something for you.”

“That would help. Thank you.”

Charissa’s mind reeled as she looked at the supervisor. She caught a flicker of emotion in Ann’s smoldering eyes.

Am I detecting a little jealousy? You shouldn’t even be talking to this guy. What would your husband think if he knew the way you flirt around here?

A thought reared up inside her. She’d seek forgiveness later, but she didn’t try to resist such an appealing temptation.

Reaching deep and grabbing her best Southern belle voice, she said, "By the way, Ann, your husband left a message for you earlier. It's there on the desk."

Daggers flashed in Ann's eyes, but Charissa didn't care. Picking up a chart, she rushed down the hall without looking back. Lord help her if Drake found out anything. She never wanted to see or talk to him again.

www.ingramcontent.com/pod-product-compliance
Lightning Source LLC
Chambersburg PA
CBHW060555310726
48982CB00008B/1132/J
* 9 7 8 1 9 6 5 5 6 1 0 7 2 *